# Quarry

Susan Cummins Miller

Texas Tech University Press

A Frankie MacFarlane Mystery

This book is typeset in Sabon. The paper used in this book meets the minimum requirements of ANSI/NISO Z39.48-1992 (R1997). ∞

*Library of Congress Cataloging-in-Publication Data*
Miller, Susan Cummins, 1949–
    Quarry / Susan Cummins Miller.
        p. cm.—(Frankie MacFarlane mysteries ; 3)
    ISBN-13: 978-0-89672-574-4 (isbn-13 : alk. paper)
    ISBN-10: 0-89672-574-X (isbn-10 : alk. paper)
    1. MacFarlane, Frankie (Fictitious character)—Fiction. 2. Mojave Desert (Calif.)—Fiction. 3. Hit-and-run drivers—Fiction. 4. Women geologists—Fiction. 5. Missing persons—Fiction. I. Title.
PS3613.I555Q37 2006
813'.6—dc22                                                      2005023692

Printed in the United States of America
06 07 08 09 10 11 12 13 14 / 9 8 7 6 5 4 3 2 1
T S

Texas Tech University Press
Box 41037
Lubbock, Texas 79409-1037 USA
800.832.4042
ttup@ttu.edu
www.ttup.ttu.edu

This book is a work of fiction. Names, characters, places, and incidents are either products of the author's imagination or used fictitiously. Any resemblance to actual events, locales, or persons, living or dead, is entirely coincidental.

*For Charles A. Repenning, Michael O. Woodburne,
and the UCR Vertebrate Paleontology Gazetteers,
who circled the wagons in the Cady Mountains
and elsewhere in the desert West*

**Quarry:**

1. [*n.*] A bird or animal hunted; prey; game. Any object of pursuit.
2. [*n.*] An open excavation or pit from which stone is obtained by digging, cutting, or blasting, usually for the extraction of stone [or fossils]. [tr. *v.*] To cut, dig, blast, or otherwise obtain (stone) from a quarry.
3. [*n.*] A square or diamond shape.

—*The American Heritage Dictionary*
*of the English Language*

# PROLOGUE

What's past is prologue.

—**William Shakespeare,** *The Tempest*

And nothing can we call our own but death,
And that small model of the barren earth
Which serves as paste and cover to our bones.

—**William Shakespeare,** *The Tragedy of King Richard II*

## Cady Mountains

Mojave Desert, California
Monday, December 13, 1:00 p.m.

The winter sun, eight days shy of the solstice, held no warmth. But inside, Dora Simpson felt a lightness start low in her belly and rise slowly to gather in her chest. Happiness. A new experience—or a very old one. How long had it been since she'd last felt happy? Ten years? Twenty?

Dora sat back on her heels and looked over the fossil quarry. The outcrop, no more than twenty feet square, was now barren of bones. Her fieldwork was finished.

In just under two weeks, working dawn till dark, she'd exposed the upper surface of the sandstone bed, plotted fossil locations, excavated bones, and discovered clues to their ancient habitat. The bones represented a decent cross section of the animals that walked and ate, slept and mated here eighteen million years ago when volcanoes sporadically spewed basalt flows and fiery clouds of gas and ash into the trough of an old rift zone. No one would ever know the number of animals that had died during those eruptions. But this pocket in the rock had held antelope, rhino, kangaroo rat and beaver, camel, horse, and dog. The mammal bones had been swept into an ash-choked pond, settling among the frogs, snails, clams, and plants that lived there.

Standing up on the gently dipping ledge, Dora leaned into the wind, counterbalancing against the icy gusts. It had been blowing all day, howling in the canyons, eddying in the quarry, peppering her skin and eyes with fine white sand. She dusted off her pants, stretched her back, flexed her hands in their blue-striped work gloves, shivered as the wind found openings under her fleece jacket and down vest. Her ears and nose were numb. She'd never warmed up today. Like yesterday and the day before, the temperature would reach no higher than the low forties. It would freeze tonight. She didn't care. She'd be long gone by then. But she prayed the rain would hold off until tomorrow, until she'd navigated the drift sand and washboard roads back to the highway.

Smiling, Dora strapped on her field belt, stuck the rock hammer in its leather loop, slipped the small digital camera into the pocket of her shirt, and stuffed her field notebook and maps in her backpack. It was odd to feel so happy here in the bone-dry center of the Mojave Desert. Barstow was nearly forty miles away, Baker about the same. That left her alone in the middle of a rugged, desolate circle of sand and rock roughly twelve hundred square miles in area. No one but the occasional rock hound, biologist, or geologist ventured into the Cady Mountains.

For two weeks she'd had the place to herself. She didn't count Killeen, who'd helped her clear the site that first weekend . . . or Jed, the archaeologist working on the eastern fringes of the Cadys. He'd driven up to her campfire the first evening after Killeen left, introduced himself, and offered to show her the prehistoric site he was mapping. She'd seen him only once more. She preferred it that way. She'd been fearful at first, never having worked alone. But she'd come to love the isolation.

Dora stashed her paintbrushes, chisels, and glue in the old plastic bucket; checked to make sure her compass, GPS unit, and penknife were in their cases on her belt; then took one last look around. Only another geologist or paleoecologist would know she'd worked here. That was as it should be.

Shouldering into the backpack, bucket in her left hand, she picked her way carefully off the ridge that splayed, like a hand, into the main wash. The narrow ravine below led downstream to her base camp in the shelter of an outcrop of Peach Springs Tuff. The layer of pink and purple ash and rock fragments had exploded from a caldera two hundred miles away, flowing out and over the old landscape. The particles fused as the tuff cooled, creating a dense, glassy rock layer. It had been one volcanic event among the many that had formed this piece of the earth's crust.

The ravine was in shadow, though it was only one fifteen. Dora circumvented the angular boulders, clambered awkwardly down the dry waterfall. The wind was picking up force. Through the roar she heard something scrape stone behind the ridge above her. A hoof? No, it was early for the desert bighorns to be heading down to Afton Canyon for water.

Dora set down the bucket, fingering the rock hammer at her side as she turned a full circle . . . Nothing. She picked up her bucket again, eager to be on the road back to Del Rio. That Mac-Farlane woman's defense was tomorrow. Dora had heard a lot about her. It couldn't hurt to introduce herself, network a little. In a few years, she'd be looking for a job. Maybe MacFarlane could help.

The wind paused, as if an unseen hand had thrown a switch. The quiet grew in the sinuous canyon. She heard a rock trickle down off the thin limestone and sandstone beds into the bottom of the watercourse. Just the wind, she thought. Just the wind dislodging a stone. Happens all the time. But she hurried now.

That sound again. A pebble plopped at her feet. She looked up. A skull-like human face peered down, grinning. She dropped the bucket and started running through the soft sand.

# PART I

Let's talk of graves, of worms and epitaphs.

—William Shakespeare, *The Tragedy of King Richard II*

# 1

## Del Rio, California

Monday, December 13, 4:00 p.m.

The Del Rio police station on Main Street was built fifty years ago. Even then, it couldn't have been an imposing structure, I thought, as I found a parking space across the street. I turned off the engine and sat for a moment, savoring the relative silence at the end of a long drive. The quiet was appropriate: the ivy-clad brick building in front of me housed the coroner's office, or so the sign said.

Del Rio was established, as its name implied, near a large river—the Santa Ana. Before the Spanish arrived this was the traditional homeland of the Serrano and Cahuilla Indians. The Californios—first Spanish, then Mexican—displaced the indigenous tribes and received vast land grants from crown and state for their sheep and cattle herds. In the latter half of the nineteenth century, Euro-Americans planted the valley with citrus trees. Canals brought water from the river to the groves, most of which had given way in the last forty years to suburban housing tracts. The river was now a dry wash and floodplain, except when carrying winter snowmelt or runoff from major storms. Even at flood stage, the wash didn't flow as it once had. The water, nowadays, rarely reached the ocean.

Getting out, I stretched my tired body and spotted the parking meter farther down the block. The state-of-the-art ticket dispenser accepted cash, coins, and credit cards. I fed it a dollar, just enough to cover me till free parking began at five. Tucking the ticket on my Jeep Cherokee's dashboard, I picked up the field bag I use as a purse and jaywalked across the street to the police station. Nothing like living dangerously.

The scratched glass doors to the police station slid open electronically. Behind a Plexiglas window on the right sat a civilian receptionist. She did not return my smile. I asked for Detective

Leonard La Joie, rhyming the name with *the toy* as the officer had done when he'd introduced himself by phone two days ago. The receptionist jotted down my name and Arizona driver's license number, then ordered me to take a seat. I resisted the urge to salute, and chose a vinyl upholstered chair near the door to the office wing. My position had the advantage of being outside the dragon lady's direct line of sight.

The reception area was old and scuffed, with minimal attention paid to comfort. I had the room to myself. I picked up a copy of *National Geographic,* eight years old, missing the cover. Someone had torn out the article on African dinosaurs.

The clock on the wall was broken, I noticed, when I tried to set my watch to California time. The clock said 11:45. Was that a.m. or p.m.? It was right twice a day, but I was sure now wasn't one of the times. I asked the dragon lady. "4:06," she said, without looking up.

I sat down again and adjusted my watch, an inexpensive Timex. Fieldwork was hell on watches. I'd ruined one last summer, another last week. Recognizing a pattern, I stuck with cheap sporty brands from Target or Wal-Mart. I was strapping the watch back on my wrist when the door to the inner sanctum opened.

An officer on the shy side of forty glanced at me. Palest blue eyes I'd ever seen. Direct gaze. Unreadable expression. Heavily muscled through the shoulders and chest. He was wearing a short-sleeved gray-striped Oxford shirt, navy slacks, and a navy silk tie. His dark blond hair was clipped short at the sides, left a little longer and curly on top, and gelled to stay in place. He strode quickly, his torso leaning forward as if he were just about to break into a run.

"Cardoza drop off that package yet, Brenda?" he asked the dragon lady.

"An hour ago." She pulled an envelope from under her desk and pushed it through the slot in the window.

"I asked you to buzz me," he said. His tone was as cold as a January Mojave night.

She shrugged. "I was on break. Lefty signed it in."

He ran fingers through the short hair at the back of his head, smoothed it down again, and massaged his neck muscles. Taking a deep breath, he tucked the manila envelope under his arm and looked at a note in his hand. He nodded curtly in my direction.

"Francisca MacFarlane? I expected you earlier." His voice was clipped, impatient, as if he had better things to do than talk to me. "I'm Detective La Joie."

I was ten minutes early. I'd just driven nine hours from Tucson. He'd asked *me* to drop by for a chat. I decided to rattle his cage. I stood up. I was six two in my Ariat boots. He was four inches shorter.

"Sounds like this isn't a good time, detective," I said. Neutral tone; innocent eyes. "Why don't I call you after I get back to Tucson?" I slipped the strap of my field bag over my shoulder.

"Wait," he said. "Sorry. I just have a full plate today." He turned on his smile. It was nice, full of bright, white, even teeth that glowed in his tanned face. I bet he flossed twice a day. Only problem was, the smile was just for show. His name was a misnomer.

Well, I wasn't there to discuss a joyful subject. I was there to discuss a body.

# 2

Detective La Joie pushed open the doors to the heart of the building. It was quieter than I'd expected. He stepped into a small break room. "Coffee?" he asked.

"Decaf, please." I added cream to mine, then followed him upstairs. The second floor was one large room partitioned into cubicles. He led the way through the maze to an office just spacious enough to contain a desk and two chairs. The fabric-covered partitions were devoid of decoration that would give a hint of his personal life. I saw only a city-issue calendar, holidays circled in red, topped by a photograph of a bronze monument to fallen officers. La Joie's workspace gave the impression that he lived for the job.

He sat directly across the desk from me, consciously or unconsciously emphasizing his authority. The former, I decided. His desk was orderly, files neatly stacked in the in- and out-boxes. No coffee rings. No Twinkie wrappers. He pulled two files from a left-hand drawer, slapped them down in the middle of his desk, pushed one to the side, and opened the second. His hands were short fingered and square, with calluses on the knuckles, as if he'd been punching buckets of pea gravel. He leafed slowly through the pages, glancing up now and then to gauge my reaction. As power plays go, his wasn't very original. But I wondered, all the same, why he'd started this pissing contest. Maybe he didn't like women who were taller than he was. I sipped my coffee and waited for him to toss out the first pitch.

At last he tapped the file with his pen. "You've been a busy girl."

I raised an eyebrow. I'd turned twenty-nine last month. Only relatives over fifty called me *girl*.

"I have copies of reports from Nevada, Arizona, and California that contain your name." His tone implied a question.

"I thought I was here to discuss Geoff Travers." Geoff was my former fiancé—a fellow geology grad student at UC–Del Rio. He'd disappeared last spring.

"I'm just curious—are you unlucky or do you look for trouble, Ms. MacFarlane?"

"Someone once called me a catalyst."

"That I believe," he said, looking at the purple weal on my left hand. Six weeks before, a bullet had grazed the skin. I'd been lucky. "You've been helpful to the police, though, I'll give you that."

Don't do me any favors, I wanted to say. But I bit my tongue.

"Looks like the Tucson detective—Toni Navarro, is it?—tried to make it semi-official. Afterward you filed paperwork as an unpaid consultant," La Joie said. "Covering her ass?"

When I didn't rise to the bait, he closed the file with a snap and said, "Did you bring me something?"

I pulled a clear plastic bag from my purse and set it on the desk. Inside was a black hairbrush with a few strands of sandy brown hair caught in the bristles. "I had to go through my storage locker—found it in the last box."

"One of Murphy's Laws." La Joie picked up the bag and held it up to the light on his desk. "There should be enough for a DNA comparison. Thanks." He labeled the bag and tucked it in a desk drawer. From another he fished a microcassette recorder. "Any objection to my recording this conversation, Ms. MacFarlane?"

"If you have no objection to my doing the same, Detective La Joie." I took a tape recorder from my jacket pocket and set it on the edge of his desk. Two could play this game.

La Joie gave another of those curt nods and slipped the tape into the recorder on his desk. We punched the on buttons simultaneously, as if this were a quick-draw gunfight. He stated the date/time/participants, turned a page in his notebook, and picked up his Bic pen. "When was the last time you saw Geoffrey Travers, Ms. MacFarlane?"

"May 8 of this year."

"What was your relationship?"

"He was my fiancé. I broke the engagement that day."

"Why?"

"He plagiarized several draft chapters of my dissertation."

"Why would Travers do that?"

"I can only speculate, detective."

"Then speculate, Ms. MacFarlane."

"Geoff and I were working in different parts of the same mountain range in Nevada," I said. "He started a year ahead of me. He wanted to finish his degree before I did, but he couldn't seem to get the words down on paper. It was easier to take my rock descriptions and geologic interpretation and use them as his own."

"What did you do when you found out?"

"I went to our major advisor, Sarah Barstead—"

"That would be Dr. Barstead, present chair of the UC–Del Rio geology department?"

The man was a stickler for titles and rank, it seemed. "Yes," I said. "We spoke at length. I presented my evidence, and then I went home and asked Geoff to move out."

"What was his reaction?"

"He wasn't happy about it."

"What do you mean?"

"At first he denied everything . . . Then he turned verbally abusive."

"Can you remember what he said?"

"He told me I'd be sorry—that he'd get even."

"Where did this encounter take place?"

"At the townhouse we'd shared for nine months."

"That would be 135-B Franklin?"

"Yes."

"Was anyone with you when you last saw him?"

"A witness, you mean?"

"Correct."

The tapes hissed quietly as I thought back to a scene I'd refused to dredge up for months. "Molly McCarthy, the woman who lived next door, came over after Geoff left. She wanted to make sure I was all right. So she must have heard the yelling."

"Did you report Travers's threats to anyone?"

"I told Molly, and then Sarah."

"You didn't call the police?"

"There didn't seem to be any point. Geoff was blowing off steam. And I was leaving town for good a week later."

"You went from Del Rio to Tucson?"

"No. I had my stuff shipped to Tucson and put into storage while I went to Nevada to complete my fieldwork. My teaching job in Tucson didn't start till late August. Before the blowup, Geoff had planned to join me there."

"The department decided to allow him to finish his dissertation?"

Biting back the old resentment, I nodded, then remembered that tape recorders can't see. "Yes, though they required additional work."

"And you were okay with that?"

I shrugged. "They were going to put it under a microscope before accepting it."

"You didn't see him again in the week before you left?"

"No."

"Did you hear from him? Receive threatening e-mails? Letters?"

"No."

"Did anyone else in the geology department see him after that date?"

"Not after his hearing. They convened the day before I left."

"Did his disappearance surprise you?"

"Not really. I assumed he'd gone off somewhere to cool down and lick his wounds . . . the beach, maybe. I figured he'd come back, do the extra work, finish up his dissertation, and find a job. He had too much time and energy invested to let it all go to waste."

La Joie ran a finger down the edge of the second file on his desk. "So you worked in Nevada from late spring to late summer?"

"Yes."

"Any side trips? R and R?"

"There wasn't time. That was the last opportunity I had to tie up loose ends."

"Any witnesses?"

I smiled. "You know there were. It's in that file."

"Humor me."

"The entire population of Pair-a-Dice, Nevada."

"Surely not *all* the population?"

"There can't be more than fifty people in town, and that's on a good day. Admittedly there were two fewer when I left, but if you want the sordid details, talk to Elko County Sheriff's Deputy Buddy Montana."

"I already have." He made a check mark in his notes. "When did you learn that remains identified as Mr. Travers had been found?"

"I received a note and newspaper clippings from Sarah a couple of days before I left Nevada."

"What did you think happened to Mr. Travers?"

"That he'd either committed suicide or slipped off the cliff."

"Was Travers suicidal?"

"I didn't think so. An accidental fall made more sense."

"Did you think he might have been murdered?"

"Only if he happened to be in the wrong place at the wrong time."

"How did you react to the news?"

"I was stunned, of course. And confused. But I'd realized in May that I'd been living with a manipulative, unpredictable stranger. The Geoff I thought I knew didn't exist." I smiled. "Love isn't blind, Detective La Joie. Sexual attraction is."

There was more, but it was personal, too revealing to share. Geoff's betrayal had haunted me all summer. It had taken me months to begin to trust my judgment of people again.

"You weren't the only one taken in by Travers," said La Joie.

"That doesn't make me feel any better."

La Joie paused, as if searching for the precise way to phrase his next question. I held his gaze the way I'd learned to do when my brothers and I used to have staring contests. My scalp tingled. The big question was coming.

"When did you learn that the remains had been . . . uh, misidentified?"

"Last month."

"Who told you?"

"A private investigator."

"His name?"

I knew the answer. La Joie had to have Philo Dain's name in his file. But I wasn't about to be pressured into bringing Philo's name into a taped conversation. "I didn't specify gender, Detective La Joie."

La Joie's jaw muscles clenched. "All right," he said finally. "My mistake. What is his *or her* name?"

"The contract between us was confidential. The name isn't relevant to your investigation." I kept my tone and body language nonaggressive.

"I'll determine what's relevant."

"All communication between us remains privileged. Shall I call my lawyer to join us? It might take a day or so for him to get here from Tucson."

He shrugged his shoulders to loosen the muscles and took an exaggerated breath. "That won't be necessary, Ms. MacFarlane. Let's move along. What did your investigator tell you?"

"That Geoff's brother supplied the dental records that ID'd the body. That the remains were cremated and released to the brother, to be taken back to England for burial. There was no local memorial service, no obituary in the local paper . . . But Geoff had no brother."

"So we learned, after the fact. That all you have?"

"The emergency contact number in Geoff's school file didn't belong to his parents. It was a cell phone. Geoff's parents didn't find out about his death until they received a visit from my parents, who were—are—in England on sabbatical. Anyway, Geoff's parents weren't convinced their son was dead. They contacted you, sent his dental records, a hair sample, and a couple of baby teeth for DNA testing. The dental records didn't match the X-rays you took of the remains, so you reopened the case. You don't know who the victim was—at least you didn't at the time my investigator looked into it."

I took two folded sheets of paper from my bag and passed them across the desk to La Joie. "I presume you have copies of these?"

He looked at the first page, a missing person's report with a California driver's license photo of a student named Bernard Venable. He'd disappeared from an apartment complex near the UCLA campus last December, just after moving there to attend graduate school. The second was a photocopy of a Mexican police report, translated into English. Bernard Venable had been arrested in Tijuana, Mexico, after an altercation following a minor traffic accident. He paid a fine and was released. The accompanying photo was not the same as the one with the first report. This was a photo of Geoff Travers, dated last Memorial Day.

La Joie studied the pages. "Where'd you get these?"

I didn't want *agente de policía* Gallegos-Martínez's name on the tape any more than I wanted Philo's. "Does it matter?"

"I guess not."

I pointed to the Mexican police report. "According to that, Geoff was alive at the end of May."

"Yes."

"How long had the body been there?" I asked.

"Three months or more. We're working on it."

The remains had been found in late July. I did a rapid mental calculation. The body had been there since late April—at least. "The remains you found . . . were they Bernie's?"

"I don't know. I hadn't seen these reports until five minutes ago. Whoever gave them to you has better resources than I do."

He started to put them in the folder, then stopped. "You called him Bernie. Do you know Venable?"

I noticed his use of the present tense. "He was in a field geology course I TA'd eighteen months ago. He graduated last fall and moved on to UCLA. I didn't know he was missing till I saw that report a few weeks ago."

"So you knew both Travers and Venable."

"The entire geology department knew them."

"But no one knew Travers as well as you did."

I raised one eyebrow. La Joie waited me out. "I don't think anyone knew Geoff," I said at last. "May I see the photos you took at the scene?"

La Joie weighed my request. I was either a potential suspect or a potential witness. "Have you looked at crime scene photos before?"

"Pictures can't be worse than the real thing."

# 3

I was wrong. I hadn't counted on my body's reaction to the reality and finality of the twenty-four photographs La Joie laid out on a worktable.

Blood rushed to my head. I took a deep breath and looked away. Beyond the double-paned glass the short twilight was fading quickly. Rush-hour traffic was a steady hum I barely heard above the pulsing against my eardrum. I took another calming breath and looked down again.

The black-and-white prints captured a brush-choked ravine eroded into granitic hills. I recognized the place, an arroyo on the edge of campus—a home for rattlesnakes, a pathway for feral dogs, coyotes, bobcats, and packrats. On the hilltop above, among boulders and eucalyptus trees, Geoff and I had picnicked on warm spring days when the air smelled of orange blossoms. It was our spot—secluded, private. I could understand why it took so long to find the remains.

*Remains*—an appropriate word. Scavengers and insects had done their work well. Only bones were left, and a lot fewer than the body'd had during life. They'd been scattered over the arroyo—some, no doubt, dragged back to a coyote or feral dog's den to feed the pups. The skull was crushed in the back—a jagged wound, as if the head had landed on rock. Or vice versa. The disarticulated spine protruded from the gnawed and torn remnants of a T-shirt, flannel shirt, and jeans. Socks and underwear were gone, probably lining a packrat's nest.

"We were lucky we found the skull so we could compare dentition," La Joie said. He was standing just behind my left shoulder.

I concentrated on the clothes, shredded as they were. I knew I'd recognize anything of Geoff's. We did laundry together for nine months.

"That's a lot of clothes for April," I said. "A flannel shirt? That's winter wear. And I don't recognize the plaid. Definitely not Geoff's. Bernie was shorter and heavier than Geoff—probably a

34- or 36-inch waist, maybe 30-inch pant length. Looks like there's enough left for you to check."

"We'll do that—and contact Venable's family for hair and DNA samples." La Joie was taking notes in a small spiral-bound notebook. I wasn't. I heard a click from my tape recorder, followed by one from La Joie's. As if choreographed, we turned over our tapes in unison.

"What was his name—the so-called brother?" I asked.

La Joie didn't have to check his notes. "Harold. Harold Travers. He didn't ask me to call him Harry."

"Do you have any photos of Harold?"

"By the time we realized our mistake, the building's surveillance tapes had been reused."

"How about fingerprints off the dental charts he supplied?"

"They were clean. We're still trying to figure out how he managed it."

"Who talked to Harold?"

He stiffened. "I did."

Perhaps that accounted for the earlier curtness. I suspected that La Joie hated falling short.

"Geoff didn't like to have his picture taken," I said. "But you have his California driver's license photo and the one I gave you from Mexico. Was there a family likeness between him and Harold?"

"You mean, could it have been Geoff who picked up the ashes?"

"The thought crossed my mind."

"Well, it's hard to tell. Harold Travers was bald or had shaved his head. He wore a well-trimmed beard and mustache—dark brown, almost black."

"How tall?"

He thought for a minute. "My height. His eyes were level with mine."

"What color?"

"I'm not sure. He wore an older version of those glasses that darken when you're outside. They were never completely clear."

"Well, the height's right, but Geoff didn't wear glasses," I said. "He had hazel eyes and light brown hair, cut short, like in the photo ID. And he hated facial hair. He shaved even when he was in the field." I watched La Joie write this down, then asked, "What was he wearing?"

"Gray dress slacks and a pink shirt."

"Geoff wouldn't have been caught dead . . ."

"In pink?" La Joie finished for me.

I nodded. "Did he say where he lived?"

"Reading. England, not Pennsylvania. But we checked. There was no Harold Travers on any flight to or from England around that time."

"Impasse," I said.

"Until today," said La Joie. "Please thank your contact for these police reports. We'll follow up."

I picked up my tape recorder and was about to turn it off when something hit me. "Geoff said he and his parents were estranged. How long had it been since he talked to them, did they say?"

"Nine years. They had a row about his leaving England to go to school in Ohio. He was an only child. He sent them Christmas cards for the first four years, then nothing."

"Geoff came to UCDR from Ohio State. He cut ties with his alma mater, too. Didn't keep in touch with anyone, didn't go to any of the professional meetings—Geological Society of America and such. He said he didn't have the money."

I wasn't sure how to phrase the next question, so I just tossed it out. "Bernie Venable went missing in Los Angeles last December. Geoff disappeared in early May, surfacing in Mexico a couple of weeks later using Bernie's ID. What's the possibility that the real Geoff Travers never left Ohio?"

La Joie closed his notebook, slipping it into his chest pocket along with the pen. He stood there, hands on hips, brow furrowed. Indecision made him seem more human, more approachable. Then, straightening his shoulders, he said, "I'll have his parents fax me a photo, and get his original passport photo, too. And I'll contact Ohio State. Where will you be staying—in case I have any more questions?"

"Sarah Barstead's." I gave him my card. "You can reach me on my cell. I'm leaving early Wednesday morning."

"With luck, I'll have some answers by then."

# 4

Outside, I sat in my Jeep, struggling to calm my mind and switch gears. The rush-hour traffic had lessened as the heart of the city bled out its workforce. Only the restaurants, hotels, and a bookstore on the corner showed signs of life.

I hit the speed dial on my cell phone.

"Dain," said Philo. He sounded as if he were right next to me, instead of somewhere inside the Washington, DC, Beltway. He was a private investigator—mostly white-collar crime, background checks, and security issues, a booming business in this age of terrorism. Today he'd had to testify before a congressional subcommittee.

"It's me," I said.

"I know."

"Is this a good time?" I asked.

"Perfect." Paper rustled in the background. "Where are you?"

"Del Rio. Sitting in the Jeep outside police headquarters."

"Before or after your session with La Joie?"

"After," I said.

"How'd it go?"

I searched for the right words. "Tougher than I thought it would be, considering I knew ahead of time that the remains might not be Geoff's. I've got him checking to see if the man I knew might not be Geoff Travers at all."

"Did you tape the interview?"

"We both did—thanks to your recorder. And I managed to keep your name out of it."

"I appreciate that."

I heard the sound of water running in a sink and the clatter of dishes. I knew he'd planned to stay in a residence suite in Tysons Corner. "Did I interrupt your dinner?"

"I'd just finished. I ordered Ethiopian."

"Good?"

"Cold. I should have cooked my own."

"How'd your meeting go?" I knew he couldn't discuss the subject, except in generalities, especially on a cell phone whose signal could be intercepted easily. I knew only that he'd been doing background security checks on a government contract when he was called to Washington.

"They didn't get to me till after three. I'm on again in the morning."

"Then by Wednesday we'll both be heading home."

"God willing and an ice storm doesn't hit." A dishwasher began to hum, the sound fading as Philo walked away. "Good luck tomorrow. Wish I could be there."

"I know."

"Call me tomorrow afternoon, after it's over?" He paused, as if he didn't know what to say, but didn't want to lose the connection. "I miss you," he said at last.

"Me, too." In the rearview mirror, I watched police officers enter and exit headquarters. Another pause. I was beginning to feel like a teenager.

"Anyway, Philo," I said, "If you want me tonight—"

"I'll want you tonight."

"Seriously," I laughed, "I'll be at Sarah's. I'll leave the cell on."

"Lot of good that will do me."

"Poor boy."

His laugh came from somewhere deep in his throat.

"Later, Philo." I pressed end and speed dialed Sarah Barstead's office number. Her hello sounded harried.

"It's Frankie," I said.

"Good trip?"

"Exhausting." I wasn't just referring to the drive out. But the explanation could wait till I saw her. "Want to meet me for dinner at Casa del Sol?"

"I'm stuck at the office. Still grading historical geology finals."

"I could bring you something from the restaurant."

"I'd rather just plow ahead."

I heard the scratching of her pen. "Want me to feed Zoey?" I asked. Zoey was her cat.

"She's on a diet. Doctor's orders. But you could check her water bowl."

"Will do."

I was about to hang up when she said, "On second thought,

Frankie, if you could pick up some chicken enchiladas for me, that would be nice. If you don't mind."

"You know I don't."

"Then I'll see you at the house around ten—eleven at the latest."

# 5

I drove the short distance to Casa del Sol, a family-run place on University Avenue, a few blocks from campus. A large asphalt parking lot surrounded the small saffron-painted building. The lot was nearly full—too many people for the few tables inside. Most of the clientele would be waiting for take-out orders.

The restaurant focused on food rather than decor. Inside, the yellow walls displayed framed reviews from thirty years ago and Maya-reproduction mosaic masks. The cook and servers smiled and joked with the customers, many of whom I recognized as regulars. Was it only six months ago I'd left Del Rio for my last field season in Nevada? It felt like years.

I took a seat at the only unoccupied table, a rickety thing with metal legs and a scarred Formica top. The waitress plunked down a basket of tortilla chips next to a bowl of homemade salsa that was hot as sin on a summer night. "Hi," she said, pencil poised to take my order. "Long time, no see." She scanned the tiny restaurant. "Geoff with you?"

I felt as if she'd dumped a bucket of ice water over my head. It figured that she'd remember Geoff. He'd charmed women of all ages—including me.

"We split up," I said, and stumbled through an order for a Burrito Aguirre—green chili and pork, not the deep-fried version—and a Negra Modelo.

"That all?" she asked. I gave her Sarah's take-out order. "I'll tell Roberto to hold off on that till you're ready to leave," she said, and moved on to the next table.

The beer came first. I picked at the label with one hand, wolfed down chips with the other. The day, which had begun before dawn in Tucson, seemed endless. Geoff's shadow sat across from me at the small table. When the food came, I didn't dawdle as I might have done if Sarah were with me. Within thirty minutes, I'd demolished the burrito, paid the bill, and picked up Sarah's enchiladas in their Styrofoam container.

Sarah Barstead lived only a couple of miles away, behind campus, in an enclave populated by professors. Her street climbed the pediment of Azucar Mountain, the eastern edge of a granitic semicircle that curved around the campus like an embrace. I drove through a poorly lit subdivision dating back to the sixties. But Sarah's home, at the far end, was fifty years older. In daylight the structure, built of granite and gneiss cobbles from the Santa Ana riverbed, seemed to grow out of the mountain itself. The old farmhouse had once overlooked acres of citrus groves that spread like a gingham apron down into the valley. When the campus site broke ground in the fifties, the state co-opted the lower orchard lands for dormitories and classrooms. Two-story homes now flanked the foothill road, but those on the east side stopped well before Sarah's property. Her house crowned a granite knob, surrounded by the remains of an orchard—orange, grapefruit, pomegranate, lemon, peach, apricot, and plum trees. In late winter and spring, I remembered, the place smelled heavenly.

Sarah and her partner, Tona Skarstaad, a radiologist, had purchased the house five years before. Three years ago, Tona was diagnosed with advanced ovarian cancer. She died six months later.

Sarah had dealt with the loss and loneliness by training for and running marathons—and by throwing herself into work. When Peter Snavely, the department chair, died in a car accident last June, Sarah had been offered the position. She'd jumped at the opportunity. It helped fill the empty hours.

I turned right off Azucar Road onto Sarah's rutted gravel driveway. California was on the cusp of winter, crisp air heightening the tangy scents of grapefruit, lemons, and orange blossoms. On the south side of the house, a few creamy camellia blossoms, caught in the glare of my headlights, nodded in the onshore breeze. Yesterday's rains had saturated the ground. Tonight, once the wind died, fog would rise.

I parked in back, next to the detached garage, where climbing roses and wisteria, barren of flowers, clung to the walls. I pulled my computer case and overnight bag from the Jeep, tucked the take-out box in the crook of my arm, and closed the door, plunging the yard into darkness. The back-door light was out. I jumped when a lemon hit the concrete patio. It sounded like a bomb. I gripped the bags more tightly. I'd been too close to bombs six weeks ago. I wanted nothing more to do with them.

Something brushed my ankles. I dropped my overnight bag and barely held onto the enchiladas. Just Zoey—short for Paleozoic—

Sarah's gray cat, welcoming me. But I still felt jittery. Maybe the effects of my interview with La Joie, the conversation about Geoff, or viewing photos of someone's remains. Maybe I was nervous because my dissertation defense was only fourteen hours away. Or maybe the pitch blackness of a city yard made me feel vulnerable. I'd always been more comfortable in desolate places. Mountains and deserts are reliable. Rocks don't lie. They may quake, fall, or slide, but never out of malice.

I used the tiny light on my key ring to find the back-door key under the welcome mat and let myself in. Zoey used the cat door.

Sarah's house smelled of cat food and banana bread. I set down my bags and flicked on the kitchen light. The floor, a linoleum checkerboard in black and white, dominated the room. The black iron stove, white cupboards and refrigerator retained the ambience of the old farmhouse. Zoey sniffed at my pant legs, catching the scent of Philo's dog, Penelope. Satisfied that the threat was not close by, Zoey wound herself around my ankles, begging for attention—and food.

"Just let me put my things away," I said. She preceded me into the guest bedroom off the living room, watching as I deposited my bags. Only then did I pick her up. She was heavier than I remembered. No wonder she was on a diet.

The house had two small bedrooms downstairs, one serving as Sarah's office/den, and a large bedroom upstairs. Nothing had changed since I'd been here last. Tona's reading glasses still lay on the table next to the wooden rocking chair. So did Thomas Moore's *Care of the Soul,* the book she'd been reading when she died. Pictures of Sarah and Tona—smiling faces with different backdrops around the globe—adorned the walls and the antique organ in the corner. Christmas music sat on the organ bench, left there two Christmases ago. Although I didn't go upstairs, I suspected that that room, too, remained locked in time. For Sarah, comfort and joy lay in the past.

But other, happier photos documented practical jokes attributed to "Hard Rock Sam." Geology's a demanding field, requiring course work in physics, chemistry, biology, and math, in addition to geology, geophysics, geochemistry, and paleontology. Students live at the department. Given the pressures and exhausting hours, a sense of humor is de rigueur. In the wee hours of the morning, Hard Rock Sam stalks the halls. Sarah's photos documented a few of his pranks: a wall of beer cans blocking the entrance to her office; a scale-model reproduction of the Matterhorn, surrounded by a moat, constructed in her lab while she was doing fieldwork one weekend; a wooden outhouse door, with carved sickle moon, disguising the entrance to Peter Snavely's office just before his death; a working distillery set up in the rock lab. Hard Rock Sam's identity changed with the prank, but the tradition continued through each successive generation of faculty and students.

The wind picked up outside. Branches scratched the roof and screeched against the windows. The night had grown chilly. I turned up the thermostat, put in a CD, and sat on the worn leather sofa. Zoey curled up in my lap, purring as I stroked her back. She closed her eyes. A minute later, so did I.

The crunch of tires on gravel woke me. I was on my feet, Zoey protesting as she landed in the middle of the room. She flung me a hurt look before turning tail and disappearing up the stairs.

I stretched and rubbed my eyes. The clock on the mantle said 10:49. Another late night for Sarah, I thought, as I opened the kitchen door.

Sarah's elfin face looked thinner, if that was possible. Below close-cropped silver hair, the muscles in her neck stood out in bas-relief above her rhodonite pink sweater.

I gave her a hug. "It's good to see you, Sarah."

Her intense brown eyes looked me over. "You've grown a couple of inches," she said. Her Kiwi accent had a faint Oxford veneer. "And you've lost weight."

Judging by the narrow wrists exposed as she shed her black wool blazer, her runner's body didn't carry an ounce of spare flesh. I gave her the Look.

"Too right," she said, setting her briefcase on the kitchen table. "The pot calling the kettle, and all that. Sorry." She opened the briefcase, took out the official copy of my dissertation, and handed it to me. "Everyone's read it," she said. "No problems. How could there be? It's excellent. Tomorrow will be a breeze."

"I just wish it were over," I said.

"It's as good as." She hung her key ring over a coffee cup hook in the cupboard and turned toward the door.

"Forget something?" I asked, taking the enchiladas from the refrigerator.

"The mail."

I was the one who'd forgotten. Like most of us, Sarah was a creature of habit. She'd drop her briefcase, hang up her keys, say hello to Zoey, and jog down for the mail. I'd watched the ritual at least fifty times in the last four years. "Sit, Sarah. I'll get it tonight."

"I've been sitting so long I've got boils on my bum. I could use the exercise. Besides," she grinned at me over her shoulder as she picked up a flashlight and opened the door, "the enchiladas will be hot when I get back." The door closed softly behind her.

Two minutes later, just as the timer on the microwave dinged, I heard an engine rev. Tires peeled out and accelerated. A thud cut off a yelp. Brakes squealed, then the engine revved again. I grabbed a spare flashlight from above the kitchen sink, my cell phone from my purse.

Sarah's mailbox was enclosed in a square pedestal of granite cobbles across the street from the driveway's entrance. The wind had died. The temperature had dropped. Fog wrapped the hillock in a damp gray blanket that obscured the valley, distorted shapes, and diffracted the yellow light from the lamp atop the pedestal, the only light on the street.

"Sarah?" No answer.

I ran down the hill. The mailbox was a black hole. The door was gone. Had it been attached when I arrived? I hadn't looked.

"Sarah?" I called again. The fog absorbed my voice. I shined my flashlight up the street, then down. Nothing.

Had she been abducted by the car with the squealing tires? Was she lying injured nearby?

I walked down the street shining my light from side to side. Maybe forty feet away, Sarah lay, chest down and unmoving, half under an oleander hedge. Fresh tire tracks in the dirt verge led to—and over—her lower body. Both legs were bent at unnatural angles. Her face was turned toward the street, her eyes were closed. She looked dead.

"No," I think I said, and then, "Sarah?"

She didn't respond. Dropping to my knees beside her, I felt for a pulse at her neck. It fluttered faintly. She was barely breathing, but she was alive.

With shaky fingers, I punched 911. Then I cradled her hand in my lap, talking softly to her, willing her to hang on till help arrived.

# 6

The street at the end of Sarah's driveway was controlled chaos. A squad car with two officers arrived at the same time as the ambulance, paramedics, and fire truck. Sarah didn't regain consciousness. She looked small and fragile as they strapped her to the gurney. An oxygen mask covered half her face. I asked to go with her. The paramedic said there wasn't room. The red lights blurred as I watched the ambulance pull away.

Uniformed police stretched crime scene tape around the site as nearby houses emptied of people. Officers were taking names and statements, mine included, when the crime scene unit arrived. Detective La Joie parked right behind them. He and another man stepped out of the car, La Joie slipping on a dark jacket as they walked over to me. La Joie's eyes quickly scanned the scene, then rested on my face. I sensed a gibe coming.

"Don't," I said so sharply he stepped back a pace. "Sarah's in that ambulance."

La Joie exchanged a look with the albino-pale, freckle-faced man beside him—his partner, I presumed. "Dr. Barstead?" asked La Joie.

"Yes." I turned and started up the street toward Sarah's driveway.

The detectives were a step behind me, La Joie repeating Sarah's name to his partner. "Where are you going?" La Joie asked me.

I stopped by the boulder that marked the beginning of the driveway. "To the hospital, of course." I said it patiently, as if to a small child.

"I don't think so," La Joie said. "We have questions." The three of us formed an odd triangle of tension. "Detective Mick Mulroney," La Joie said, "meet Ms.—soon to be Dr.—Francisca MacFarlane."

I didn't take Mulroney's hand. My knees gave out, and I sank onto the boulder. My whole body shook. Delayed reaction.

"Is there anyone in Dr. Barstead's family we can call?" Mulroney asked, notebook open, pen poised.

"Sarah's parents are dead. She broke ties with her other relations years ago, or so I understand. It was mutual. The department is her family, now. You should call Janet Nakata, the assistant department chair. Campus police will have the number."

Mulroney took a couple of steps away from us and pulled out his cell phone. I tried my legs again. They'd hold, at least for the short walk to the house.

La Joie put his hand on my arm. The grip was light, but firm. "I'd rather you didn't go just yet, Ms. MacFarlane."

"She needs me."

"She'll be in surgery for a while. You'd just be waiting around. At least here you can do some good—fill us in on the details." The foggy darkness robbed his eyes of color. "You're a witness to a crime, Ms. MacFarlane," he said, anticipating my objection. "So, no, you don't have a choice."

"I'm allowed one phone call?"

"You aren't under arrest. Take two."

It was the first attempt at levity I'd heard from him. "Your generosity—" I started to say, then gave up. "Forget it."

La Joie gave me a piercing look. "Wait here," he said, letting go of my arm. "I'll be with you in a minute." With a not-so-subtle flick of the head, he signaled Mulroney to keep an eye on me, then jogged back to the crime scene.

I took my cell phone from my pants pocket and scrolled through the address book until I found my friend Killeen's pager number—a private number, known only to a few. I knew he slept with the damn thing.

I'd met E. J. Killeen, U.S. Army (Retired), as I was winding up my fieldwork in Nevada. He'd helped me find the last piece of the geologic puzzle that was my dissertation research. I'd helped him solve a family mystery. We'd helped each other survive a rock slide and attempted murder. And it was largely because of Killeen that I'd regained something of the trust Geoff had destroyed last spring.

When Killeen told me he was looking for a place to roost and a job that suited him, I'd recommended him for a factotum position in the geology department. He cut and ground rock thin sections, stained rock slabs, ordered supplies, and maintained department equipment and vehicles. Though Killeen was well read and spoke several languages fluently, he preferred to present himself as a simple mechanic. Being a mechanic had been a cover for his operations with military intelligence. He'd worked in Latin America, Vietnam, Korea, the Middle East, and God only knew what other zones of conflict. He was unflappable—a good man to have on your side in emergencies. Taking a deep breath, I punched the send button.

"What's wrong, Frankie?" Killeen's bass voice cut right to the problem.

"Sarah's hurt," I said without preamble. My mind wasn't functioning on all cylinders.

"Where? When?"

"Hit-and-run, here—outside her house, I mean. Less than an hour ago, while she was getting her mail."

"How bad is it?"

"She stopped breathing once while they were loading her onto the gurney." I took another deep breath to steady my voice. "She's at the hospital by now."

"Which one?"

"University."

"I'll meet you there in fifteen."

"I can't. Not yet. The police want to talk to me."

"Tell them they can talk to you at the hospital."

"I tried that. Detective La Joie won't budge. Small world that it is, he's handling Geoff's case. We crossed swords this afternoon."

"Imagine that," Killeen said softly.

"And besides," I said, as if he hadn't spoken, "the police have blocked off the street."

Killeen considered this in silence. I heard the rustle of him putting on clothes.

"Don't worry, Killeen. I can handle La Joie. But once you get to the hospital and check on Sarah, will you call the professors and department staff? And keep me posted on Sarah until I can get there? I'll keep my phone on."

"I'll call you back within the hour," Killeen said. "And Frankie?"

"Yes?"

"Hold onto your temper."

"What temper?" I asked. But he'd hung up.

I settled down on the boulder to wait for La Joie. The bronze house numbers set into the granite seemed to burn through my heavy denim jeans. Fog drifted and swirled, turning the portable police lights to amorphous globes. A man detached himself from the crowd of onlookers and walked toward me. Even in the dim light I recognized his Afro, a holdover from the sixties. Dr. Phillip Grover. I'd taken a class from him my first year at UCDR.

"We've met, haven't we?" Grover asked in that slow, sonorous voice I remembered. "You sat in the front row. I tried to talk you into ditching geology for physical anthropology." He looked up the driveway behind me. "I run with Sarah several times a week, and keep an eye on the place when she's in the field. I'd be happy to feed Zoey until Sarah's out of the hospital."

"Yes," I said, grateful to him as much for believing Sarah would pull through as for the offer of help. "Thank you, yes. I'll call you when I leave."

"Good," he said, patting my shoulder. "I know where the key is. If you need anything while you're here, just holler. I'm three doors down on the right." He pointed. "3516."

Grover's kindness was almost my undoing. His figure blurred as I watched him walk back to rejoin the remnants of the crowd. I rubbed my eyes on my sleeve. La Joie was talking to a chemistry professor holding two barking dachshunds on leashes. Her voice, accustomed to reaching the back row of an auditorium, carried easily. She told La Joie she'd noticed a truck parked a few doors up from her house when she walked the dogs about ten. No one was in the driver's seat, she said. She pointed up the street.

I followed La Joie's gaze. "The engine I heard could have come from there," I said half to myself, half to Mulroney, who was standing next to me. He hunkered down, one knee in the dirt, while I described the motor sounds I'd heard. "It tore out and headed downhill—as if the driver'd just had an argument."

"Please," he said, "wait here, Dr. MacFarlane." I didn't bother to correct him.

Mulroney collected La Joie and they trudged up the road, black outlines against the flashlight beams that danced along the road-sides, looking for evidence. Four doors up, La Joie squatted, his flashlight beam fixed on the dirt verge. Mulroney joined him for a moment. Then, rising, he walked back and took a couple of orange cones and a roll of yellow crime scene tape from the trunk of their car. Without being asked, one of the uniformed officers grabbed a second roll of tape and hustled after him. While Mulroney cordoned off the site, La Joie disappeared through a gap in the box-wood hedge that hid the house. I heard a faint knock.

"Ma'am?" said Mulroney a few minutes later. He was perhaps five years older than I, but he made me feel ancient. "Why don't I take your statement in the house? Detective La Joie will join us there in a few minutes."

It was an order. Mulroney watched me closely, tensed to counter any protest—physically, if necessary.

I hesitated. It would be easier talking here, where I wasn't surrounded by Sarah's things—favorite books, fossils, all those photos, and file cabinets full of class notes and research, each a memory. But for the first time, I noticed I was coatless and shivering. Even with my arms wrapped tightly across my chest, the cold sifted through my cotton turtleneck. I did an about-face and started up the drive.

The heavy, damp air carried the faint wail of a siren. Mulroney walked two paces behind me. He didn't attempt conversation. We were among the fruit trees when I remembered why Sarah had left the house. I stopped.

"Ma'am?"

"Sarah's mail," I said. It seemed important. "That's what she was doing on the street—getting her mail."

I guessed that La Joie had told him not to leave me alone. "Okay," he said.

When we were nearly to the bottom of the hill, Mulroney shone his flashlight beam into the oversized mailbox. His hand came up like a crossing guard's. "Stop," he said to me. "Wait right here."

I stopped. Mulroney walked across the road and peered carefully into the box. "Get La Joie," he called to a uniformed officer.

"What's up?" La Joie said a minute later.

"A package addressed to Dr. Barstead." Mulroney directed his flashlight beam into the yawning mailbox. "Brown paper. Block lettering. No return address."

# 7

Mulroney cleared the area and evacuated the two nearest houses while La Joie called the bomb squad.

*This can't be happening,* I thought. Only six weeks before, a colleague had been killed with a pipe bomb. That bomber was history. I'd watched him die. There couldn't be a connection.

Mulroney finally noticed me standing in Sarah's driveway. "Officer Rivera will stay with you at the house," he said. "I'll be there shortly."

This time I didn't hesitate.

Officer Rivera was of average height and stocky build. Neat French braids restrained her curly dark hair, except for the wisps that escaped at her neckline and around her widow's peak. In her mid-thirties, I guessed. A competent woman with a noncommittal expression.

We walked in silence to the house. The front door was locked, so I led her around to the back. "Oughta fix that light," she said, as our flashlights found the doorknob.

I didn't answer. In the kitchen, I stood in the middle of the chessboard floor, trying to corral my thoughts into some kind of order. I felt like a pawn, moved by an unseen hand, and wondered if La Joie felt the same.

I wanted something warm and comforting. Unfortunately, Philo wasn't around. Even Zoey had deserted me.

"Coffee?" Rivera asked, as if she'd read my mind. She was holding the carafe from the automatic coffeemaker. She'd already filled it.

"Yes, thanks. That'd be great." Then I realized she didn't know where the coffee was. Like a Stepford wife, I ground the Kona beans and measured them into the basket, pressed the on button, and took the heavy cream from the refrigerator. "Sugar?" I asked her.

"Not for me. But Mulroney'll want the works."

While the coffee brewed, I rummaged in the hall closet for lightbulbs. Nothing. I finally tracked down Sarah's stash in the den closet. She had enough spare bulbs to light Del Rio. I wondered why she hadn't replaced the bulb.

Rivera pointed the flashlight while I replaced the bulb and switched it on. "Much better," she said, and nodded approvingly.

I took Sarah's favorite tray—black plastic with the USS *Constitution* inlaid in wood, coral, and mother-of-pearl—from the top of the refrigerator. I poured the coffee into a metal thermos, added four mugs, teaspoons, and the cream and sugar, and started to pick up the tray. The spoons clattered to the floor.

"Here," said Rivera, "let me do that."

I tossed the spoons into the sink, pulled four more from the drawer, and followed Rivera into the living room. In the hall, I paused to turn up the heat. I couldn't seem to get warm. My cell phone rang just as I sat on the couch.

"Sarah's in surgery," Killeen said. "They're estimating it's gonna take four to five hours."

*If she can hang on,* I thought, but refused to say it aloud.

"How long before you can get here?" Killeen asked.

"There's been a complication. The bomb squad's on their way."

Officer Rivera looked up sharply from a photo she was studying. With short, quick movements, she set down her coffee cup on the table beside the rocking chair, stripped off her jacket, and took out her notebook and pen.

I could almost hear Killeen's astonishment: Hit-and-run *and* a bomb? Finally he asked: "Where's the bomb?"

"In the mailbox—though so far it's just a suspicious package. Anyway, La Joie won't be able to question me till they arrive." As I spoke, Officer Rivera scribbled.

"Where are you?"

"In the house. Officer Rivera is keeping me company."

"Your watchdog?"

"In a word."

"Sounds like Detective La Joie's got a lot of sense."

"Whose side are you on?"

"I thought we settled that last summer."

"Well then?"

"Want me there to run interference?"

"Thanks, but no thanks. Just keep me updated on Sarah. Did you reach any of the faculty?"

"Nakata's here already. Marsh and Rudinsky are still at school. They'll stop by on their way home. Couldn't reach Rhys-Evans.

Abrams and Rizzo are in the field . . . And Dean Crouse just walked in. Did you call him?"

"No. One of the neighbors did—Phillip Grover, anthro."

"We've met. Nice guy."

"Yes," I said. "He is." And my eyes did that teary thing again. Killeen must have heard it in my voice. "Call me if you need me," he said.

"I've got you on speed dial."

"Who was that?" Rivera asked. Her notebook had a lilac cover. For some reason that seemed incongruous.

"E. J. Killeen. He works for the department."

"What department?"

I realized she had no idea who Sarah was. "The UCDR geology department. Sarah Barstead, the woman who was hit tonight, the woman who lives here, is the chair of the department. Killeen is at the hospital. He's keeping me posted on Sarah's condition—since the police won't let me leave."

Rivera ignored the dig. "How's she doing?"

"It's in the hands of the surgeons, now."

"And God's." Rivera put away her notebook and, reaching under the cuff of her left sleeve, slid a beaded bracelet over her hand. It was a single decade of rose quartz rosary beads strung on an elastic band; a tiny crucifix dangled from the middle. "Do you mind?" she asked.

"If you pray for her? No. Sarah needs all the help she can get." I didn't tell her Sarah was an atheist.

We were both quiet, then, just the clicking of the beads, the sipping of coffee, the ticking of the clock. Zoey padded down the stairs, sniffed Rivera's pant legs, and accepted the foreign hand on her back. For ten seconds. Then she jumped into my lap, crying softly, like a newborn kitten searching for its mother.

Oh, hell. Why not? I carried Zoey into the kitchen and filled her bowl with Sarah's uneaten chicken enchiladas. Zoey was partial to ethnic food.

In the living room, I refilled my coffee cup, took a pen and yellow legal pad from my briefcase, and created a time line for the past eighteen hours: *@6 a.m.—Dep. Tucson. 10 a.m.—Gas up in Quartzsite . . .*

I paused in the middle of the list to consider whether I should include my phone call to Philo. No. If this fell into someone else's hands, Philo's name would be dragged into the situation. He wouldn't thank me.

The clock struck midnight as I finished. A new day. The day I was supposed to defend my dissertation. The day Sarah decided to live—I hoped.

I don't cry easily. And I never cry if I have an audience. "I'm going to take a shower," I said to Rivera, and sprinted from the room.

# 8

## Mojave Desert, California

Dora Simpson awoke to a darkness lit only by starlight, to a silence broken only by a bitter wind. She was alone. Which day—which night—was it? Where was she? What had happened?

She remembered nothing.

The cold dry air sucked warmth from her face. She couldn't seem to move her limbs. Her wrists and ankles were tied or taped. Her body lay wrapped in a sleeping bag on a hard uneven surface . . . Her own bag? No. It smelled of a man's sweat, a familiar smell that tickled her memory. But she couldn't quite grasp it. Her mind felt as if it were encased in layers of cotton wool. Her head throbbed. Her eyes wouldn't focus. Nausea hit her in waves.

She felt herself drifting off again. Maybe if she slept, just for a little while, she'd be able to remember . . .

PART

'Tis in vain to seek him here that means not to be found.

—William Shakespeare, *Romeo and Juliet*

# 9

## Del Rio, California

Clean of body, organized of mind, and with emotions under control, I emerged twenty minutes later from the steamy guest bathroom to find La Joie and Mulroney drinking coffee. In the gentle light of the living room, Mulroney's platinum hair had a touch of red. His eyebrows and eyelashes, nearly colorless, framed gray eyes five shades paler than my own. The veins in his temple showed through translucent skin that would never tan. Mulroney was meant for night work.

Upstairs, in Sarah's bedroom, Zoey yowled in outrage, tore down the stairs, and leapt into my arms, her claws biting through my black turtleneck and Shetland sweater.

Zoey eyed La Joie suspiciously as I said, "What's going on?"

"The bomb-sniffing dog, I imagine," La Joie said, while Mulroney tried to contain a smile. "A precaution in case the package in the mailbox was just a decoy. I didn't know there was a cat in the house." La Joie drained his coffee cup and set it back on the tray.

"Have they checked the guest bedroom?" I asked him.

"They started with the outside perimeter and then did the first floor—all except the bathroom."

I carefully detached Zoey's claws from my clothing and skin, took her to the guest room where I put her on my bed, and closed the door. "Well?" I said.

Somehow La Joie made the mental leap with me. "It wasn't a bomb. They'll open the box in the lab and call me with the results. It shouldn't be long."

Despite the shower, I felt cold. I made a fire in the grate while we waited. The dry pine tinder crackled and flared, eating quickly into the kindling. I added split oak logs from the stash in the woodbox. The flickering glow, the heat, and the mix of scents grounded and comforted me. For the moment.

A German shepherd/Labrador mix came down the stairs towing his handler. Rivera brought up the rear. "All clear," she said, opening the front door.

"Thanks for coming out," La Joie said to the handler, and watched them disappear into the fog. He turned back to me, notebook at the ready, as if to say, *Coffee break's over. Time to get down to business.* "How did Dr. Barstead look when she came home?"

"Tired and hungry." I described the scene in the kitchen. Then La Joie led me through the rest of the events.

"I've been thinking," I said, tucking stray strands of my damp hair back into the ponytail.

La Joie looked at Mulroney. "Oh?" they said in unison, making it sound more like, *Oh, joy. What now?*

I broached the conclusion I'd reached in the shower: "It couldn't have been an accident. I think it was a crime of passion."

"What makes you say that?"

"After the driver hit Sarah the first time, he or she ran over Sarah's legs."

"He or she?" Mulroney said.

"Dr. Barstead's a lesbian," I said.

Rivera left her position by the front door, picked up a photo of Sarah and Tona Skarstaad, and handed it to La Joie. "A commitment ceremony—or a marriage, depending on where and when it took place."

"Commitment ceremony," I said. "In San Francisco, two years ago . . . Tona died a few months later."

"Has Dr. Barstead had any relationships since then?" La Joie asked.

"Not that I know of. She buried herself in work—and in training for marathons. She'd qualified to run Boston. That's why I said it was a crime of passion. Something to do with love, hatred, or revenge. The driver wasn't content with hitting Sarah. On the off chance that she survived the impact, he or she wanted to make sure Sarah didn't run another marathon."

"So we have to broaden our search to include women—"

"And girls." Mulroney interrupted La Joie before I could. "Some of the UCDR students are under eighteen."

"Okay. Women *or* girls," La Joie conceded. "Anyone who might suffer from unrequited love—or obsession." His cell phone rang. He answered with his name. A series of "Yups" followed, ending with, "Roger. Thanks." He looked down at his scrawled notes, then up at us. "The box contained a message, same lettering as on the outside."

"Which said . . . ?" I prompted, as La Joie hesitated.

"We want to keep it under wraps," he said.

"You think I'd talk to the press?"

La Joie studied the note. "'One, two, and the third in your bosom,'" he read.

Rivera and Mulroney looked at him as if he'd lost his mind.

But I knew. "Were the numbers written out?" I asked.

La Joie punched numbers into his cell phone. "Spell that message for me . . . Got it. Hold on a sec." He looked at me. "Written out."

*"Romeo and Juliet,"* I said. "Copied verbatim. I don't remember which scene."

*"Romeo and Juliet."* La Joie didn't bother to jot it down. Apparently Shakespeare wasn't required reading at whatever military academy he'd attended as a youth. "You're sure?"

"I was fed the classics along with breast milk. My mother's a literature professor at the University of Arizona."

La Joie shrugged, relayed the tip, and slipped his phone back in its holster. He closed his eyes and massaged the muscles at the nape of his neck.

"But was the note meant for Sarah?" I walked as I thought aloud. "Was it just chance that Sarah didn't open the package before she was hit? Or were the box and message meant for the police who'd investigate the accident?" I was speaking so rapidly, I didn't give La Joie a chance to reply. "If the note means that Sarah was the first victim, and the package was meant to be opened by the police, then there will be two more attacks, the last hitting very close to home. If Sarah was the second—or third—victim, then there have already been one or two attacks that haven't been linked to this person."

"There's at least one more option," said Mulroney, when I stopped and took a breath. La Joie and I watched Mulroney pour out the dregs of coffee from the thermos and add cream and sugar to his cup. "If the driver knew you were going to be here, Dr. Mac-Farlane, and Dr. Barstead was the *second* person attacked, then the note could have been meant for you. *You* could be the third person."

"There's a problem with that," I said. "Who would expect me to open a package addressed to Sarah? Even if . . . if—" I stopped, not wanting to follow my thought to completion.

But La Joie was already there. "Besides the police, who else would open Dr. Barstead's mail?"

"Her lawyer. She has written power of attorney. When Tona was dying, she and Sarah both signed limited POAs and DNRs. They wanted their choices in writing. That's another reason I need to get to the hospital—to inform them of Sarah's wishes. And I need to call her lawyer."

I went into Sarah's office and rummaged through her files until I found the one marked "Wills, etc." I used the phone on her desk to call Geraldine Robinson, Sarah's lawyer. She was surprisingly gracious about being awakened after midnight, and asked for Sarah's doctor's number. I located Sarah's medical file, found the physician's name and number, and passed them along. Geraldine said she'd take it from there, which put her in my good book forever. I pocketed both her card and the physician's and went back to the living room.

Mulroney had torn my time line from the tablet and was studying my notes. La Joie had the legal pad. He'd written the Shakespeare quotation at the top of a blank page. He stared at the message as if it were Einstein's theory of relativity. Maybe it was.

"Mind if I keep this?" Mulroney held up my notes.

"To compare the handwriting to the message in the box?"

Color flooded his face, mottling his skin and making the freckles stand out. He looked like a fourth-grade boy caught peeking into the girls' locker room. "To attach to my report," he said, but he shot La Joie a glance. I didn't doubt they planned to lift my fingerprints from the paper before they compared the handwriting.

"Just let me make a copy." I reclaimed the time line and, with Mulroney watching over my shoulder, fed it into the combination copy/fax/answering machine in Sarah's den. I slipped the original into a plastic bag Mulroney held open. He zipped it closed and tucked it into the breast pocket of his jacket.

Back in the living room, La Joie was still mulling over the quotation. "This seems to support your crime-of-passion hypothesis," he said.

"But the hit-and-run was carefully planned, implying premeditation," Mulroney said. "It's an odd mix of passion and intellect. Almost a game. And if the assailant had time to leave one note, he might have left more."

"Clues to his identity?" La Joie looked skeptical.

"Just go with it for a moment," Mulroney said. "If the assailant wanted to play us, where would he have us look?"

I thought for a minute or two. "If he sticks to the *Romeo and Juliet* theme, then there are plenty of quotes to choose from."

La Joie rubbed the back of his neck again. "I don't suppose Dr. Barstead has a copy of *Romeo and Juliet?*"

# 10

In the den, the built-in pine bookcases, dark with age, contained only Sarah's scientific books and journals. The living room held Tona's medical books and a few essay collections, dusty now. I climbed the stairs to Sarah's bedroom, feeling as if I were invading her soul.

It was a large room tucked under the pitched roof. Two dormer windows looked out through the bare branches of the orchard. But tonight, fog blocked the lights of the valley—blocked everything except the crime scene lights on the street below. The illusion was one of total isolation. I preferred this to the activity one floor lower. Here, I could think.

I flipped on the overhead light. The bedroom looked as if Sarah had just dashed out for an early morning run. A quilt—an Irish Chain pattern in shades of teal, cream, pale aquamarine, and amethyst—half-covered the bed's rumpled sheets. I'd pieced the top before returning to school for my doctorate, and quilted it in hours snatched from work or sleep over the following two years. It had been my "wedding" present for Sarah and Tona. The colors matched those in the Tiffany-style stained-glass bedside lamps Sarah had given Tona. I ran my hand over the quilt, felt the four-leaf clover stitching that held the layers together. Despite my good wishes, it hadn't brought luck to either of them.

Tona had covered the window-seat cushions with teal fabric to match the quilt. Sometimes, Sarah told me once, Tona sat here, hour after hour, staring out across the valley—too depressed to speak, too depressed to fight the cancer, just waiting for the end. Which proved, Sarah said, shaking her head, that doctors make the worst patients.

I shook myself out of my reverie. Sarah was fighting right now. She was still alive, or I'd have heard from Killeen. I needed to be there.

I glanced at the titles on the bookshelf to the right of the door— old whodunits, yellowed with age, alphabetically arranged: Allingham, Chandler, Christie, Hammett, Marsh, Sayers, Stout. Only two authors from the last twenty years—Claire McNab and Laurie

R. King. No Shakespeare. But I found a well-thumbed copy of *Bartlett's Familiar Quotations*. I tucked it under my arm, reached for the light switch, paused.

On top of the bookshelf, next to a photo of Tona, was one I'd taken in the mountains west of Pair-a-Dice, Nevada, nearly two years ago. I picked it up. Geoff, Sarah, Peter Snavely, Dai Rhys-Evans, Janet Nakata, Rudy Rudinsky, and a couple of under-grads—Bernie Venable and Deirdre "Dee" Marsland—were leaning against tilted beds of Permian limestone and dolomite. Everyone was smiling. Even Geoff. He had his arm draped casually across Dee's shoulders. I remembered the day. Geoff and I weren't a couple then. I'd led the trip through my field area. We'd visited Geoff's the day before. Geoff had taken a picture of the group with my camera; I'd taken one with his.

I started to set it down, then looked again. "Dear God," I said. I switched off the light and carried the photo downstairs. La Joie was on a cell phone—*my* cell phone.

"Killeen," he said, handing it to me. "I introduced myself."

"It's me," I said to Killeen, and held my breath, waiting for the bad news.

"The internal damage is more extensive than they thought," Killeen said. "Surgery's going to take maybe twelve more hours. Nakata's still here. Rudinsky and Marsh stopped by and left again. They want us to call them if anything happens."

"I'll be there as soon as they'll let me leave," I said, and punched *end*.

"What's that?" La Joie asked, pointing to the photograph in my hands.

"A hunch. I may be way off base." I gave him the photo, naming each face in turn.

"I don't see anything odd," he said.

"Of that small band of merry geologists, one—Peter Snavely—is dead. His car went off the road near Crestline. Two—Bernie and Geoff—are missing, and may be dead. And a fourth—Sarah—is in critical condition. What are the odds?"

"About the same as your being able to recognize a random quote, I imagine. But that doesn't make you right—or wrong," said La Joie. "I'll check Dr. Snavely's accident report. And I'd like to borrow the photo. I'll return it tomorrow."

"Fine," I said.

La Joie bagged the photo and labeled it. When he finished, I handed him the *Bartlett's*. "Not the complete play, but these excerpts may help."

Mulroney came in from the kitchen as La Joie opened the "Index of Authors," then flipped through Will's section till he found *Romeo and Juliet.* I looked over his right shoulder, Mulroney over his left. Mulroney pointed to the second entry: "A pair of star-crossed lovers." La Joie nodded but didn't look at me. I didn't volunteer that there was a quicker way to search for the quotation in the message. That would have been overkill. But he found it soon enough, in Act II, scene iv. Word for word, as I'd said.

Smiling, I watched La Joie move his finger back up the page till it stopped on "Lady, by yonder blessèd moon I sweare / That tips with silver all these fruit-tree tops."

"Do me a favor, Mulroney," said La Joie.

"You want me to search all those trees in the dark?" Mulroney asked.

"Rivera will help. Take a camera. If you find something, call me. And check the rosebushes while you're at it."

"Excuse me?"

"'What's in a name? That which we call a rose / By any other name would smell as sweet,'" La Joie read, pointing to the page.

"There's a climbing rosebush out back," I offered.

"You think the bad guy'll give us his name?" Mulroney said, closing the back door with authority.

La Joie turned back to me. "What now?"

I pointed to another line in Act II: "For stony limits cannot hold love out."

"The entire house is built of stone!" La Joie said.

"But at least it's well lit," I said in a reasonable tone.

He gave me a black look.

Outside, there was a shout. I went to the bedroom to grab my coat and scarf. Zoey was curled up in the soft, plaid-flannel nest. She didn't appreciate the disruption and told me so before streaking out through the open door.

"No." La Joie blocked the door. "We'll wait."

I shed my coat again and sat on the sofa.

"Did you see anything suspicious when you arrived here?" he asked.

"No. The light over the back door was out, which meant it was dark as sin back there. I replaced the bulb when Officer Rivera came back with me."

"What did you do with the used bulb?"

"Put it in the kitchen trash."

He was already moving, pulling on plastic gloves. "Cupboard

to the left of the sink," I called. I heard the squeak of the cupboard door, the rustle of paper. No plastic garbage bags for environmentally conscious Sarah. The back door opened. Mulroney and Rivera spoke to La Joie. They stayed in the kitchen. I heard the water running in the sink, followed by the sound of paper towels being torn. La Joie joined me in the living room. He carried the bulb in a small brown paper bag. "Doesn't sound like it's burned out," he said, shaking the bag near his ear. "Did you check it?"

"No. I just toggled the light switch a couple of times." I picked up my copy of the time line and read: "*7:15 p.m.—Arrive Sarah's house (back porch light out) . . . @11:35—come inside Sarah's house with Officer Rivera; make coffee; replace back porch bulb . . .'*"

"So one of two things happened," La Joie said. "The attacker disabled the bulb before 7:15. Or the bulb burned out or loosened on its own. If the former, then the assailant probably also placed the package in the mailbox before you got here."

"That might have happened later," Mulroney said from the kitchen doorway. His shoes were muddy. He had leaves and twigs in his hair. "The actions at the house, which took advantage of the darkened yard, could have been independent of what happened on the street."

"'Actions'?" I stressed the plural. Apparently there was more than a burned out bulb to worry about. "You found something?"

"One under the climbing rosebush," he said. "Another in a notch of a lemon tree. And a third in an old stone barbecue pit with a spit big enough to roast a whole goat. All packages identical to the one in the mailbox."

"You think they could have been put there while I was snoozing on the couch?" I said. "Scary thought." I picked up *Bartlett's* again. Three pairs of eyes watched as I searched for a relevant quotation. "It could be 'One fire burns out another's burning, / One pain is lessoned by another's anguish,'" I said. "Or maybe something else."

"Call back the dog," La Joie said to Mulroney. To me he said, "You didn't hear anything?"

"I'm normally a light sleeper, but I was exhausted. Zoey was purring on my lap. I had a CD on."

"What CD?" La Joie asked.

"Jobim's *Wave*."

La Joie went over to the CD player and checked. It's the little things that catch people up, I thought. "Okay," he said.

Though I was dying to know what messages, if any, those packages contained, the search could take hours. In the meantime, Sarah was in surgery. I needed to get to the hospital, where Nakata would be waiting. And Killeen. I picked up my coat and scarf from the couch, my purse from the floor where I'd left it nearly six hours ago. "You don't need me here while the dog searches. May I go now?" But La Joie didn't answer. He was staring at the photo again. "What is it?" I said.

La Joie fixed me with that direct, assessing gaze. "The bad guy kindly stashed every clue we need to solve this case in or around this house," he said.

"Convenient," said Mulroney from the kitchen doorway.

La Joie nodded. "Officer Rivera will drive you to the hospital and stay with you tonight," he said to me. "We'll play tomorrow by ear." He opened the front door. Rivera was already on the porch. She'd removed any trace of mud from her shoes, I noticed. "Lose Ms. MacFarlane," he said to Rivera, "and I'll have your badge."

"Won't happen," she said. As she closed the door gently behind us, I saw La Joie putting the *Bartlett's* in a large paper bag.

Rivera and I walked in silence down the hill and past the crime scene to her cruiser. I avoided looking at the spot where Sarah'd been struck. Instead, I pictured her running up the steep mountain road. *Think positive thoughts, Frankie. Positive thoughts.*

In the squad car, I scrolled through my cell's address book, wondering if La Joie had made notes of my frequently called numbers while I was upstairs. Probably. I punched Killeen's number.

"I'm on my way," I said. "Be there in ten." I didn't give him a chance to reply.

It was then, as the silence flowed over me, broken only by the occasional crackle of the radio, that I realized I was somewhere near the top of La Joie and Mulroney's suspect list: no apparent motive, sketchy on means, but loads of inside knowledge and opportunity . . . and an uncanny aptitude for recalling lines from relevant Shakespearean tragedies. It was my word against a nameless specter.

So why had La Joie let me go so easily?

# 11

## University Hospital
Del Rio, California
Tuesday, December 14, 1:35 a.m.

The glass doors of UCDR University Hospital opened automatically, closing behind us with a grating noise and shutting out the wail of an arriving ambulance. In the foyer, white snowflakes cut from tissue paper dotted the redbrick walls. In one corner stood a twelve-foot Douglas fir, decorated with blue lights, blue-glass ornaments, and a dreidel or two—just for political correctness. Instrumental Christmas carols played softly through speakers. Christmas lights twinkled on the arch above the deserted information desk. No staff at the patient admittance desk, either. Officer Rivera and I continued straight past the bank of elevators and through the double doors. Three corridors branched off. My mind couldn't seem to decipher the signs hanging from the ceiling.

At the best of times, hospitals have that effect on me. They give form and substance to nebulous dread, and highlight the thin line between life and nonlife. My only experiences with them have been painful. I respected, but couldn't empathize with, my brother Jamie's choosing to spend his days and nights in settings like this. I needed rock and air, sun and water and distances around me.

"This way," Rivera said.

I followed her into the labyrinth of gray-tiled corridors, through four sets of double doors, to the small surgical waiting room. The floor was of slate blue and white tiles. Charcoal chairs alternated with the occasional love seat—nothing long enough to stretch out on. Inhospitable signs on the wall told us that food and drink were not allowed. They weren't encouraging friends and family members to stick around.

Dr. Janet "Nono" Nakata, the department's igneous and metamorphic petrologist, sat in a corner chair, briefcase on the adjoining end table, laptop computer open on her knees. The lamplight emphasized the gray in her very short, spiky hair and her pitted, coarse-textured skin. She didn't look up. I gave her thirty seconds, then cleared my throat. She raised her head, but it took another few heartbeats for her mind to return from whatever stratum she was in and focus on me.

"Frankie," she said, as if expecting someone else. Her voice tones were soft and pitched higher than my own. "You look like hell."

Nono Nakata looked the same as always—a youthful sixtyish, as square of face and body as a carved alabaster chess piece. A rook, I decided. Her nickname, bestowed during her graduate school years at Berkeley, derived from her habit of contradicting colleagues and students. Also from her no-nonsense approach to life and teaching.

"I feel like the bottom of a latrine," I said, offering my hand. Nakata gave it a perfunctory shake. She wasn't the hugging type.

I waved in the general direction of where Rivera stood, guarding the door. "Officer Rivera, Dr. Janet Nakata." Nakata glanced over and nodded. Rivera remained impassive. "How's Sarah doing?" I asked Nono, taking a seat across from her.

"Still in surgery. No word yet. They suggested Killeen and I go home, but we wanted to wait for you."

"I'll see what I can find out," said Rivera. "Don't go anywhere, Dr. MacFarlane."

The doors closed noisily behind her. "Is she protection or escort?" Nakata asked.

"A little of both," I said. "Killeen's in the cafeteria?" E. J. Killeen's massive body was a furnace that needed stoking at regular intervals.

"Where else?" Nakata looked at the clock on the wall. "He'll be back soon. Just give me a minute to finish this section, and I'll be able to talk." She started typing again. Nothing threw Janet Nakata. Not even this crisis. Knowing her background, I understood why.

Nakata was born at Manzanar, the relocation camp in California where her parents were interned during World War II. She'd arrived on New Year's Day, while the wind whistled down from the top of Mount Williamson, carrying snow that blanketed the fifteen-by-twenty-foot pine and tar-paper barracks assigned to her family. She was named for the month she was born. And for the two-headed god Janus, who looks both forward and backward at the same time—as the family did, during the long days at Manzanar. Her parents came to America via Hawaii at the height of the Depression. Her father had been a chemist in Japan. He became a gardener in Pasadena . . . until Pearl Harbor was attacked. Four months later they were in a relocation camp in the Owens Valley. After their release from Manzanar, they went back to Hawaii. So Nakata's first mountains were the bare granite shoulders of the Sierra Nevada; her second, the volcanic craters of the Big Island.

Nono Nakata studied igneous rocks, such as granite and basalt, and metamorphic rocks that had "changed form" when subjected to elevated pressures and/or temperatures. She'd studied Tertiary vulcanism in the Great Basin for her doctorate, Hawaiian island vulcanism for her post-doc. Since coming to UCDR, she'd worked with Rudy Rudinsky on the volcanics of the East Pacific Rise and the Russian Kamchatka Peninsula. She and Rudy detested each other. I tried not to take sides.

Three minutes later Nakata saved her work to her portable USB thumb drive and closed down the laptop.

"What are you working on?" I asked.

"Notes for a class next quarter," she said, slipping the computer into her briefcase. "I'm asking the students to read and comment on some of the classic papers of the last century or so—Bowen, Eskola, Lindgren, Buerger. I'll send you my notes when I'm finished, if you'd like."

"That's very generous, Nono. I'd appreciate it." It seemed odd to be discussing a mundane subject while Sarah was fighting for her life a short distance away. But I didn't know what else to do. The room was so quiet I could hear the clock ticking on the wall, an eternity within each second. "How's Simon?" I asked, to drown out the sound of the clock.

"Same as always," Nono said. "Lost in space."

Nakata was married to a tall, skinny, theoretical mathematician. Opposites attract. They'd met at MIT, where Nono had done a post-doc. It always surprised me that Simon came down to earth long enough for sex, but they'd produced a son who was currently at Oxford. Simon taught only graduate level courses at UCDR. The math department tried giving him undergrad courses, but he couldn't communicate with the students. He lost them the first day. I think the university would have let him go if he didn't bring in oodles of grant money to study fractal geometry patterns.

The sum total of my knowledge of fractal geometry had to do with pineapple "eyes," nautilus whorls, and cactus spines—practical knowledge. So at the rare social functions Simon attended, I steered the conversation in that direction and let him ramble. He didn't seem to remember we'd had the same conversation at least a dozen times before—or he was too polite to mention that I must be a dolt for not retaining the information.

Nakata stood, stretched, and resumed her seat. "We need to talk about your dissertation defense."

"You want to cancel it?"

"No, no. Maybe postpone it." She saw the look on my face. "Just a day or so, if you can stick around."

I didn't have much choice. "Who's taking Sarah's place?"

"Rudinsky."

A groan slipped out before I could stop it. Rudinsky was my nemesis as well as hers.

"I know," Nakata said. "But he's available."

"There's no one else?"

"We haven't yet replaced Snavely. Marsh hasn't been to your field area. The same can be said for Abrams and Rizzo. Besides, the geophysicists are all in the field—though Rizzo might make it back in time. The good news is that Rudinsky doesn't want to postpone—even till tomorrow afternoon. Says he can read the manuscript in two hours. He left here an hour ago to get my copy."

"Did Dai weigh in?" David "Dai" Rhys-Evans, our Welsh structural geologist, was the third member of my committee. Bearded, barrel-chested, short-legged Dai reminded me of Clarence King, the first director of the U.S. Geological Survey. Like King, he enjoyed mountaineering in his spare time. Dai had an exquisite collection of rock and mineral specimens and did a little side business in precious stones. He also talked to trees and rocks.

"He's not answering his cell phone. Tara says he's working down in the rock lab tonight—has a new shipment of sugilite." Tara Rhys-Evans was Dai's Nepalese wife. "He's making book ends and coasters as Christmas presents for the family back home. He may not be able to hear his cell above the saws."

Just then Nakata's own cell phone played Beethoven's "Ode to Joy." It was Rudy. "Did you check the rock lab?" Janet said. "Uh-huh. No, no. I'll try his cell again." There was a long pause. "Okay," she said. "Tomorrow at ten." Her face wore a resigned look when she ended the call. I waited as she punched in Dai's number. She reached the voice-mail box and left a message.

"Dai wasn't at the lab?" I said.

"Rudy said the door was closed and locked. No lights or noise."

"He's probably on the way home and turned off his phone."
She looked at her watch. "I'll let him sleep. He'll be in at six, as usual. And Tara will give him the news in the morning." She looked at me. "You do have a vote, you know, Frankie. Do you want to go ahead with the defense, or postpone it until Sarah's out of the woods?"

What did I want? My Tucson job was contingent on completing my degree. Even if Sarah pulled through, she'd be recuperating for a long time. That would mean another trip to Del Rio. I didn't want to wait. I wanted my life back.

I'd eaten/lived/slept/dreamed this project for four years. I wanted to finish what I'd started. I wanted to stand up before my committee, recount the story I'd deciphered from clues in the rocks, and answer their questions. At this moment, I knew more about that patch of earth than anyone else in the world—including Geoff, wherever he was. I let my mind drift there for a moment. Geoff and I had shared an office at UCDR, discussions on the outcrop, a bed, and, for a few months, a future together. But because he stole my data, the dissertation work had left an ugly taste in my mouth. Getting those three signatures on my magnum opus would sever forever my emotional and mental ties with Geoff and with the past. I was ready. I'd functioned on little sleep before. I could rest later.

"You name the time, I'll be there with bells on," I said to Nakata.

"That's the spirit," said Nakata. "But I'll try to postpone it till one. That'll give Rudinsky time to read it, and you time to get a few hours' sleep. And we'll have to tamp down the usual bash."

And hope the celebration didn't turn into a wake for Sarah.

# 12

Officer Rivera returned, carrying a cup of coffee. "No word yet," she said. Taking a seat under the No Food or Drink Allowed sign, she pulled the lid off the cup and took a sip. The smell of coffee turned my stomach.

"Is there a watercooler?" I asked.

"Around the corner," Rivera said.

I left her there, listening to Nakata on the phone leaving voicemail messages on the office phones of Rhys-Evans, Rudinsky, the dean, and a few other faculty members. The drinking fountain was thirty steps down a white-painted corridor that led to the surgical wing. The fountain made a humming sound, loud in the quiet hallway. It was built for children or people in wheelchairs. Bending down, I closed my eyes and drank deeply. My body felt dehydrated. I couldn't seem to get enough.

I sensed a presence behind me. Something substantial. Straightening, I stepped to the left and turned, my body tense. It had been that kind of night.

"Hey, Frankie," said Killeen.

I hadn't heard him come in. Killeen always walked softly. But he didn't need to carry a big stick—or a gun—though he sometimes did. And he knew how to use both.

I tried to smile. The muscles had forgotten how. My face felt as if it were cracking. Killeen enveloped me in a bear hug. I felt my tension dissipate, leaving me calm and clearheaded.

Rivera stepped into the corridor as Killeen let me go. Her hand rested casually on her hip, just above the gun. I introduced them. She nodded and disappeared around the corner.

"She's detailed to watch me. She'll be nervous as long as I'm out of sight," I said.

Killeen smiled. "Lead on, MacFarlane." It was an old joke between us.

"Macduff."

"Whatever," he said amiably, and followed me back to the waiting room.

Nakata was still on the phone. Killeen settled his massive frame on one of the love seats. He was shorter than I by four or five inches, but broad as a beehive fireplace. None of the bulk was fat. Rivera studied him as if she were memorizing his features for a future report. Or maybe it was his bizarre appearance that drew her eyes. Looking at him, as if for the first time, I saw what Rivera saw: rust-colored wiry hair cropped close to his light brown skin; slightly protuberant dark olive eyes in a misshapen face. Broken nose. Lobeless right ear. Scar from an old burn curving down in front of his right ear to his neck. Rivera would have stared harder if Sylvie, his significant other, were here with him. She was as pale and blonde and delicate as he was dark and solid. Beauty and the Beast. But this beast hadn't turned into a handsome prince—at least not on the outside. Sylvie had looked beyond the ugliness. She was that rare person who sees past facades.

"How are Sylvie and Tommy?" I asked. Tommy was Sylvie's four-year-old son.

"Tommy started preschool, but he was so far ahead in basic skills that we found a prekindergarten class for him. He loves having other kids to play with. Sylvie's working part-time at the university and taking a couple of courses. She wants to teach."

"It's working out then."

He smiled. "You could say that. We're getting married on Saturday." He looked around the sterile waiting room. "Not the best time or place for an announcement, but there it is. We waited till you could be here. It'll be just the three of us—plus Sylvie's boss and you—if you can stay."

I leaned over and touched his hand. "I wouldn't miss it."

All of a sudden, despite what was happening in surgery, the night seemed brighter.

"How's the job going?" I asked.

"Interesting. Fun. I'm learning a lot. Sylvie, Tommy, and I have gone on several field trips. I'm in demand. I can carry a lot of rocks, as you recall. I helped clear overburden from a fossil quarry in the Mojave a couple of weeks ago." Killeen shifted on the love seat. It was barely large enough for him. "It's been a good time for all of us. But we're planning to move to Tucson over Christmas break."

It was the best news I'd heard all day. "You've seen the light?"

"I don't know about that, but I liked what I saw of Arizona when I was stationed at Fort Huachuca. We thought we'd try Tucson. Smog's bad here, and it's too damn crowded. Better to move now than later. We want Tommy settled before kindergarten starts. And Sylvie can go to school there just as easily."

"Have you thought of putting your intelligence training to use?"

"You got an idea?"

"A friend—a private investigator—could use the help. His background's similar to yours."

"How good a friend?" Killeen's grin transformed his face from downright ugly to almost homely.

I wasn't about to go there with Rivera watching. But my silence and answering smile said, *Let's save it for later.*

Killeen nodded, then turned serious again. "With Sarah incapacitated, what happens to your defense? Do they postpone it?"

"Just till one o'clock—if Rudinsky agrees." I looked at Nakata. "That's what Nono's trying to set up now."

Nakata closed the phone and slipped it back into the case clipped to her belt. "I'm going to go rattle a few cages and see if I can find out anything about Sarah."

But just as Nakata stood up, we heard quiet footsteps in the corridor. A young doctor in surgical garb appeared. A paper cap covered his hair. He wore a tiny silver cross in one pierced ear. His face gave nothing away as he looked at our small group. "You're Dr. Barstead's family?"

Sarah was an only child, single, orphaned, and childless. We were her family. "Yes," I said, before Nakata could deny it.

"We've managed to stop the internal bleeding, but the damage is extensive. The repairs will take another ten hours, at least. But for now, she's holding her own." He saw the exhaustion on our faces. "Go home. If you leave me your numbers, I'll call when we have news."

He gave us his business card: Nolan Tensing, MD. I scribbled my cell number on my business card and handed it to him. Nakata and Killeen followed suit. So did Rivera. This was a police case.

"Anything else we can do?" I asked Tensing.

"Pray," he said, and left as quietly as he'd come.

"I'll be taking the morning off," Killeen said to Nakata. "Wedding preparations. But I'll be at the department by noon to help Frankie set up."

"No problem," Nakata said, collecting her briefcase.

In the lobby, I hugged Killeen. "My best to Sylvie and Tommy," I said. "And tell her I'm delighted with your news."

Rivera and I climbed into the police cruiser parked in the no parking zone at the main entrance. While Rivera reported in, I watched Killeen and Nakata walk toward the visitors lot. Half of me felt bereft. The other half wanted desperately to be alone. It wasn't going to happen.

Back at Sarah's house, Officer Rivera made herself comfy on the couch. La Joie and Mulroney were just finishing up. Nothing more outside. The packages were at the lab. Again, not bombs. Again, messages from *Romeo and Juliet*. But not all the messages were included in *Bartlett's Quotations* . . . My brain couldn't process the new information. I was suffering from sensory overload.

"And there was this," said La Joie. He handed me a smashed beige plastic rock in a closed plastic bag.

"Uncle," I said.

"It's a motion sensor—from a kid's spy kit. It's supposed to beep whenever something moves within six feet of it."

"Okay," I handed it back.

"Crime scene unit found it by the mailbox."

"You think a beeping rock distracted Sarah?"

"I think she would have paused to find the source of the sound. It's only natural."

"Paused just long enough to be struck, you mean."

"Yes," said La Joie. Mulroney nodded eagerly, as if this had been his idea.

"That's diabolical," I said.

"But very simple," said Mulroney. "The best plans are simple."

"It couldn't have been there all evening," I said. "People walking their dogs would have heard it. The driver would have to have placed it there after Sarah went up the driveway."

"Right," said La Joie. "Plan A hinged on her coming back down the driveway. There must have been a Plan B, as well."

"I offered to get the mail for her," I said. "But Sarah wanted a little exercise."

"I wonder if he would have struck you, instead." La Joie put the fake rock into a carton with other little paper and plastic bags. "Puts a different light on things."

"I can't deal with this tonight." I picked up my briefcase.

"We'll talk tomorrow," La Joie promised.

Tired, but too keyed up to sleep, I carried my briefcase into

Sarah's office, set it beside her desk, and pulled out three copies of the dissertation. Four years' worth of research and work. Three hundred and seventeen pages of text, figures, and photographs, plus colored geologic maps, cross sections, paleogeographic reconstructions, measured sections. All it needed was the imprimatur of three signatures.

I took out my thumb drive, slipped it into Sarah's computer port, and changed the title page on the dissertation text to reflect the new lineup of professors. I revised the acknowledgments section to comment on why Sarah's signature wasn't on the front page. Lastly, I added a dedication to Sarah Barstead. Would she live to read it?

The printer spit out the new pages. As I was replacing the old ones in the three copies, Rivera knocked on the door and handed me a cup of hot cocoa. It was an unexpected kindness. I felt my emotional walls start to crumble.

"They're gone," Rivera said. "I'll be staying the night."

I nodded, unable to speak. I put the dissertation copies away, retrieved the thumb drive, turned off the computer, straightened up Sarah's desk, and turned off the light. Carrying my cocoa and briefcase, I sought the refuge of the guest room. Zoey lay curled in the center of the afghan that covered the double bed. Tona had crocheted it. When I pulled back the covers, Zoey snorted, jumped down, and deserted me. The sheets were freshly laundered and smelled of lavender. I stripped quickly, donned a cotton nightshift, and slid my weary body between the sheets. Snuggling down, I felt something hard under the pillow. A box.

"Officer Rivera?" I called. My voice sounded raspy. "Would you come in here a minute, please?"

"Something wrong?" Officer Rivera asked from the doorway.

"There's a box under the pillow," I said.

It couldn't be a bomb. We both knew that. The dog had been all through the house. Still, Officer Rivera was cautious as she lifted the pillow. Beneath was a present, tied with a silver ribbon. The card bore my name: Dr. Francisca MacFarlane. The Dr. was underlined. Sarah's writing. Rivera handed it to me.

*Dear Frankie,*

*Tona asked me to give this to you after your defense was over. It was her way of saying thanks for all the help in those last months—and congratulations for all you've achieved.*

*I bought it for her in Coober Pedie ten years ago, after I finished the Australian Trek. We both thought it would suit you.*

I didn't wait to open the box. I no longer felt sure that the sun would rise, that my defense would take place.

It was an opal pendant and earrings, set in white gold. When I lifted the pendant from its satin bed, the colors caught the light from the bedside lamp. I heard Rivera's sharp intake of breath.

"What is it?" she said.

"Black opal. And pearl." The natural outline of the pendant was a woman's form, like the most ancient figurines unearthed in Eurasia. Gaea. First Woman, in aboriginal creation stories. She was holding up a large dark gray pearl, like the new moon, above her head. The matching opal earrings were simple oval cabochons that dangled from pearl studs. Tona was wearing the set in their commitment photo, the one in the living room. She'd been wearing the pendant the last time I'd seen her, the day she died.

"It's beautiful. Try it on," Rivera said. Her voice held no covetous note. Before I could say no, she'd undone the clasp and fastened it around my neck. "It does suit you. The pearl matches the color of your eyes. You should wear it tomorrow."

"I don't know," I said, taking off the pendant and returning it to its black satin bed. "I don't know."

"I think Dr. Barstead would like to know you were wearing her gift. It'd be like she was there. Now, get some sleep. I'll wake you at eight."

When I looked up to thank her, the door was closed.

*It's a luxury in this world to be protected while we sleep,* I thought as I slid between the sheets. We haven't evolved much from the ages we walked the savanna with the other apes or decorated cave walls in the Pyrenees . . . or carved "Venus" figurines on midwinter nights.

Safety reminded me of Philo. It was six thirty in DC. I should call him before he left for Capitol Hill. But I felt myself drifting. Later, I thought, I'll do it later . . .

# 13

## Cady Mountains

Mojave Desert, California
Tuesday, December 14, 4:30 a.m.

A coyote's howl woke Dora Simpson.

She was still alone. The nausea had subsided, but now she was aware of a great thirst. Feeling was returning little by little to her bound limbs.

A fat quarter moon hung in the western sky. What time was it?

Keeping track of time was vital. She couldn't get to her pocket watch, but the moon, she remembered, would have risen at nine. It must be around four in the morning. But which morning?

Tuesday. If it were Wednesday, she'd be hungrier, thirstier. So she'd had her last insulin injection about fourteen hours ago. She didn't remember having eaten anything since, so her biochemistry was okay. For now. But ketoacidosis—her body breaking down its own proteins—could be a problem before long.

Her eyes were focusing better. Black shadows, thrown by the ridges, turned the tilted conglomerate beds the color of bleached bones. She recognized the outcrop. She was lying on the sand at the mouth of Baxter Wash. How did she get here?

She went back to the last clear images and struggled to fit them into a pattern . . . Picking up her tools on the outcrop. Starting down the small tributary canyon. The face on the ridge above her . . . Jed. Jed Strong. He'd scared her. His smile said he'd enjoyed scaring her.

He'd dropped down into the ravine and carried her bucket back to camp. She smelled beef stew as they neared her campsite. A Dutch oven was buried in the coals of a campfire. He was leaving in the morning, he said. He just wanted to have a celebratory meal with her. He was wearing excitement like a second skin.

Jed seemed vulnerable and eager. His enthusiasm was contagious. He'd finished photographing and measuring the archaic rock alignments he'd shown her. He said he just needed to share the news with someone who'd understand.

Dora was all packed, except for her field gear. She needed to reach Del Rio where her next insulin shipment was waiting. She'd brought extra insulin into the field, but she'd used much more than she'd planned. Now she was cutting it close—only one dose was left in her insulin-delivery "pen." But she agreed to stay for thirty minutes. She'd share his meal and have just half a glass of wine. She'd been on insulin so long that she knew what her body could and couldn't tolerate—and how to compensate. She'd still be back in Del Rio by five thirty—six at the latest.

Dora loaded her gear in the back of the truck, tested her blood sugar, and gave herself an injection. But what had happened next?

She'd taken a picture of Jed at the fire. Jed, intent on pouring the wine, didn't notice. Then she must have eaten—though Dora's memory was hazy. Afterward, wanting to pee before she started home, she'd walked around the pink finger of the ashflow tuff at the entrance to the canyon. She felt uncoordinated, woozy. Something was wrong. Seriously wrong. Had she injected herself with too much insulin? Was she hypoglycemic? While she could still function, she tested her blood. It was okay. But her sight blurred. She placed her used insulin pen, GPS unit, cell phone, and camera in the shadow of the outcrop, where someone would find them—if they were looking.

She remembered stumbling back to the truck, pulling the insulin case and tester from her pocket, and putting them in her purse. The fire was out. The campsite was clean. She fell. She couldn't move her limbs. Jed called her name. She couldn't answer. That was all she remembered.

Jed must have left her here. But why? Where was he? Would he come back for her? What if he didn't come back?

Dora knew the answer to the last question. She might die before she could be rescued . . . unless she could get away while she was still able to function.

Her left arm was asleep. She'd been lying on that side. She rolled to her back. If she could just work her bound hands under her buttocks and then around her legs and feet.

Dora pulled her knees to her chest. Her wrists were bound with some soft material that nonetheless cut into her flesh as she curled her body into a ball and wriggled her buttocks through the circle of her arms—one cheek, then the other. For the first time, she was glad that she was small and fine-boned, that she'd inherited her mother's long arms—arms that had battered Dora from frustration, drunken rage, or just because . . . arms that had never held her with love. Now she blessed her mother's genes. She blessed the fact that she was as slim as she'd been at fifteen, when she'd gotten pregnant with Annie . . . Annie, who was now twenty-two and with a child of her own on the way.

Dora used her teeth to work on the soft cotton rope that bound her wrists. This was going to take a while. She heard muted sounds from the ridge above. Hooves on desert pavement. More than one animal.

The wild burros of the Mojave? They hadn't been reported in the Cadys—at least as far as she knew. And on a ridgetop? No. They'd follow the washes to the water and grass in Afton Canyon.

The hoofbeats came closer. No one but Jed knew she was here.

He'd come back.

# 14

Dora stayed limp—eyes closed, breathing regular—as she was lifted in the sleeping bag and slung like a sack of grain over an animal's back. She needed time to plan. Straps crisscrossed her back to hold her in place. Only when they were moving did she peek. Jed, astride one burro, led hers.

They scrambled over the ridge, turned south, and crossed a series of small washes. They covered a mile, maybe two. The jolting pace made her bladder ache. The trip seemed to take forever. They entered a small canyon so narrow her head and feet brushed the walls. The level trail turned back on itself again and again, as if they'd entered a maze. It was all she could do not to swear when her head glanced off a jutting outcrop. And then it was over. The trail ended in a space wide enough for the burros to stand side by side without touching.

"Sorry about that," Jed said, removing the straps and putting Dora down on the sand.

So he knew she was awake. Dora opened her eyes. Steep rock walls led to a low mesa above. The rocks were different here, though they were capped by the same old alluvial unit, leached by the moonlight.

Jed ran a hand over her hair, touched the tender spot. She winced and jerked away.

"I'll be back in a minute," he said, and led the burros around a corner further up the wash.

One of the burros brayed. The other answered. Jed must not be worried about someone hearing, Dora concluded, as she worked at the rope that bound her ankles. If she could just get her feet free . . .

Jed was behind her. He picked her up, tossed her sleeping-bag cocoon over his shoulder, and strode toward the black wall of rock at the side of the canyon. Despite the darkness, he found the base of a narrow trail. It slanted gently up toward the top of the mesa. Jed settled her weight more evenly across his shoulders, then took the trail at a rapid pace. His breathing grew more labored, but he didn't stop until he reached a shelf just below the top of the mesa. There he pushed aside a net curtain. The stiff material brushed Dora's neck like a rough caress as Jed stepped into a walled-off recess in the cliff.

He set her down on a foam pad against the wall and lit a candle. The room was roughly circular, maybe nine feet across. A fire pit lay to the right of the opening.

Jed unbuckled his belt. The strap of Dora's leather purse slipped off his belt. The purse landed with a thud on the floor. Jed kicked it out of the way.

Dora tensed. Her head touched the wall. Inside, fear fought with confusion and anger. She tamped them down. She had to stay clearheaded, focused. She tried to gauge his mood. Should she fight him, or placate him?

"Relax," he said, rebuckling his belt and stepping back. "I didn't rape you when I had the chance. That's not why you're here."

"Where's *here*?" The question came out in a raw whisper.

"I call it Taliesin Mojave," Jed said. "Do you like it?" She didn't answer. "You don't know Frank Lloyd Wright?" he said.

"Not intimately. Why did you drug me, Jed? Why am I here?"

He shrugged. Crouching down, he unzipped the sleeping bag, staring for a moment at the bound hands that were now in front of her. "Getting ready to run?"

Without waiting for a reply, he shackled her right ankle to a steel peg buried in the floor. Only then did he untie her hands and feet. "Take off your boots."

Dora's fingers struggled with the double knots in the laces. She held up her middle finger. A Band-Aid covered the tip. "What happened?"

"I borrowed a few drops of your blood," Jed said. He finished undoing the laces, tugged off her boots, tied them together, and hung them around his neck. "Don't worry. I put antibiotic ointment on it," he said, standing up.

"That's reassuring."

The air was frigid. Jed made no move to light a fire, though a woodpile stood near the hearth. Dora crawled back inside the sleeping bag. The chain attached to the shackle prevented the bag from being zipped. "I'm cold," she said.

Jed took a striped Hudson Bay blanket from a chest near her

feet. Crouching down, he tucked it in around her. "You can scream if you want," he said. "There's no one for miles in any direction."

"They'll search for me," Dora said.

"I know. But not yet," he said. "Not till this afternoon."

"We have a problem."

"You do. I don't."

"I'm diabetic. Type I."

"So?"

She digested this for a moment. "You mean, whether I live or die doesn't matter to you?"

Jed gave her an odd, penetrating look. "We all have to die sometime."

"Well, unless you want me to starve to death in the meantime, I'll need insulin injections and my testing equipment whenever I eat," she said. "I used up my last insulin just before you . . . What did you give me?"

"Rohypnol."

*A date-rape drug,* Dora thought. Of course. He'd put it in her wine. It would have worked within thirty minutes. No wonder she'd blacked out.

Jed smiled. "Did you know it's legal in Mexico?"

A rhetorical question. Dora didn't bother to answer.

He took a gym bag from atop the footlocker, and put the bag by the opening. From the footlocker he removed something dark. He stripped quickly out of his moccasins, dark turtleneck, and sweatpants, and stepped into a one-piece uniform. By the flickering light of the candle she could read a name sewn over the pocket. *Ben,* it said.

"Who *are* you?" Dora said.

"Who do you want me to be?" he said. Dora shook her head, confused by the question. "You have more insulin and needles at home?" he asked.

"A shipment arrived while I was gone," she said. "My roommate put it in the refrigerator."

"What about testing strips?"

"There's a meter. In my purse."

He picked up her purse. It took him a minute of pawing to find the meter and her black insulin case. He held up the meter.

"That's it," she said. "There should be enough strips left for three days."

"It'll be over by then," he said, dropping the meter and case in her lap.

He pulled her key ring from his pocket. She noticed the department truck key was missing.

"This your house key?" He held up one with a hexagonal head. When she nodded, he said, "What food do you need?"

"Nuts, cheese, meat, trail mix, dried fruit. Some fruit juice in case I miscalculate and become hypoglycemic. And water."

He placed a few strips of beef jerky, a couple of apples, and a pottery mug by the sleeping bag, then pointed to the corner. "There's water in the cistern. You can reach it. There's a piss pot by your feet."

He took her driver's license from under its plastic sleeve and looked at the address. "Does your roommate work?"

A dilemma. Dora didn't want to put Stephanie in danger. But did she have much choice? "She teaches first grade."

Jed put the driver's license and wallet back in the purse and tucked the purse under his arm. "I'll be back in, oh, ten hours or so." He lifted the two sides of the net curtain and draped them over hooks in the wall. "Hope you're not afraid of the dark," he said, and snuffed out the candle.

His bulk blocked the moonlight for a moment, and then he was gone. She heard no footsteps, just snatches of a tuneless whistle. It was hauntingly familiar. From a movie her mother watched over and over, a movie about obsessive love. And murder . . . "The First Time"—that was the song. From *Play Misty for Me*.

Dora heard a motor start up in the distance. He must have a vehicle, then. He didn't have to rely on burros to come and go. Something to remember.

She used the chamber pot and climbed quickly back into the warmth of the sleeping bag, pulling it and the blanket over her head. She took the watch from her pocket and pressed the nightlight. It was nearly five.

She had to wait until daybreak. She needed light to free herself. Only then could she deal with Jed—or Ben, or whoever he really was . . .

# 15

## Barstow, California
Tuesday, December 14, 6:30 a.m.

Loretta Stanton's shift was nearly over when Ben stopped for a coffee to go at the Barstow Bun Boy. It was forty degrees outside, but he wasn't wearing a jacket over his janitor's uniform—the one that reminded her of her father's old filling station uniforms, consigned to the rag box when she was small.

Loretta had met Ben last summer. Sometimes he went home with her. She made it worth his while. A slow shower and shave and blow job, in return for company. Sometimes he'd even sleep for a few hours in her rented mobile home. It was enough. Dreams died a quick death in Barstow.

Loretta was forty-five, self-sufficient, and lonely. She'd come to terms with her narrow, pockmarked face, crooked teeth, and hooked beak of a nose. She wasn't looking for Prince Charming anymore. She took what she could get from life.

"What, no breakfast today?" Loretta asked Ben.

"No time," he said, giving a little shrug.

Loretta handed him coffee in a Styrofoam cup. Leaning over the counter with his change, she whispered, "I'm off in five. Want to come over?"

When he smiled, his eyes crinkled at the edges and burned bright as tiny Christmas lights. "I'm bushed," he said.

"Me, too," said Loretta, and winked.

"Rain check?"

"Tomorrow?"

"I'll rest up."

"You'll need it," she said, and watched him leave. He was chuckling as he waved to her from the doorway. He didn't laugh often enough, she thought, untying her apron.

. . .

The eastern sky was tinged with gray. Pulling into her rutted driveway, the headlights picked out Ben's ancient Land Rover parked deep in the drooping carport. She made him wait while she walked back to pick up the paper and searched for her house key.

"Change your mind?" she said.

An awning threw deep shadows over the front steps. He was sitting in a rocking chair, screened from the narrow lane by tall potted plants in terracotta containers.

"Depends." He crumpled the coffee cup and tucked it in his pocket.

"I know—you're a little short on time. How about I do you today, and you do me tomorrow?"

"The Loretta special?"

"What's your window?"

"An hour."

"That's enough," she said, unlocking the door. "You got what you need?"

Ben lifted a gym bag from the concrete deck, holding it out for her to see.

"Comin' right up." She pulled him into the house and closed the door.

Loretta's living room was furnished with a lounge chair, a lamp attached to a small side table, and a TV on a chipped metal cart. A king-size mattress covered most of the floor. Nothing on the walls. No pictures of loved ones. No knickknacks here or in any other room. Loretta reserved the tiny bedroom, with its two long tables and chest of drawers, for her beading projects. She'd placed earrings, necklaces, and bracelets in stores all over Barstow and as far away as Las Vegas. She wasn't a social person. Beading filled the empty hours between shifts at Bun Boy.

She closed the heavy gold drapes and turned the lamp on high. "Back in a sec," she said, and went into the tiny bathroom.

From the bag he took a rubber hospital sheet, a can of shaving cream, and three disposable razors. He stretched the rubber sheet over the top of her mattress, finishing just as she returned with a bowl of warm water, a towel, and a washcloth. She was naked. She stripped him quickly, almost roughly, and pushed him down on the mattress, straddling him. She started with his head, shaving the top and sides, each stroke of the razor a caress, then moved down to his face and neck. Her pendulous breasts touched his eyes as she worked, but he didn't move.

"Roll over," she said.

He turned. The razor glided over the back of his head, down his neck, over his shoulders and back and buttocks, each arm and leg in turn. She was silent, letting the razor strokes speak for her. She slapped him once on the rump and he rolled again beneath her.

"Careful," he said, as she picked up a fresh razor.

"I'm always careful." Her smile transformed the pitted face with its flat black eyes. "Now shut up and let me concentrate."

The razor slid across his chest, circling each nipple in turn. Sliding off to the side, she continued down his abdomen, then down each leg. "Spread 'em," she said.

He opened his legs. She picked up the flashlight to make sure she'd gotten every hair, then ran her hands over his body. "Smooth as a baby's butt," she said, standing up and pulling him after her.

Together they stripped the rubber sheet from the bed. He rolled the sheet, razors, and shaving cream into a ball, and placed it next to the mattress. He took out a lipstick in a pale green case and handed it to her.

"This one's almost gone," she said. "Want me to use one of mine?"

"No." There was a hardness around his mouth she didn't like.

"Well, you'll have to get a new one for next time," she said.

"It won't be a problem." He watched her circle her lips with the bronzy color.

"Good?" she asked.

"Perfect," he said, leading the way into the white-tiled bathroom. He turned on the shower and stepped into the tub. She followed him in, helping the warm water rinse away the last of the lather. Then she poured a dollop of liquid soap into a fresh washcloth and ran it over his body. When she slipped the condom on, which he'd insisted on from the first time, Ben raised his arms and held onto the showerhead for support. She dropped to her knees and quickly brought him to climax.

"Jesus!"

"Amen." She smiled up at him.

He toweled off while she finished her shower, and left her the small space in the bathroom.

"A friend's letting me use his cabin up at Big Bear for a few days," he called from the living room. "Want to go with me?"

"Really?"

"Why don't you call the restaurant and get a sub while I dress."

"Screw them. I was ready to quit anyway. Let's just leave." She twisted her hair up into a knot on her head and secured it with a clip.

Ben's reflection joined hers in the bathroom mirror. "It's never good to burn your bridges, Loretta."

"I said screw them, Bennie."

He shrugged. "Have it your way."

She was reapplying the lipstick. Most of the original coat had been left on the condom. The few traces on his groin, he'd been careful not to towel away.

"I wish you hadn't done that," he said, taking the lipstick away from her. He moved one hand to cup her jaw, the other to her temple.

Loretta's black eyes widened. Her mouth opened. But the words never came.

# 16

Jed snapped Loretta's head to the side, heard her neck pop. When he threw her to the floor, her head cracked against the side of the tub. He took the lipstick tube, wiped it clean of prints, and impressed it with her thumb, forefinger, and middle finger, before dropping it on the floor next to her body.

"I really wish you hadn't done that, Loretta," he said, looking down at her crumpled form. "But it's simpler this way."

He poured a little water on the floor and on the soles of her feet. Maybe the police would think she'd slipped. Stepping over her, he wiped his fingerprints off the showerhead, scrubbed his footprints off the tub. He took the condom and wrapper from the trash and walked back into the living room. He rolled his towel and washcloth in with the rubber sheet, stuffing them in a plastic grocery bag he found under the sink in the kitchen. He tucked his janitorial uniform in the gym bag, pulled out a denim skirt and navy wool turtleneck, and slipped into them. From the bedroom closet, he took one of Loretta's wigs, a shoulder-length chestnut affair, and spirit-gummed it to his head. Under the ankle-length skirt he wore navy knee-high ski socks and unisex slip-on leather shoes. No makeup. But he added a pair of dark glasses. If the police stopped him, and didn't look too closely, he could pass for Loretta.

Lastly, he found the number for the restaurant, picked up the phone, and called. "This is Loretta Stanton," he said, mimicking her voice and inflections exactly. "I'm leavin' town for a while. You can take your job and shove it."

He left the lamp on. Taking Loretta's keys and purse, the grocery bag, and his gym bag, he went out the front door, locking it behind him. Smiling, he took Dora's purse from the Land Rover and tucked it under the front seat of Loretta's Escort. The bags went into the trunk. He parked the Rover in a minimarket lot a block away and walked back. He'd pick it up on the return trip.

He knew exactly what would happen next. The police were predictable. He just wanted to be there to watch the fun.

The sun was clearing the horizon. A few miles west of Barstow, he stopped at one of the blue emergency phones placed every mile along the interstate. Mimicking Loretta's voice, he reported an abandoned truck in the Cave Canyon campground.

He declined to leave a name.

# 17

## Cady Mountains

Mojave Desert, California

Tuesday, December 14, 7:40 a.m.

The cold rays of the rising sun struck Dora full on the face. The light held little warmth, but lifted her spirits. She felt as if she'd been blind during the long night. Blind and disoriented. Now she knew which way was east. Her internal compass had been reset.

She tried not to think about how hungry she was. The apples and jerky sat by the sleeping bag, but she didn't dare eat the apples until she had more insulin. Her body had long ago used up the insulin from her last injection. To dampen the hunger pangs, she chewed on a little of the jerky and filled a cup with water from the cistern, a large, handmade earthenware bowl. She sat in a pool of sunlight in the middle of the floor, taking stock of the situation. It didn't look good.

Who *was* Jed, and what were his plans for her?

Before he came back she had to learn as much about him as she could. Know your opponent. She'd learned that as a child, when she had to cope with her mother's storms. Dora was a survivor. Now she had to prove it. But first things first. She had to find a way to free her ankle.

Jed had taken her purse, and with it her penknife and diamond nail file. No great loss—the links were too heavy for either of them to be effective. But maybe, if she could get the pin out of the floor, she could drag or carry the chain with her. It was only two feet long . . . No go. He'd set the pin deep in the rock floor and encased the first few links in inches of concrete. It would take forever to dig it free. She didn't have forever.

Maybe Jed had left a tool in the trunk. It was a footlocker from an army surplus store in Del Rio. The store bar code was on one end. It contained a few clothes, neatly folded, and a coat, which she put on over her own vest and jacket. His coat hung down to her knees. She'd have to leave it behind if, by some miracle, she freed herself. She'd never be able to run in it.

She found a geologist's field belt with a Brunton compass, but the loops for knife and rock hammer were empty. A yellow field notebook was in its pouch. She took it out. The pages were filled with detailed descriptions, measurements, and drawings of the rock alignments on the mesa below, notes about myths and legends associated with the constellations, and seasonal star charts. On the inside flap was a detailed drawing of a tarantula hawk wasp.

Dora shivered. She knew about *Pepsis* wasps from her child-hood in Texas. They sting their tarantula prey, drag it back to their den, and lay eggs on the paralyzed victim. When the eggs hatch, the larvae begin to feed . . . That's what Jed had done to her—paralyzed her and dragged her off to his hole in the hill. Now she was chained to the floor, unable to leave.

She put the field notebook back in its pouch. The only other object in the footlocker was a marbled black-and-white notebook. She set it aside for later and searched the rest of the room for anything that could be used as a tool.

The room was a semicircular cavity with a smoke-blackened ceiling. The recess, no more than seven feet high, was eroded into a softer layer under the caprock. Jed had extended the natural opening by building two rock walls, six feet high and a foot thick, of carefully fitted, unmortared cobbles. They came from the old alluvial unit. Jed had used what was at hand. Something to think about.

A tent of military-surplus camouflage-patterned net was suspended from the cliff face just above the recess. The net draped over the stone walls of the semicircular addition. The shackle and chain were just long enough to let her touch the apex of ceiling—if she stood on tiptoe. But she couldn't reach the top of the wall. It was as if Jed had measured her sixty-three inches and figured out her reach before he'd cemented the peg into the floor, before he'd attached the net. Maybe he had.

This was war. Dora stretched out on the floor as far as she could. The top of her head didn't clear the outside edge of the wall. Lying on her back, she let her fingers walk along the curving walls to the left and right of the opening until they touched a metal tent peg, fastening the net to the ground. A tent peg was a tool. She pried, tugged, dug with her fingernails until her muscles were shaking. The peg didn't budge. She didn't have enough leverage.

Turning over, she put her chin on her arms and stared out at the vista before her: the Mojave River Wash, interrupted by low hills, in the foreground, the northern reaches of the Bristol Mountains beyond. A playa stretched south, its surface reflecting the sun's rays. Nothing moved. It was as if she were alone on earth.

The sun had moved south far enough that the rays no longer came through the opening. The netting overhead made the room a place of twilight. Worse, if planes or helicopters looked for her, she'd be invisible from the air. She had to find a way to strip it away.

She pulled the footlocker to the center of the room. The chain was long enough to allow her to step onto the chest. The net was knotted around a metal ring that was attached, she supposed, to a spike driven into the face of the cliff. Her numb fingers worked on the knot. It was so tight that it wouldn't budge. She kept worrying the rough twine. A knife would be so much easier.

She sat down to rest her arms. The cut on her finger was bleeding again. Sepsis would set in if she weren't careful.

Maybe she could make a knife—at least something with a sharp enough edge to cut through material. She needed a rock high in silica. The Cady Mountains was an old volcanic center, the source of andesite and basalt flows, but no obsidian layers, unfortunately. So she wouldn't expect to find obsidian cobbles in the alluvial unit. And the only chalcedony she'd seen had been small cavity fillings in local basalt flows . . . But the Peach Springs Tuff was siliceous, and the intense heat during eruption had welded portions of the rock layer as it cooled. The dense parts were resistant to weathering. There should be samples in the wall.

Jed hadn't left matches for the candle, but he'd left his compass. It had a mirror to reflect light onto the walls. And she could dig with the sharp end of the sighting arm. Why hadn't she thought of that before?

She took his compass out of its leather holster and closed the trunk lid. Lying down on her back with her head by the opening, she caught and reflected the sunlight slowly over the inner walls, starting at the top . . . There—where the stone wall met the cliff face. The cobble was dark mauve, the color of a desert sunset. Sanidine and quartz crystals sparkled in the redirected light. Silica in the groundmass would give flakes a concave fracture. She wouldn't get as fine an edge as she'd get from obsidian, but it would do. And the sanidine might have other uses. The problem was, it was out of reach.

She took off her belt, made it into a loop, and fastened it to Jed's field belt. Mounting the footlocker again, she began tossing the lasso over the stones at the top of the wall. It was like fly fishing—a lot of solitary work, often for little reward. She kept casting for twenty minutes, thirty, forty . . .

Dripping with sweat, she took off Jed's coat and her own. She was feeling lightheaded. She drank some water, rested for a few minutes, and started again. Finally she hooked a stone and pulled it down. It wasn't the welded tuff, but it could be used as a hammer. One by one, she roped rocks, moving ever closer to the tuff. When it fell at last, she was so relieved and exhausted she started to cry.

This wouldn't do. It was already after nine, and she didn't know when Jed would be back. She chose the densest of the stones littering the base of the wall—a rounded andesite cobble—as her hammerstone. Within the welded tuff, compressed pumice fragments and biotite grains aligned in flow layers. She struck parallel to the layering. Short, quick strokes. The andesite broke first. She picked up another andesite cobble and began again. A sliver, perhaps three inches long, flew off. She could have stopped there, but she didn't. Jed might not leave her alone again—at least not long enough to make a weapon.

So she kept knapping until she'd reduced the tuff to a pile of curving slivers. She tucked one of the larger slivers in a pocket of her cargo pants. She hid several others around the cave. He might find one or two. He wouldn't find them all.

She rested, drank more water, used the pot. She didn't have time to fashion a more elegant knife. Taking a shirt from the footlocker, she cut off a sleeve and wrapped it around her hand.

Her hands were still shaking from the knapping when she stood on the chest again. One by one, she slashed the thread of the webbing until the entire net fell. Light poured in. The sky was the color of Annie's eyes. Would she see her daughter again? Would she see her grandchild?

Dora wrapped the knife in the sleeve and stuffed it in her pocket with the other sliver before she stepped stiffly down from the chest. Jed would find the knives in her pocket. Maybe he'd stop there.

She pushed the footlocker back against the wall, picked up the journal and notebook, dragged the blanket to a patch of sunlight, and collapsed. She lay there, watching clouds drift past, relishing the unobstructed view of the sky. Just a few minutes, she said to herself, closing her eyes. And then she'd read . . . Just a few . . .

PART

A kind of excellent dumb discourse.

—William Shakespeare, *The Tempest*

# 18

## Del Rio, California
Tuesday, December 14, 8:30 a.m.

"I let you sleep in," said Officer Rivera, handing me a heavy earthenware mug. She looked just as crisp and neat and placid as she had six hours ago. I felt grubby by comparison. "But don't worry," she said. "You've plenty of time to get ready."

I inhaled the scent of coffee liberally dosed with cream, and took a sip. "Bless you—on both counts. Did you sleep?"

"I'm leaving in a few minutes. I'll sleep when I get home." She slipped into her jacket.

"Who's your replacement?"

"There isn't one. I offered to stay, but they didn't feel it was necessary."

"And they didn't want to pay the overtime," I said.

"That about covers it." She turned at the bedroom door. "I already fed Zoey and cleaned the cat box."

"That was kind. Thank you. Did the hospital call?"

"No." She handed me her card. "Call me if you can't find somebody to watch Zoey when you go home. She's a sweet little thing . . . And good luck with your talk today."

And then I was alone in the old farmhouse that creaked as it expanded in the sunlight.

I picked up my cell phone and called the hospital. Sarah was still in surgery. No news. I punched in Philo's number. It rolled over into voice mail. He must be testifying still, or in the air, on his way to Tucson. I left a message that said that someone had tried to kill Sarah last night, that she was still in surgery, that my dissertation defense was going on as scheduled with another professor taking Sarah's place, and that he shouldn't worry about me. Killeen and Sylvie were getting married on Saturday, I added, so I wouldn't be home till Sunday. And I'd call this afternoon, after the defense. By then I'd be able to tell him more about Sarah.

Even as I finished the message, meant to reassure Philo that all was okay, the words seemed to fall short, like a volleyball serve hitting the top of the net and dribbling down. I'd never been a skillful liar. I wasn't fine. I was worried about Sarah. And I was nervous about having to deal with Professor Rudolf Rudinsky's questions.

Zoey jumped up on the bed, looking for loving. I held her face and kissed her nose, saying, in a poor imitation of Rudinsky's cultured Russian accent, "Kindly explain again, please, Ms. MacFarlane, the evidence supporting your interpretation that the mountain mass was transported southeast along post-Jurassic, low-angle faults? Either your evidence is flimsy, at best, or I somehow missed the corroborating points."

I shooed Zoey off the bed. She complained. "I've a date with the black knight, Zoey. And I have to shower and eat before I don my chainmail."

Nakata called as I stepped out of the shower. "Bad news," she said. I held my breath. "No, not about Sarah," she was quick to add. "But Rudy refused to postpone the defense. He has a handball date at one. He says he can't reschedule."

"Or *won't* reschedule," I said.

"You know Rudinsky."

What Rudinsky wanted was to keep me off balance, to set me up to fail. Nakata knew that. What she didn't know was why. And I wasn't about to explain that I was hip deep in sludge because I hadn't slept with Rudinsky when he offered me the opportunity—on more than one occasion. Nor had I kowtowed to his brilliant intellect. I hadn't reported the harassment because each episode was a he said/she said situation, impossible to prove. I'd discussed it with Sarah. She'd talked to Rudinsky privately. After that, we'd avoided each other whenever possible. But recent events had provided Rudinsky with the perfect opportunity for payback. I should have expected it.

"The sooner it's over the better," I said.

"There's one other thing," said Nakata.

"What else does he want?"

"To move it to PS 400."

I didn't ask Nono if Rudinsky could do it. I knew the answer. When the audience was too large for a classroom, the defense was moved to a lecture hall. But by choosing the physical sciences lecture hall, one of the oldest on campus, Rudinsky seemed determined to intimidate me. The room seated four hundred, was cold and drafty, and had terrible acoustics. The place echoed, even when every seat was filled. But I'd given lectures and presentations under worse situations. I'd manage.

"He, er, strongly recommended that all the students attend," Nakata continued. "None of the classrooms can accommodate that many."

"Rudy expects them to attend even though they're on winter break?"

"He's making phone calls as we speak. He's offering one unit of seminar credit if they show up and ask questions. He'll be keeping track."

"Tell the—tell him we can have it on the mall at the foot of the carillon tower if he wants."

Nakata laughed. "I don't think I will. He'd pick up the gauntlet, and you'd be trying to make yourself heard over the deafening sound of bells."

She had a point. "Okay," I said. "But I'm going to have to move it to get there on time. Will you call Killeen for me? I could use his help setting up."

If she recognized how steamed I was, she didn't let on. "Will do. See you in an hour," she said.

In thirty minutes I was headed down the gravel driveway. Sarah's home floated like a rocky island in the dissipating fog. Radio towers sprouted atop the granitic arms that cradled the University of California, Del Rio. Red fire retardant stained the hillsides. Slabby foliation threw striped shadows over the gold C above the campus. During orientation week each fall, freshmen climbed the mountain to give it a fresh coat of paint. It was tradition. So was the kegger that followed.

The Del Rio campus had begun as a citrus research station fifty years ago. From the beginning the curriculum was strong on liberal arts and the physical and life sciences. The focus had changed with technological advances. Bioengineering, computer sciences, medicine, and public administration now helped attract more than 14,000 students from across the country and around the world. But change had a price tag. Since I'd returned to school for my doctorate four years before, the place had been under constant construction. Parking was at a premium. So was housing. Most of the avocado and orange groves had fallen to the bulldozer; only the botanical garden remained. The phallic carillon clock tower on the central mall—locked, urban legend has it, since the Texas tower shootings in the sixties—poked through the fog. Nearly every day, the carillonneur practiced old tunes that echoed in the far corners of the campus. That sound, like the painting of the C, linked generations of students.

For once, because of winter break, parking wasn't a problem. I fed six dollars into the machine to buy an all-day pass. Better safe than sorry, I decided, especially the way things had been going since I arrived back in town. I tucked the ticket on my dash, grabbed my computer bag, purse, and briefcase, and trotted across the street. The path took me between the physics and chemistry buildings and into the geology building.

Aerial photographs from the fifties lined the wall near the entrance. Except for the addition of a wing, the exterior of the old brick building hadn't changed in half a century. But inside, the old physical sciences library had been converted to lab space, and areas under the stairwells had been enclosed for use as grad student offices. When I went to Nevada to finish my dissertation fieldwork last summer, I gave up the one I'd once shared with Geoff. Because I'd had a job waiting in Tucson, I knew I'd return to Del Rio only to defend my dissertation and visit friends. So I yielded my space to the next crop of grad students.

Killeen was waiting for me in the department office. He'd brought a cart to carry the projector, laptop, and a backup computer. "Murphy's Law," he said. "How're you doing?"

"Okay. Sorry about this, Killeen. I know you had plans for this morning."

"Nothing that can't wait. You'll want one friendly face in the front row."

By the time we'd gotten the screen down, set up the PowerPoint presentation with the projector, and double-checked that everything worked, perhaps fifty people had trickled in. Rudinsky's gambit had worked.

The mountains near Pair-a-Dice, Nevada, were far from the campus. Only one other student in the room, Dee Marsland, had gone through the section with me. For the rest, this was new ground. If Rudy required them to ask questions, I hadn't a clue what they'd be.

I'd dressed for the occasion in a black-wool pantsuit, rose-colored turtleneck, low heels, and Tona's opal necklace and earrings. A suit is like psychological armor. I'd need it this morning. I'd defended my master's thesis at Stanford seven years before, but that had been a small affair—just four professors and a few grad students. I'd taught classes and given plenty of talks and presentations in the interim, but never before a stacked audience . . . and after only a few hours of sleep. My stomach churned.

Cassandra Belman, a German student studying under Rudinsky, strode down the aisle. Zev Rothstein, Dee Marsland, and Ryan Fitzpatrick trailed behind her, forming a semicircle between me and the audience.

"Rudinsky's a bastard, Frankie," Cassie whispered, giving me a hug. "We will not let him detrain the proceedings." She held a stack of papers. Taking one off the top, she folded it and tucked it into my jacket pocket. "From all of us."

"We brainstormed this morning." Ryan's grin was infectious. "But that's how we do our best work, as you know."

"Trust us, Frankie," Zev said, tugging on a strand of my hair. "We have your spine."

"*Back,* you idiot," said Dee, not bothering to keep her voice down. "We have her *back.*"

"Well, I could use a little spinal support, too," I said. "Thanks, guys. What'll this cost me?"

"The first two rounds," said Cassie.

"Deal . . . Excuse me for a few minutes, okay? I need to check out the stylolites."

I caught Killeen's eyes and held up five fingers. He nodded. I slipped out a side door. The closest restroom was at the other end of the building. In the privacy of an old stall, separated from the other two by polished slabs of dolomite, I pulled the folded paper from my pocket. It was a list of questions about my dissertation topic, with a note at the top that said: *Please forgive the spelling errors. My English needs work. (German is* so *much easier!)*

I read quickly through the list, as if I were cribbing for an exam. They were straightforward, logical questions, the kind you'd expect from any audience of geologists: clarification of rock unit correlations, the strength of fossil evidence used to date the rocks, the differences between the rock units and equivalent formations in Idaho, Utah, and elsewhere in Nevada. No surprises. No spitballs or sliders like those Rudinsky would throw. These were topics I'd cover in my presentation, but ones that could be discussed in greater detail. And the grad students could be counted on to "encourage" the undergrads to follow the program. It was the teaching assistants, after all, who graded lab reports and quizzes, helped lead field trips, and recommended course grades. Undergrads learned early on to nurture those relationships.

Seven minutes later I was back in the lecture hall, flashing a smile of thanks at the geology students clustered in the center section. I felt much better. Though the battle lines were drawn, I had enough soldiers on my side that my army had a fighting chance.

Most of the professors were in their seats. Rudinsky's eyes bored holes in my skull. My mind went blank.

"Take a couple of deep breaths," said Killeen, softly. "They're free."

"I have that deer-in-the-headlights look?"

"More like a deer about to bolt."

"It's tempting."

"You haven't run from anything in your life," said Killeen.

"There's always a first time." I took the prescribed deep breaths and looked at my watch. Five minutes to go.

The professors left an empty chair for Sarah, a nonverbal tribute to her struggle a few miles away. To the left of Sarah's chair sat Rudinsky, mid-forties, a mineralogist and geochemist. He was tall, with a Goyaesque face, soulful brown eyes, and elegant carriage. Today he was wearing a charcoal vested suit, formal attire for a casual department. He could have been the model for the song "You're So Vain."

Born to Russian immigrant parents—intellectuals, defectors during the cold war—he spoke five or six languages fluently. A graduate of the University of Chicago, he worked on the mineralogy of vents from the East Pacific Rise for his dissertation, then turned to the radiometric age-dating of igneous rocks. Primarily a lab geologist, he was more comfortable with his mass spectrometer than with the rigors of fieldwork. Geoff and I used to joke that he preferred dating rocks to dating women. Women were conveniences, nothing more. Yet he was the only professor whose students—at least the females—took regular advantage of his office hours. Go figure.

He also preferred to be called Professor Rudinsky, or at the very least, Dr. Rudinsky. I called him Rudy. He retaliated during my oral qualifying exam by asking me to determine the mass of the Earth from first principles, and to describe in detail all the methods (past and present) used to date the age of minerals, fossils, rocks, the Earth, the solar system, and the universe. He also wanted to know who'd discovered the methods, when, and what the limitations were of each. It took a long time. He tried to flunk me for leaving out dendrochronology—tree-ring dating.

Rudinsky had initially supported Geoff during the departmental disciplinary hearing. Nakata hadn't, adding fuel to their conflicted relationship. Today she sat to the right of Sarah's chair, as if Sarah's spirit were still acting as referee. Next to Nakata sat Theo Marsh, a paleoecologist and vertebrate paleontologist who'd worked in Panama on Miocene land mammals for his dissertation. He was only six years older than I—a man of middle height, built like a gymnast. He had thick shingled brown hair, streaked with early gray, and leathery sun-browned skin. Extremely myopic, he wore contacts that turned his hazel eyes turquoise—his one vanity, other than an encyclopedic memory. He looked younger than his years, not much more than a teenager. But he had a short fuse when life's details went awry. Once, when a transfer student cheated on a midterm exam, the entire building reverberated. Marsh wasn't a voting member of my committee, but he could ask questions. So could Dean Crouse, sitting behind him.

I didn't know the dean well, had never taken a course from him. He was an organic chemist, but one of his degrees was in geochemistry. He often served as third or fourth committee member of grad students focusing on petroleum geology. It's all in the hydrocarbons.

I was grateful to Crouse for showing up today. With my major professor in the hospital, he could act as the home plate umpire and keep the proceedings on task. There was a lot at stake, for both sides, in a dissertation defense. The awarding of a doctoral degree by a department, school, and university meant their reputation was riding on the preparedness and performance of the candidate. Knowing this, I'd been surprised that the department had been so soft on Geoff when they could have sent him packing. What had saved him, Sarah explained, was that he hadn't published the information and thereby publicly embarrassed the department. By dealing with the situation quietly, in-house, the department saved its scientific reputation.

Dai Rhys-Evans's chair, to Rudinsky's left, was empty, too. The structural geologist was notoriously late. He was terminally curious about the world, and would lose himself for hours or days in esoteric scientific digressions—or in his mineral collection. But despite thirty years of teaching, he'd not become disillusioned. I loved that about him.

The final faculty member in attendance was geophysicist Chip Rizzo. Rizzo was stocky, casual, crude, his conversations and lectures liberally laced with profanity. It was habit. He couldn't seem to remember that he wasn't on a drilling rig. This morning, wearing dusty Levis and a navy workshirt with sweat stains under the arms, Chip looked like he'd just gotten in from the geothermal field in the Salton Trough. He slouched in his chair, mud-caked field boots stretched out on the royal blue carpet patterned with gold rhombohedrons—UC colors.

When we'd waited ten minutes for Dai to show, I walked over to Nakata. She anticipated my question.

"Haven't spoken to him this morning. Let me check with Tara and see if he's running late." Nakata pulled out her cell phone.

Tara hadn't seen her husband, Nakata told us after a short conversation. Dai had stayed at school last night. But in the windowless lab, night was the same as day. If he were ever to win the Nobel Prize, he'd be late to the ceremony.

"I'll get him." Killeen moved quickly up the aisle and through the double doors.

The rest of the audience sat, murmuring among themselves. All except for a woman sitting in the last row, next to the aisle. A stranger. Our eyes met. She rose, paused just inside the door, smiled, as if to wish me luck, and opened the door. For a moment she was backlit against the courtyard beyond. The tilt of her head seemed familiar, I thought, but I couldn't place her.

Killeen took his time. Rhys-Evans must not have been in either his office or the rock lab.

I went up and sat with the students, who updated me on how well their work was progressing (or not), which relationships had dissolved, and who had hooked up with whom. My former students, those who'd been in classes I'd TA'd, told me who'd dropped out, interrupting each other with caustic comments. The course work, both within the department and from the required physics, math, chemistry, and biology classes, led to a 30 percent attrition rate. Each fall, incoming freshmen and community college transfers infused new blood into the program and kept the overall enrollment stable. Those who survived the lecture, lab, and fieldwork, especially the boot camp called Summer Field Geology, were battle-scarred veterans and blood brothers. The bonds were strong. No one got through it alone. And the teaching assistants became translators, defenders, counselors, intermediaries, drinking buddies, and, at grading time, wielders of Fate's axe.

I realized, right then, how invested I'd become, and how much I'd missed them. I realized, too, just how much that teaching position in Tucson meant to me.

I'd been hoping that Killeen would return in time to spare me from the students' inevitable questions. He didn't cooperate. I looked at my watch. He'd been gone for fifteen minutes. The gods only knew into what hole Dai had disappeared. So now it was my turn to share news. I gave them the abbreviated version of what had happened to Sarah last night, watching their faces for any sign that someone wasn't surprised by the information or might know more about the hit-and-run than they should. Not a flicker seemed out of place.

The questions tapered off, so I excused myself and called the hospital for an update. Dr. Tensing answered on the first ring.

"I was just going to call you," he said. "Dr. Barstead's out of surgery. She's been moved to the critical care unit."

I gave a thumbs-up to the group of students. "What's the prognosis?" I asked.

"It's early going yet. We'll know more after the anesthesia wears off." Tensing's words and tone were guarded.

"What about visitors?" I asked him.

"Not till late this afternoon—at the earliest," he said. "And even then, Dr. Barstead might still be in a coma. You might want to call ahead to make sure you can see her."

"Will do," I said, and disconnected. Nakata had joined the group, and I passed along the news.

"Good," she said. "I'll tell the others."

The back doors of the lecture hall opened, and two campus security officers stationed themselves just inside the exits. Uh-oh.

"Storm Troopers," said Zev Rothstein. He didn't specify whether he meant the German or the Star Wars variety.

Killeen came in a moment later. No David Rhys-Evans. But La Joie and Mulroney were right behind him. I was the only one in the room who knew what their presence signified.

I stood and made my way to the aisle, intercepting the three men. Nakata and Dean Crouse were right behind me.

"No," I said to Killeen. "Damn it, no." But the look on his face told me that this time there was no hope.

"Where's Dai?" Nakata said.

"Don't tell me Dai's gone fuckin' AWOL," said Rizzo. "Just like him to leave us high and dry." Some of the students laughed.

"I'm sorry, but Dr. Rhys-Evans is dead," said La Joie.

# 19

Stunned silence greeted La Joie's announcement. Confusion, disbelief, and bewilderment rippled across the faces in the room. Rudinsky's expression was impassive; Nakata gaped, as if she'd aborted a lecture in midsentence.

"You're shittin' me," said Rizzo, breaking the logjam.

Bedlam ensued as everyone shouted questions. I looked at Killeen. He gave the slightest hint of a nod. Dai had been murdered.

La Joie and Mulroney waited patiently until the faculty had reduced the noise to a murmur. It took five minutes.

"I'm Detective La Joie. This is Detective Mulroney. We'll need to interview each of you. It would help if you spread out in the lecture hall, leaving a chair or two between you. You may use your laptops, but please don't go online or converse with each other until we've released you. If you have an appointment, you may call and cancel. Otherwise, turn off your cell phones."

Rudinsky closed his notebook, stuffed it in his briefcase, and stood up as if to leave.

"I believe he means faculty, too, Rudy," Dean Crouse said.

Rudy gave him a frosty look, then shot his cuffs, exposing gold cuff links on his crisp white shirt. He brushed imaginary lint from his sharply creased pants, settled back into his seat, and crossed his legs.

Mulroney assessed the number of people in the room. "If we don't get some help, we'll be here till Friday."

"You read my mind, Mick. See what you can do."

"In the meantime," said La Joie, turning to the rest of us, "I'd like the faculty and staff to sit down front. I'll interview you. Detective Mulroney will take the students."

Rank has its privileges, I thought, as I walked down to collect my gear. But once there I stood and stared at the blank screen that covered the blackboard—which wasn't black at all, of course, but a dull faded green. I felt a hand on my shoulder. Killeen. I put my hand over his and squeezed gently. In silence, he helped me disconnect power cords, put up the screen, and pack my equipment. Behind us, accompanied by the squeaking chairs, banging of folding desktops, and scuff of boots and shoes, the audience sorted themselves out.

I didn't know where to sit—with the faculty and staff, or with the students. I was a woman without a country. Yet I'd committed no crime.

La Joie noticed my indecision. "I'd like to interview you last, Dr. MacFarlane."

"*Ms.* MacFarlane," said Rudinsky. "She hasn't satisfied the requirements."

No one in the room missed the underlying note of pleasure in his voice. It was a very public slap in the face. I rarely blush. I did then. I was so angry I couldn't have spoken if I'd tried.

"Duly noted, Dr. . . . ?" said La Joie.

"Rudinsky. Rudolf Rudinsky. I have an appointment. I'd appreciate it if you interviewed me first."

La Joie looked at the rest of the faculty, who were now spaced two seats apart in the center of the front row. He didn't know who was nominally in charge. They were all looking at Nakata and Crouse, the top dogs in the pecking order.

"I have no problem with that," said Crouse.

Nakata shrugged. "Fine by me." But her stiff shoulders and bland expression said that it wasn't fine at all.

While La Joie and Mulroney began creating a list of names of those present, I selected a seat at the end of the front row, as far from the others as I could get. Killeen sat directly behind me, a reassuring presence. Leaning back I closed my eyes, still stinging from Rudinsky's barb. He was right, of course. My dissertation defense was effectively dead in the water. But that was a paltry thing compared with Dai lying dead nearby or the loss Tara and the children had suffered.

I pushed aside my hurt and Rudinsky's pettiness and focused on breathing evenly and deeply, searching for that calm place where healing begins. I found questions instead: Could the attack on Sarah and Dai's murder be related? If so, could they have something to do with me? I wasn't sure I had the stomach for it, but suddenly I needed to know the details.

Noise. I opened my eyes to see three more officers making their way down the aisle. They conferred with La Joie, divided the students into groups, and made new lists of names. Mulroney left the students and went to help La Joie with the faculty and staff. I noticed they left Killeen alone, as if by tacit agreement. I wondered why.

A pall settled over the normally rambunctious students. The ivory tower had been breached. Sarah Barstead and Dai Rhys-Evans were favorite professors and mentors, respected for their knowledge and experience, teased for their idiosyncrasies. They were family. And the students grieved as only the young can grieve. I watched them deal with their personal loss: Cassie snuffled and swiped at her eyes; Zev pounded furiously on his laptop keyboard; Ryan stared dazedly at the ceiling; Dee slouched in her chair, eyes closed. I saw an undergrad I didn't know sending a text message on her cell phone. The hall had wireless, so no doubt others sent e-mails. There weren't enough officers to stop them.

I didn't know whether to curse La Joie or thank him for putting me last. At least it gave me time to organize my thoughts. I took out my laptop, opened a new file, set the font to Arial 14, and zoomed to 150 percent. I might not be able to speak to Killeen about what had happened, but he could read over my shoulder what I was typing. I no longer cared about La Joie's rules. I'd moved from shock to anger. An interview was a two-way street. I had questions. I wanted answers. So I created a list of my movements that morning and then composed questions for La Joie.

Where was Dai Rhys-Evans killed? When? How? Why? Did the murderer leave notes behind? Was it the same person who struck Sarah? And how did Dai's murder fit into the sequence of violent incidents that recently had befallen the department?

Dai had no enemies that I knew of. He was genial, absent-minded, never petty, and perennially supportive of his students . . . with one exception: Dai had been on Geoff's dissertation committee. He'd agreed with the rest of the department faculty that Geoff's plagiarism warranted serious disciplinary action. They gave him until the end of fall quarter to measure, describe, and correlate additional sections, and completely rewrite his dissertation. The due date, I realized, would have been this week.

Because of their edict, I'd expected Geoff to arrive at some point last summer, during my final field season in the mountains west of Pair-a-Dice. And then Sarah had sent me the news that they'd found his body.

But the remains weren't Geoff's. The photos I'd received from a Mexican police officer proved Geoff was alive the last weekend in May. But where was he? And did the scattered bones belong to

Bernie Venable? Had La Joie received Bernie's dental records? Bernie disappeared from Los Angeles in December. If he died then, where was his body till spring? Could the remains have been on the hillside for eight months? What had La Joie said about the time of death?

I hauled Philo's tape recorder from my briefcase, put in the earphone, and skipped forward and backward until I found that part of our conversation from . . . yesterday? Good God—so much had happened in less than twenty-four hours.

My voice sounded tinny and flat on the recording: "How long had the body lain there?"

La Joie: "Three months or more. We're working on it."

I turned off the recorder. I'd reported Geoff's plagiarism on May 8. He was last seen at the department hearing a few days later. The remains had been decomposing, at a minimum, from late April till late July, when they'd been discovered. But eight months' exposure—from December through July—could not be ruled out. Yet. So the body could have been left on the mountainside soon after Bernie disappeared in December. But who, I wondered for the umpteenth time, had claimed the remains, and what had happened to them? The only thing I knew for sure was that they hadn't reached Geoff's parents in Reading, England. And if the remains belonged to Bernie Venable—or someone else—then that was a good thing.

Where was Geoff last December when Bernie disappeared? With me, at least for part of the time. I forced myself to picture my movements a year ago. My calendar was in the computer. I opened it and went back twelve months. My only classes were a seminar on tectonics, with a final term paper due on the tenth, and Independent Studies, a euphemism for research and dissertation writing. I'd taught Historical Geology, an introductory course, and Stratigraphy and Sedimentary Petrography, an upper-division course. Final exams were on the eleventh and twelfth, respectively. On the twenty-first, the winter solstice, Geoff had asked me to marry him. I'd taken him home to meet my parents on the twenty-third. We'd stayed in Tucson for four uncomfortable days. Geoff didn't like my family, though he'd tried to hide the fact. He'd sat silently in the corner most of the time, letting the hubbub swirl around him. He'd responded when addressed directly, but he'd appeared sullen. He'd told me later that he hadn't liked sharing me with my family, especially not so soon after our engagement. I took that at face value. A large extended family gathering can be a shock to anyone brought up in a quiet, small, nuclear family. I felt I should have prepared him better . . .

But where was Geoff during those first three weeks, when I was writing a paper, grading final exams, and turning in chapters of my research? The calendar didn't say.

I remembered that he hadn't yet moved in with me—not officially anyway, though we'd shared an office and spent most of our free time together. On Thanksgiving weekend, he'd been grinding rock thin sections in the lab and describing mineral composition and geologic history, while I worked on a term paper about faulting in the overthrust belt. He'd finished with his course work the spring before, so he had no finals of his own to take. At the end of finals week, after he'd graded exams for the class he TA'd, he'd taken off to putter around in the Mojave Desert. I hadn't thought anything of it. Geoff would often disappear into the desert for a bit of R and R. Sometimes he took students along. He liked guiding field trips to isolated places.

I flashed on the framed picture at Sarah's house, the one I'd taken on a ridge northwest of Pair-a-Dice more than two years ago. Of that smiling group, Bernie Venable was missing and presumed dead. At the very least, Geoff was guilty of stealing his driver's license . . . Peter Snavely and Dai Rhys-Evans were dead; Sarah nearly so. They'd made up Geoff's dissertation committee, and they'd all participated in the faculty committee meeting that resulted in Geoff's reprimand. Janet Nakata and Rudy Rudinsky were also on that faculty committee. So were Marsh and Rizzo. Everything circled back to Geoff.

I had so much information swirling around inside my brain that I felt dizzy. I typed a summary of where my brainstorming had taken me, ending with the questions: If Geoff was on the warpath, were Nakata, Rudinsky, Marsh, and Rizzo also in danger? Was I?

My summary was short on facts, long on supposition and inference. The same bits of information could be rearranged in an infinite number of ways. Maybe La Joie could connect the dots in a more coherent pattern.

I looked up. La Joie and Mulroney were more than halfway through the faculty and staff. They hadn't yet called Killeen. I went back to the drawing board, typing questions that I could reasonably expect La Joie to answer.

Was there any news about Sarah's case?

Did DNA from the hair samples I gave him match the remains on the hillside?

Had he received a photo of Geoff from Ohio State? How about one from Geoff's parents? Did they match Geoff's driver's license photo? In other words, was my Geoff Travers the original Geoff Travers? I thought I might know the answer to that one. But I wouldn't, *couldn't,* face that specter unless I had to . . . And lastly, if my Geoff wasn't who he claimed to be, what had happened to the Geoff Travers from Ohio State?

I found a fresh tape and slipped it into my microcassette recorder. I was ready for La Joie. But I wondered if he was ready for me.

I heard the sound of a chair bottom squeaking as it flipped up. La Joie was finished with Nakata. She collected her things, but instead of using one of the aisles on either side of the center tier of seats, she detoured over to me. The lines in her face had deepened; she looked haggard, as if the events of the last twelve hours had depleted her reserves.

"You're going over to Tara's?" I whispered.

"Soon as I can get away," she said, making no effort to keep her voice down.

La Joie and Mulroney looked over to see who'd broken the rules. *I should have known,* said the look on La Joie's face. Nakata ignored them.

"Please give Tara my condolences," I said.

"Will do." And then Nono surprised me by saying, "Friday at ten."

I wondered if she'd lost her mind. They couldn't have planned a memorial service that quickly. "What?"

"Your defense." She had her pocket calendar out and pencil poised, as if sanity lay in mundane tasks.

It took me a moment to change gears. "Who's the third man?"

"Marsh, though I had to twist his arm. Rizzo offered, but he's dyslexic. It'd be tough for him to get it read in time."

"Ms. MacFarlane," said La Joie, attempting to bring the stray doggies back into the herd.

"Call her 'Doctor.' She's earned it," said Nakata.

She gave me a pat on the shoulder, shoved open a side door, and disappeared into the watery sunshine.

# 20

Time passed. Voices droned on—question, answer, question, answer—until at last the auditorium was empty except for La Joie, Killeen, and me. The additional officers left with the last of the students. So did campus security. Mulroney went to check on progress at the crime scene, wherever that was. La Joie picked up the plastic stacking chair he'd been carrying from person to person during the last ninety minutes, and set it down in front of me.

"Mr. Killeen," La Joie said. "Would you move down next to Dr. MacFarlane, please?"

"You're interviewing us together?" I asked, turning on the tape recorder.

"We've ascertained the time of death. You have an alibi."

"Oh?"

"You were speaking with police and paramedics at the time."

"Dai was killed last night? When?"

"Around midnight, we think. We'll know more after the medical examiner finishes."

So Dai was killed shortly after Sarah was hit. I thought back to the scene on the street below Sarah's house. "I paged Killeen last night while I waited for you to interview me," I said to La Joie. "Sylvie Kingsley's a witness."

"Yes. He answered from home. We've checked. He also made calls to other faculty members from there. And we know when he arrived at the hospital. We've also checked out his background."

Killeen squeezed his bulk into the seat next to me, accompanied by the alarming creaks and groans of chair springs. He said nothing. We both believed in listening much, speaking little. But, unlike me, he was succeeding. I wasn't sure why.

"Okay, then," I said, squaring my shoulders and straightening my spine. "Let the inquisition begin."

La Joie smiled. "Feeling like Joan of Arc?"

"I, too, have wars to fight."

"But not on an empty stomach," he said as Mulroney came in, holding a brown paper bag and large cups of coffee.

"With cream," Mulroney said, handing me a tall disposable cup.

"You remembered," I said. "Thank you."

"I brought extra cream, in case you need it . . . Black?" he said to Killeen, handing him a second cup.

"My father was."

"I didn't mean—"

"He knows that," said La Joie. "He's just trying to throw you off balance."

"Yes, well, it's working," Mulroney said, passing out deli sandwiches. Mine was turkey and avocado. I'd had only coffee and a banana since dinner last night. No time for breakfast. Till now, I hadn't realized I was starving.

I demolished the sandwich before slowing down to sip the coffee. "I called the hospital while we were waiting for . . . for you," I said to Killeen. "Sarah's out of surgery. They're not making any guesses at this point. I can see her later this afternoon."

"I'll go with you," said Killeen.

"What about your wedding preparations?"

"They'll wait."

"You're sure?"

"I'm sure."

"Then, about Sarah," I began, paused, raised one eyebrow, and looked at La Joie.

He chewed, swallowed, took another bite, and repeated the sequence before he came to a decision. "The ME confirmed that Dr. Barstead was struck twice. So you were right—it was somebody with a beef. We were just starting to go through the list of her students and colleagues this morning when we got this call."

"Did you see the site where Dai was killed?"

"Yes."

"Who's processing it?"

"The ME was right behind us, and so was the forensic geologist we borrowed from the Department of Justice. She happened to be in town to consult on another case. I thought a geology lab would be right up her alley." La Joie looked at his watch. "They should wrap it up anytime now."

"I won't ask you for details about Dai's case, except . . ." I paused, searching for the right words. "Are the cases related—Sarah's and Dai's?"

La Joie knew what I was asking. He and Mulroney exchanged glances.

"I won't blab," I added. "And Killeen knows how to keep his mouth shut."

La Joie nodded.

"Are you agreeing with me about Killeen, or answering my question?"

"Yes," said La Joie, which didn't help me a bit.

"Yes," said Killeen, taking pity on me. "And yes." Which rescued La Joie very neatly.

I didn't need more information than that. They must have found a note at the scene, or some other similarity between the two crimes. I could get the rest of the information from Killeen later.

I finished my coffee, dropped the crumpled sandwich wrapper into the empty cup, and opened my laptop again. "I have questions—"

"Surprise, surprise," said La Joie.

"And maybe some leads for you," I added, refusing to be drawn. "But before I start, I need to use the restroom." I handed him my laptop. "It might save time if you read this while I'm gone."

"Mulroney will go with you," La Joie said, balancing the computer on his knees. And when I bristled, he added, "For your protection."

The restroom was as empty as before, but it looked different somehow. The sun was on the other side of the building; the room was darker, even with the lights on. I stopped in the middle of the floor and stared at the pale rock in the wall under the window. The stone matched the dolomite of the stall dividers. Within the rock, minerals at the ancient bedding planes had, under pressure, gone into solution, leaving behind jagged lines of intergrown crystals. The lines resembled those printed by a seismograph during an earthquake. As my eyes traced the pattern, I thought, *That's what happens when stress overwhelms fragile psyches: positive and negative emotions intergrow and fuse until . . . what? What happens next? Hate, anger, and deceit displace love . . . and murder becomes a practical, dispassionate option for survival . . .* Was I describing Geoff?

All the bits and pieces of evidence pointed back to him. I was positive now, in that way of knowing that has nothing to do with science and facts and evidence, but is as instinctive as breathing, that Geoff had attacked Sarah and Dai. Why hadn't I seen it before?

I'd spend the rest of my life answering that question. But there were others far more pressing: if everything pointed to Geoff, where was he right now; what had he planned next; and how could he be stopped?

I heard the restroom door swing open, then Mulroney's voice, saying, "Are you okay, Dr. MacFarlane?"

Was I? "One more minute," I said.

Mulroney closed the door. A minute later we walked in silence back to the lecture hall.

Janet Nakata intercepted us at the door. Her gray-streaked black hair stood out at all angles, as if a child had been tugging at it.

"I'm so glad you're still here," she said to Mulroney.

"What's wrong?" he asked, as we walked down the aisle.

She waited until we reached La Joie and Killeen before she said, "Dora Simpson's missing. The Barstow sheriff's office responded to an anonymous call about a UCDR truck abandoned in Afton Canyon. Dora's field vehicle. All her equipment was in the back. A bloody rag was on the seat."

# 21

## Cady Mountains

Mojave Desert, California
Tuesday, December 14, 10:15 a.m.

A burro brayed. Dora Simpson dropped the journal she'd been holding. A second burro answered. Was Jed back?

She put her ear to the dirt floor of the makeshift room . . . No footsteps. She started breathing again.

Clouds whipped across the sky. A dry wind pelted the rock walls with sand. Dora's body, wrapped in the sleeping bag, was in shadow. The sun had traveled. How long had she dozed?

She dug out her pocket watch, a gift from her daughter Annie on Dora's birthday last summer—the Fourth of July. The watch showed 10:19. Jed said he wouldn't be back till afternoon.

Dora ran her fingers over the chain connecting her ankle to the floor of the room, looking for a weak spot. There wasn't one. Solid forged steel. Would she ever be free again? She wouldn't let her mind wander down that path. She was alive and uninjured, except for the cut on her finger. She'd just have to stay that way.

Dora pricked her finger and checked her blood glucose level—116. Not great, but not bad considering the stress and lack of insulin. As long as he returned before long, she'd be fine—weak from hunger, maybe, but she wouldn't die.

She took a sip of water and dragged her body, the bag, and Jed's journal to a sunny spot. The temperature was dropping. The chill would be brutal in the full blast of the wind. She wished she had matches for a fire. Given time, she could start one from scratch, but she needed to conserve her energy. She couldn't eat until Jed returned with the insulin . . . if he returned. Life offered no guarantees, no happy, glowing, uncomplicated, rosy futures. Life offered only work and more work, competition and survival. She'd learned that at fifteen, when she became pregnant with Annie.

So it was a toss-up—physically exhaust herself making a fire, or conserve energy for a few more hours. If Jed didn't show by two thirty, if she'd been abandoned in this place, she'd begin the laborious process of making fire. And after she succeeded, then what?

She looked at the steel chain on her leg again. She couldn't break the chain by striking it, but maybe there were other methods . . . She tried to remember. Steel was a hardness of five and a half on Mohs' hardness scale. Quartz was seven. The welded tuff, high in silica, was probably between six and seven. She could pound and scrape for a while and see if she did any damage . . . At what temperature did steel melt? She couldn't remember exactly . . . Over two thousand degrees, certainly . . . If she made a pit fire in the middle of the floor—an impromptu oven—and buried the chain in the hot coals, could she soften the steel enough to thin it? Break it? Maybe. Worth a try, anyway. But it was attached to her ankle. How did she keep the metal from burning her so severely she couldn't run if she had to?

Dora found she wasn't concerned about disfigurement. She was concerned about surviving long enough to reach help. For that she had to be able to run—or at least walk.

She could stuff a little material between her ankle and the shackle. Asbestos would be best, but she didn't have any . . . If she heated the links closest to the anchoring pin and put the rest of the links in water, would the water absorb enough of the heat to keep her ankle from burning? She'd need to keep cooling the water and intermittently pounding at the hot, more ductile links until they became thin enough to quench with water. Only then might she be able to break them between two rocks. Heat would alter the internal structure of the metal, but she wasn't enough of a metallurgist to know how. It would be an experiment. Trial and error, with her freedom at stake.

But first she needed fire, and a container large enough to hold water *and* the chain. She had nothing at the moment. If Jed came back, she could talk him into lighting a fire and maybe letting her make coffee or tea or soup. He must have pots stashed away nearby. He'd *lived* here, for God's sake. And if she didn't expend the energy making fire from scratch, if she let Jed do it with matches, she'd have enough energy left to work on the chain—if Jed left her alone long enough.

It was odd that she hadn't felt sexually threatened by Jed. Physically, yes. But there were no sexual vibes at all. Maybe he was gay. He'd taken pains to reassure her he didn't rape women, that she wasn't here for that reason. So why *was* she here?

Dora hadn't a clue. But if the truck was parked somewhere far away, maybe Death Valley, then no aerial search would take place here. Damn. Had she wasted all that effort tearing down the netting?

She had to focus on getting away. She'd give Jed a few more hours to get back with her insulin. If he didn't come, she'd do whatever it took, whatever was in her power to do, to free herself. But she prayed it wouldn't come to that.

Dora didn't know to whom she was praying. She'd stopped believing in a Christian, loving God when she was a child. Loving gods don't give children to abusive, alcoholic parents. Faith in a belief system riddled with inconsistencies didn't make sense to her. Nor did belief systems that claimed to have the only answer, the only *Way*. Reason and science, now, they made sense. She'd learned that the hard way. But just in case she was wrong about there being some omnipotent being behind the whole Big Bang thing, she sent up a prayer—a plea for help, a plea that she'd have the strength to play the cards she'd been dealt. She wanted to see Annie again. She wanted to see her grandchild.

In the meantime, while she waited for Jed, she would read his journal. Maybe it would answer some of her questions. *Know your enemy.* She'd get to know Jed, just as she'd gotten to know her mother—and her old boss, the head of the law firm where she'd worked back in Austin. She'd documented that bastard's harassment, taken him to court. The settlement had given her the financial resources to go back to school. Sometimes, negative events led to positive outcomes. She hoped that would be true today. If nothing else, reading would pass the time.

Dora opened the marbled black-and-white cover. Inside was the name Seth Camber, written in a strong masculine hand. The pen had dug so deeply into the cardboard cover that blind fingers could have traced the letters. Was she wrong? Did this belong, not to Jed Strong, but to someone else?

The notes were dated five years earlier:

> *It seems strange to open a notebook and pick up a pen for no other reason than to record bits and pieces of my life. I've watched others keep a journal, but I've never written a letter— not to anyone, not for anyone, not as anyone. For seventeen years I've looked forward, not back. The past was a cache of meat crawling with maggots. I never wanted to lift that stone cover and look inside. It's been all I could do to learn how to*

*survive without family. My parents didn't prepare me for that.*
*I never had a chance to tell my story to the people I met*
*along the way. So I guess this is like a letter to them—a letter*
*they'll never read. But that's okay, too. Some of their names*
*will be here in black and white, and I think they'd like that.*
*Killing Quick was the beginning. I know that now. "The*
*Beginning and the End," just like it says in Revelations. Quick*
*wasn't his real name, of course. It was Abraham Baca. We had*
*the same mother. Different fathers. The only thing I know*
*about my real father is that Pa killed him in the parking lot of*
*a bar in Kalispell. That's the reason they lit out for the Moie*
*River country. Ma was already pregnant with me.*
*Ma entered Quick's name right under mine in the old*
*family Bible. But I never called him Abe or Abraham. Quick*
*was short for Quicksilver. That's what he was like, even as a*
*baby, Ma said. She loved him more than anything. So did I.*
*Pa didn't love anything or anybody, I don't think, besides*
*his guns. He looked like the picture of Noah in our Bible, and*
*spent all his time gathering stores of food and guns and ammo,*
*preparing for Armageddon. I never saw him smile. I didn't*
*mind that much. But it wouldn't have mattered if I did.*
*Our place is the Ark, a log cabin hidden away in a sea of*
*forest. No running water, electricity, plumbing, or telephone.*
*No address or P.O. box. The land was homesteaded by Ma's*
*grandfather. There's a trail in, an overgrown logging road from*
*early in the last century—a horse road, not wide enough for a*
*car or truck. We only had the two motorcycles anyway. And*
*the horses, of course. Needless to say, we never paid taxes.*
*Hunters tried to hail us a time or two, but Pa shot at them.*
*They spread the word, and we were left in peace.*
*We stayed put, up there by the Canadian border—except*
*for summer trips to sell Pa's honey, Ma's pottery, and huckle-*
*berry jam at fairs in Idaho and Montana . . .*

So Jed Strong was Seth Camber. Dora skimmed the next two
pages, the story of a boy who'd killed his brother, been banished
from Eden, and done what it took to survive. The cold, objective
words seeped into her, chilled her to the marrow. She couldn't deal
with this right now. Putting the notebook away, she burrowed
deeper in the sleeping bag. She would have given anything, right
then, for the warmth of a fire.

But questions followed her, demanding answers. Why did Seth

leave this for her to find? An oversight? No. Seth paid attention to details. Why had he let her see him, revealed his true name—a name no one else knew? Either he meant to kill her, or he meant to die soon and leave her as a witness to his work. Was there anything she could do to increase her odds of surviving?

Identify with Seth. If he saw them as two halves of the same coin, she had a chance. She must listen and feign empathy. She'd tell him bits of her own story, emphasize the similarities. There were several. They'd both been on their own since fifteen. They'd survived everything life had thrown at them. But would that be enough?

# 22

## UC–Del Rio

Tuesday, December 14, 12:25 p.m.

"Who's Dora Simpson?" La Joie, Mulroney, and I asked in chorus.

"An undergrad," said Janet Nakata. "You don't know her, Frankie. She transferred in from U–Texas this fall to work with Marsh—a senior thesis on a vertebrate quarry in the Cady Mountains. She's been in the field for a week—"

"Two," said Killeen. "I helped her get set up out there. She was due home last night."

"I called her apartment just now," Nakata said. "Got her machine. Have you heard from her?"

"She called me on her supply run to Barstow a week ago," Killeen said. "Said things were on schedule. She didn't need my help."

"Have they begun a search?" asked La Joie.

"We were their first call," said Nakata. "They weren't sure who had the truck checked out. And they didn't want to start searching if we'd left it there because of engine trouble."

"With a bloody rag on the seat?" Killeen asked in disbelief.

"She could have cut herself loading the truck," Nakata said.

"I'll check on the status," said Mulroney to La Joie, and disappeared through the side door.

"Have you called her daughter?" Killeen asked.

"Not yet," Nakata said. "I wanted to check with her roommate first. And you. Make sure it wasn't a false alarm—something wrong with the vehicle."

"Except that her route home didn't take her through Afton Canyon," said Killeen.

"You're sure?" Nakata asked him.

"Positive."

"She wouldn't have gone there to check out the rocks, or just to see the place?" said La Joie.

"No need. We stopped there on the way in," Killeen said. "And Dora wouldn't have interrupted her trip home for anything but gas and a snack. Dora's diabetic. She brought extra insulin, but she wouldn't want to push it."

"Unless her roommate forwarded her insulin supplies to Barstow," Nakata said.

"That wasn't the plan when I spoke to her last week," Killeen said.

"Easy enough to check," said La Joie.

Mulroney slipped back through the door. La Joie conferred with him for a minute and then rejoined us. "Barstow wants you to look at Dora Simpson's gear," he said to Killeen. "To see if anything's missing."

"I know what general equipment was there—camping gear and such. But I'm just learning to sort out the geologist's tools." Killeen looked at me expectantly.

"There's nothing I can do for Sarah just now," I said to La Joie. "And with my defense postponed till Friday, well, I'm at loose ends . . . If Dora's still out there in the Cadys, I'll want to help search anyway."

La Joie pulled on his earlobe while he thought about it. "It might be safer if you're out in the Mojave just now—at least until we complete our preliminary investigation on Dr. Rhys-Evans's death. And that goes for the rest of the faculty, too. So far, whoever's targeting them has stayed on this side of Cajon Pass."

"Then we can go?" I asked.

"As soon as I finish interviewing you both."

"I'll try the roommate again, and then alert the rest of the department," Nakata said. "If Dora doesn't show up by tonight, they'll want to help with the search."

La Joie didn't waste time beating around the bush. "Did you speak to Dr. Rhys-Evans last night or this morning?" he asked me.

"No," I said. "We haven't spoken since last spring. His comments on my dissertation draft were delivered via e-mail."

"Okay." He pointed to my computer. "I read your notes while you were in the restroom, and typed short replies where necessary. We don't have to discuss them now. Check them over later, and call if you don't understand anything . . . I took the liberty of e-mailing the file to my office. Saves time—and I can print out multiple copies there." He turned to Killeen. "Your turn. You've already described what you found in the rock lab—"

My small sound was enough to check his flow. I hadn't known where Dai had been killed. I hadn't been ready to know.

"In the rock laboratory," La Joie repeated. "But what exactly did you touch? We'll want to sort out those prints from any others."

"My prints are all over the room," said Killeen. "I work there every day." But he listed the places he'd touched that morning. Then, prompted by La Joie, he named the people he'd spoken to about what he'd seen in the room. I was the only one on the list who wasn't legitimately associated with the investigation.

"Fair enough," said La Joie. "That's all I have right now. We'll type up a statement from what we have in our notes, and give you a chance to add anything that comes to you after you get back from Barstow. Please keep your pagers and cell phones on, in case we need to reach you."

He was at the door when I stopped him. "It may be nothing, but . . . I saw someone who reminded me of Geoff Travers today—while I was waiting for Killeen to come back."

Silence. "That wasn't in your notes," said La Joie, coming slowly back to face me. Behind him, Mulroney came in and waited just inside the door.

"Today's been crazy."

"What happened?"

"A woman—"

"A woman?"

"A woman was in the last row of seats—by the door. She followed Killeen out. But . . . but she paused in the doorway, as if—" This was harder than I thought it would be. "Look, she paused there, under the light, as if she wanted me to notice her. And then she smiled. Something about the way she held her head, her posture, reminded me of Geoff . . . It might be nothing," I said again, kicking myself for saying anything.

"Which door?" Mulroney said. I pointed, blessing his pale freckled face. "If the crew's still here, I'll have them check it for prints," he said. "Can't hurt."

La Joie sighed and ran both hands through his short hair. "Okay," he said. And then to me, "Detective Crank." This time it was my turn to be silent. "Detective Sergeant Conway Crank's in charge of the Barstow case."

"Crank with a C?" I asked.

"Yes. And he doesn't have much of a sense of humor about his name," he said. "Call me if you learn anything in Barstow." It sounded very much like an order. And La Joie and Mulroney were out the door before I had a change of heart.

"It'll be just like old times," Killeen said, pushing the cart with my equipment up the aisle. We were careful to head for the door opposite where the woman had exited.

"Except I'll be helping *you* this time." I pushed open the door and held it till he was through. The fog had burned off, and the courtyard was quiet and blessedly sunny. Cumulus clouds skittered across the sky and cast shifting shadows on the knobby, green-washed mountainside. The carillon tower struck the hour, a single sonorous note that vibrated along my spine. *Hickory dickory dock, The mouse ran up the clock, The clock struck one* . . . It was a lovely day to be alive. I wondered if the missing girl felt the same way.

"Is Dora especially friendly with anyone in the department?" I asked Killeen as we crossed the courtyard to geology.

"She's prickly," he said. "Keeps to herself mostly."

"Who's she rooming with?"

"An elementary school teacher. Stephanie Young. But they had a falling out recently. I don't know why. Dora said she's moving out at the end of the month. She wants a place of her own."

"Expensive," I said.

"She has money. A settlement of some kind."

"Work related?"

"I guess. She didn't volunteer the details, and I didn't ask."

"How old is she?"

Killeen paused for a moment. "Mid- to late thirties, I'd say. She was a legal secretary before going back to school. Said she used to go on field trips with the museum staff in Texas. Read up on fossils, took a few community college courses. Then something happened and she quit her job—or lost it—and went to school full-time. Transferred to Del Rio because she'd been out in the field with Marsh in Texas—and because a senior thesis with Marsh would help her get into grad school. She was applying to schools all over the West this fall."

"Did you get the sense that she knew what she was doing—workwise, that is?"

"She'd been out with Marsh a few times before to get the procedures down. The site was manageable. And she was able to explain taphonomy to me clearly enough."

I must have looked doubtful because he said, "Okay. Taphonomy goes beyond just identifying the fossils. It looks for clues as to where the fossils came from and how they came to be buried there—like the orientation of the bones with respect to each other, the presence of gnaw marks from predators, signs that the bones were weathered before they were buried. Things like that."

"Remind me to find a gold star for your collar."

Killeen made a snorting noise. "Anyway, Marsh and Dora had visited this fossil quarry that was worked out thirty years ago. A student wrote a thesis back in the seventies, describing the rocks and fossils. But she didn't include a taphonomic study of the site. The science was pretty new then, apparently."

"It was . . . I take it that recent erosion exposed more fossils?"

"Yeah. The pocket seemed to extend farther into the ridge. Dora was excited by the project, totally focused. Couldn't wait to be her own boss."

"Was she leery of working under people?"

"Been burned more than once, I'd say." Killeen paused while we negotiated the door to the geology building. "Dora has your old desk, by the way," he said, as we passed the office under the stairwell. "That poster's hers."

I looked at the crimson letters that shouted *ENOUGH!* "Is that a general comment on world events, or was someone harassing her?"

"I took it as an antiwar statement. If she was being harassed or stalked, she would have said something—loudly and clearly."

"Maybe that's what she's doing with the sign," I said.

"God, I hope not." Killeen gave me a bleak look. "I hope I wasn't too busy to notice something that serious."

"I doubt it. You don't miss much, Killeen."

We turned right down the connecting hall, passing the seismograph and the reconstructed *Cuvieronius edensis* skeleton in his glass display case. Like the fossils from the Cady Mountains quarry, this representative of an ancient side branch off the mastodon line was a gift of the Mojave Desert.

"So what do you think happened to Dora?" I asked him.

"Haven't a clue," said Killeen. "Maybe someone from her past tracked her down. Maybe the truck broke down and she decided to hitchhike into Barstow for help."

"Wouldn't she have called someone?"

"You'd think so, though the reception's iffy out there. I'll be curious to see if her cell phone's in with her gear."

As we turned left into the other wing of the building, I could hear faint voices coming up the stairwell from the basement. Sounded like Mulroney and La Joie. I wondered if Dai's body was still in the rock lab. Poor Dai—

"Frankie?" Killeen's voice called me back to the vinyl floors and glass cases of the hallway. "Don't go there," he said. "Not now."

I nodded and preceded him into his office. The room smelled of dusty rocks and fossils, cold coffee, WD-40, and glue. Below us, two floors down in the subbasement, the rock lab would smell of oily water and kerosene. "How did he die?" I asked Killeen as we unloaded the equipment into the old oak lockers. This was as good a time and place as any to hear the story.

"Sure you want to know?"

I nodded. I wanted to listen, then leave the memory here, in this building, forever.

Killeen described the scene. Rhys-Evans had been perched on one of the metal stools, working at a lapidary wheel, polishing an oval cabochon of sugilite. He was wearing safety glasses, a plastic apron over his clothes, and headphones. Water spraying from the lap wheel had dripped off his plastic apron to form a puddle on the cement. He'd been listening on his Walkman to Richard Burton's rendition of *The Little Prince*. The plastic tape case was on the table by the door. He wouldn't have heard anyone come in . . . Killeen found the cabochon still on the wheel and Rhys-Evans on the floor, in the water. He'd been struck on the head more than once. A metal ammo box was by his foot.

"Jesus H. Christ." I sat down so hard in Killeen's chair that it almost tipped over.

Killeen put a hand on my shoulder to steady me. "You okay?"

I shook my head. The picture he'd created was so vivid I wondered if I'd sleep that night. "Rhys-Evans was a creature of habit. Everyone in the department knows that. The first night of quarter break he was always at school, working on his mineral collection."

"Habit makes you vulnerable."

"Yes." I took a brush from my purse and ran it through my hair, over and over. The strokes were soothing. Killeen handed me a rubber band from the top drawer of his desk. "Thanks," I said, pulling my hair into a ponytail. "You know, you're lucky the police let you go."

"If you hadn't called me about Sarah last night, they might be holding me downtown right now." Killeen picked up a hand broom and swept rock chips from his desk into a metal wastebasket. They clattered like wind-driven sand against a car door, making me homesick for the desert. "I take it your own visit downtown yesterday prompted the typed questions to La Joie," he went on. "And your 'seeing' Geoff in that woman at the back of the hall."

"You wondered if I was losing it?"

"Just for a moment." Killeen leaned against the desk, waiting for the rest of the story.

The big clock on the wall showed 1:15. I felt as if a month had passed since I entered the lecture hall to defend my work. I picked up my briefcase, purse, and computer. "Look, Killeen, the Geoff story's pretty long. How about I fill you in on the way to Barstow?"

"Deal. My place at three?" Killeen hung the broom and dustpan on nails driven into the wall, and dusted off his hands. "I'll call Barstow and see if we can look at the truck tonight. It'll save time."

I turned at the door. "Have you figured out how you're going to explain to Sylvie that you're off to Barstow four days before you tie the knot?"

He grimaced. "Not a clue."

"Flowers might reassure her that you have your priorities straight."

"Nothing," he said, "will interfere with that wedding on Saturday."

*Throwing down the gauntlet to Fate is never a good idea,* I thought, closing the door behind me.

# 23

## Del Rio, California

Tuesday, December 14, 1:40 p.m.

I hung my suit in Sarah's crowded guest-room closet, tucking Tona's opal necklace and earrings into a jacket pocket. Dressing quickly in field pants and boots, I stuffed my toiletries in my overnight bag, before looking up the number for Sarah's neighbor, Phillip Grover. I left my cell phone number and a message asking him to feed Zoey while I was in Barstow. After taking a last look around, I filled Zoey's food and water dishes and gave her a kiss. I left a light burning. Sometimes symbols are all the hope we have.

At the hospital entrance I turned off my cell phone and followed the signs to the chapel. There I lit ten candles and sat on the hard wooden pew, letting the silence wash over me. Deep red poinsettias and cream-colored candles stood on either side of the altar. They reminded me of Sarah's blood and waxen pallor last night. Today, upstairs, she'd be swathed in white, like a newborn child. If she survived, is that how she'd feel—reborn? I'd know soon enough.

I could have stayed in that quiet place all day, but I didn't have the option. When I felt composed enough to go, I asked directions to Sarah's room. They'd moved her to the third floor. A police officer was sitting to the left of the door, guarding the entrance. He called in my name, checked my driver's license, and carefully noted the information and the time of my visit. Only then did he allow me inside.

A nurse stood by the bed. Sarah's small body was swathed in bandages—head and arms and what I could see of her chest above the hospital gown and white sheet. Her legs were in casts, elevated in slings. A respirator helped her breathe; an IV fed her body.

"How's she doing?" I asked the nurse.

"Pretty well, considering what she's been though," he said. "Still in a coma. We'll have a better idea in a day or so."

"I didn't bring flowers. I wasn't sure you'd let her have them."

"Later," he said. "For now, why don't you just talk to her for a bit—in case she can hear your voice."

So I pulled up the chair, took her unbandaged hand between mine, and said in a low voice, close to her ear, "Don't you quit on me now, Sarah Barstead. Don't give Geoff that satisfaction. Don't you *dare* give him that satisfaction."

And it might have been my imagination, a muscle twitch, or spasm of pain, but I thought her fingers tightened for an instant on mine.

"Hang in there. I'll be back soon."

The only answers were the whooshing sounds of the ventilator and respirator, and the soft, regular beeping of the pulse and blood pressure monitors.

I pressed her hand one last time, kissed her bandaged forehead, and picked up my purse. To the nurse and guard outside the door, I said: "Keep her safe."

And then I went to collect Killeen.

# 24

## Cady Mountains

Mojave Desert, California
Tuesday, December 14, 2:30 p.m.

Seth Camber walked through the opening of the stone room and looked at the net canopy lying on the dirt floor. The lightness drained from his face. "Now why did you have to do that?" he said in a tone all the more fierce for its softness.

He took off his backpack and dropped it just outside the doorway. Crouching down he unpacked her insulin supplies and set them next to Dora.

"I had to see the sky," she said, checking to make sure that everything she needed was there. Adopting a more docile tone, she added, "Thank you for bringing the insulin."

"I'd rather keep you alive, you know. But it isn't necessary."

"I gathered as much." She pointed to the journal, lying at the foot of the sleeping bag.

Without acknowledging her comment, Seth sliced hard salami, handed it to her, and followed it with a handful of trail mix and a cup of water. "Enough?" he asked, a glint of humor underlying his words.

"What's so funny?"

"Ironic," he corrected.

How long had Jed—or Seth—been planning this kidnapping? Dora wondered, as she chewed slowly on the spicy meat. Since they'd spent the day down below on the mesa? He'd tell her. She'd make sure of that. But *she* had to take charge of the conversation.

"Did you ever go back to Idaho?" she asked.

He was sitting in the doorway, his face to the sun. It took him a long time to answer. "I thought they might have forgiven me. Quick had been gone a long time . . ." he said at last. "But the mark had made me invisible, even to them."

"What mark?"

"The mark of Cain, of course. Ma cursed me. Seth's dead. They're all dead now."

"So who am I talking to?"

"A ghost. A nameless, ageless ghost." He was quiet for a minute, watching Dora test her glucose level and inject insulin. "How old do you think I am, Dora Simpson?"

She'd worked it out from the dates in the journal. "Thirty-seven. We're the same age, Seth. But you don't look it."

"That's the mark—the curse and the blessing. I can look any age." He smiled, and the smile reached his eyes. "People see what they expect to see, Dora."

He'd spoken in Dora's voice. She'd heard her own voice on the answering machine often enough to know the tones and inflection were perfect. It was eerie, disconcerting. She sounded like her mother, she realized, and hated the thought.

"You think the mark will protect you forever?" she asked.

"People see what they expect to see. That's all the protection I need."

This goodly frame, the earth, seems to me a sterile
promontory . . .
—William Shakespeare, *Hamlet*

Out West . . . there is more sky than any place in the
world. It does not sit flatly on the rim of the earth, but
begins somewhere out in the space in which the earth is
poised, hollows more, and is full of clean winey winds . . .
This is the sense of the desert hills, that there is room
enough and time enough.
—Mary Austin, *The Land of Little Rain*, 1903

Far ahead of us a white line traced across the barren
plain marked our road. It seemed to lead to nowhere,
except onward over more and more arid reaches of
desert. Rolling hills of crude color and low gloomy
contour rose above the general level. Here and there the
eye was arrested by a towering crag, or an elevated,
rocky mountain group, whose naked sides sank down
into the desert, unrelieved by the shade of a solitary
tree. The whole aspect of nature was dull in color, and
gloomy with an all-pervading silence of death . . .
—Clarence King, *Mountaineering in the Sierra Nevada:
I. The Range*, 1871

# 25

## Del Rio, California

Wisteria vines, flowerless now as winter approached, cloaked the portico of Killeen's rented bungalow on Lecil Street. A stray cat fled around the corner as I climbed the single porch step and knocked on the door. Tommy Kingsley, Sylvie's four-year-old son, opened it.

"My tempracher's a hunnerd an' two," he said by way of greeting. "And my ear hurts. Mommy gave me pink med'cin that tastes like bubble gum. She says not to kiss you."

"How about a hug, then," I said.

"Mommy says I give the best hugs." Tommy demonstrated by wrapping his wiry brown arms around my legs and squeezing.

"Your mommy's right." I picked him up. "You've grown," I said, carrying him into the front hall and setting him down.

"A whole inch," he said.

Sylvie was typing a paper on a laptop at the tiny kitchen table. The university radio station was playing a bluesy jazz piece by Wynton Marsalis. "Hey, Sylvie," I said.

She jumped up and hugged me tightly. "God, Frankie—it's so awful about Sarah and Dai. I just can't believe it." Taking a step back, she scanned my face with serious blue eyes. She was twenty-four and looked sixteen. "How are you holding up?"

I wasn't sure of the answer, so I settled for a so-so wiggle of the hand.

"Give me one more minute to finish this paper, and then I can welcome you properly. There are soft drinks in the fridge," she said. "Eddie's in the garage, I think—or meditating in the front room."

Sylvie was the only one who called Killeen by his given name. "Take your time," I said. "I'll visit with Tommy."

I took a long skinny bundle from my back pocket. It was

wrapped in the Sunday comics. "I brought you something," I said, handing it to Tommy.

He held the present as if he'd never had one before. "For me? Do I have to wait till Christmas to open it?"

"No, you don't have to wait till Christmas. It's a 'just-because' present."

"What's that?"

"Just because you're special."

"We have a tree," he said, changing subjects with the speed of light. He grabbed my hand and tugged. "Come see."

A sweet-smelling pine, hung with tiny white lights, stood in the living room's bay window. The tree was decorated only as high as a four-year-old could reach. "Lovely," I said, as Tommy tore open the package. It was a soft plastic snake, about three feet long.

Tommy had a thing for animals, reptilian or otherwise. Our first conversation had concerned the biological definition of the class Mammalia. "Wait," he said, and ran out of the room.

A simple altar occupied one corner. No icons—just candles, an uncarved cube of raw green marble, a scrub jay's feather, and a cowrie shell, lying on a scrap of gold cotton cloth. In front, on the floor, was a cushion in matching fabric, large enough for one Killeen-size person to sit and meditate. I turned to look out the front window and saw Killeen toss something into the back of the Cherokee. Ten seconds later he was opening the front door. "Ready to go?"

"Almost."

Tommy came back carrying a field guide to reptiles, plopped himself down in an armchair, and flipped through the pages until he found what he wanted. "This one?"

"Good call. I have a king snake just like it in my backyard at home."

I was rewarded with another hug. "Thanks, Frankie. I'll keep it always. I'm gonna call him George."

"George? As in King George III of England? The Revolutionary War?"

"No, silly. Because snakes live under bushes."

It took me a minute. George. Bushes. Got it. "George it is," I said. I decided not to ask whether he meant father or son.

"I don't think they cover the Revolutionary War in prekindergarten," Killeen said, picking up Tommy and kissing him on the cheek.

"You never know," I said.

"Are all snakes the same, Frankie, or are there mommy snakes and daddy snakes?" Tommy asked from his perch on Killeen's shoulder.

I knew what was coming next. So did Killeen. He just grinned. "There are male snakes and female snakes," I said. "And when your daddy gets home from our little trip he'll be happy to answer *all* your questions."

Sylvie joined us just as I finished. "You're leaving already? We haven't had a chance to visit."

Killeen set Tommy down. "We'll be back soon," he said, running a hand down her flaxen hair.

Sylvie captured his dark hand between her pale ones. A silent message passed between them, but all she said was, "Promise me, Eddie."

"We're not heading off to war, honey. We're looking for Dora."

"Saturday morning," she said. "Newman Center. Noon. Don't forget."

"Have I ever let you down?" he said. "Don't worry. Frankie and I have it covered. We'll be back in plenty of time. You just focus on getting our ring bearer well." Killeen picked up an overnight bag. "Sylvie needs the truck," he said to me. "Okay if we take your Cherokee?"

"I'd planned on it."

"Good. Because I've put a few things in the back—just in case."

Sylvie gave me a hug. "Please find her," she said. "I remember how it feels to be lost."

"We'll find her," Killeen said. "How was Sarah?" he said to me.

I didn't ask how he knew that I'd been to see her. Killeen knew things. "Hanging in there," I said. "And she's protected. One officer outside her door, and a male nurse beside her bed."

"Good," Killeen said again. He kissed Tommy and Sylvie, and then we were out the door. "Just like old times," he said for the second time that day.

"Don't remind me." My cell phone rang. It was Philo, calling from Tucson. He must have gotten my message from this morning. I hadn't had a chance to call him since.

"Is this Dr. MacFarlane?" Philo asked.

"No."

"You failed your defense?" The astonishment rippled across the airwaves. I could hear my four brothers squawking questions in the background. They'd probably popped the champagne cork already.

"It was canceled," I said.

Tommy had followed us onto the porch and was watching me intently from great, dark eyes, drinking in every word. He didn't need to hear the details.

"Can I call you right back, Philo? Killeen and I need to get on the road." I dropped my keys into Killeen's outstretched palm, and followed him across the small patch of grass to the car. "I'll explain everything, I promise. You can even put me on speakerphone so the guys can hear. Where are you, by the way?"

"Your house. We'll be holding our breath," Philo said, and hung up.

I needed to collect my thoughts, so I waited until we were on Highway 60 before punching my parents' home number. I was still house-sitting for them. They'd be home from their sabbatical in England next week.

"One of my professors was killed last night," I said.

"Dr. Barstead died?"

"No. This was a second one. David Rhys-Evans. Killeen found his body this morning. At school."

"Is there a connection?"

"Looks like it."

"Are you in danger?"

"No. I'm with Killeen."

"I hope you're going to tell me you're heading home."

"Not yet. The defense has been rescheduled for Friday. The acting chair pressed another prof into subbing for Dai."

"So two of your three committee members have been attacked."

"Yes. I think it's Geoff. They were also on his committee. So was Peter Snavely. He died in a car accident last spring."

"Geoff's definitely alive, then."

"I'm not sure Geoff is Geoff, but yes—and I think I may have seen him today."

I heard him swear under his breath. "Frankie—"

"Philo, if Geoff wanted to hurt me he knew where to find me. He's always known. Anyway, I'll be out of harm's way for at least a day. Killeen and I are going to Barstow. One of the students has gone missing out in the Cadys. We're going to check out her field vehicle."

"This disappearance—you're sure it isn't related to the other attacks?"

"Dora was new this fall. She didn't even know Geoff. And her major professor wasn't on Geoff's committee."

"Still . . ."

"Dora's diabetic. She was working alone. We think she may have run out of insulin or had a reaction."

"I thought you didn't believe in coincidence, Frankie?"

"I don't, generally speaking. But there are always exceptions to prove the rule." Before Philo or my brothers could debate the point, I added, "Anyway, I won't be home till Sunday. Killeen and Sylvie are getting married on Saturday."

"I'll fly out tomorrow," Philo said. "No, don't argue, Frankie—unless you want all five of us to show up." He was telling the truth—I could hear my brothers discussing schedules in the background. "I wouldn't have missed your defense in the first place, if I hadn't had to testify. I'll call and let you know where I'll be staying. We can drive back together on Sunday. And please tell Killeen congratulations—and there'll be an additional guest at his wedding."

"You win," I said. "And you might as well drink the champagne you opened. Wouldn't want to waste it. I'll call you from Barstow. Love you all."

"Philo's flying in tonight?" Killeen said.

"Tomorrow. How'd you know?"

"It's what I'd do. And I take it he's crashing the wedding?"

"He is indeed."

"Good," Killeen said. "I need a best man. By the way, I reached Crank. He'll stay late so we can see the truck tonight. They've already dusted it for prints—nothing turned up—and they've inventoried the cargo."

My cell phone rang again. At this rate, I'd have to recharge it before we'd even crossed Cajon Pass. It was Detective La Joie.

"You're on the road?" he asked.

"Yes. Killeen's driving. I can talk."

"I spoke to Stephanie Young, Dora Simpson's roommate. Simpson's insulin supply is gone. Young thinks it was there this morning, but she's not sure. No sign that anybody broke in, so she figured Simpson must have come back either last night, when Young was asleep, or after Young left for work. But she didn't leave a note. And even though they weren't on the best of terms, Young thinks Dora would have left a note."

"Does anyone else have a key to the apartment?" I heard the flipping of notebook pages and the ringing of a phone.

"Hold on a sec, will you?" La Joie said, and the line went quiet. "Dr. MacFarlane? Thanks for holding. Let's see . . . The apartment manager has a key," La Joie continued. "But we checked. She was out all day. We checked with the neighbors, too. One said she saw a woman in an older car—faded green—let herself in. Middle of the morning, she thought. The woman came out carrying a box and a grocery bag. It could have been Simpson. The neighbor just moved in last week. She doesn't know either roommate."

"So you think she's okay?" I asked him. "Should we turn back?" Killeen looked at me, and I held up a finger to forestall the question.

"No. The Afton Canyon business bothers me. And Barstow still needs to work the case as if she's a missing person. Call me after you check the truck?"

"It might be late."

"I work nights," he said, and disconnected.

# 26

## Cajon Pass, California
Tuesday, December 14, 3:40 p.m.

"We're good to go," I said to Killeen as I reached over the seat to get my computer. While it booted, I told him what La Joie had to say.

La Joie's style of written communication, I found when I opened my file, was equally terse. To the questions I'd posed about Dai's death, he had no answers—understandable, since the investigation had just begun. Or maybe he hadn't wanted to put notes on my computer where anyone might view them. But Killeen had already answered the *where* and *how* of Dai's death, and La Joie had told me approximately *when*. What I didn't know was whether the ammo box had contained a note. Killeen hadn't touched it. A note at the scene would confirm the tie to Sarah's attack.

"When we were in the lecture hall," I said to Killeen, "why did you tell me that Dai's death definitely was linked with Sarah's attack?"

"Besides the fact that he was killed just after Sarah was hit?"

"Yes. What didn't La Joie want to say?"

"He opened the ammo box while I was there. Probably broke all kinds of rules and regulations doing it. It could have been booby-trapped . . . Anyway, La Joie nodded, like it was something he expected to find."

"It was. Was there a note inside?"

"Yup. I didn't get a look at it, of course. I was waiting just outside the door. But I saw him take it out and look at it."

"So I have at least one question to ask La Joie."

"Were there notes at Sarah's house?"

I realized Killeen didn't know any of the details from last night. There hadn't been time to fill him in. He needed to know what the faculty was facing, so I gave him the short version—timing, sequence, clues.

"*Romeo and Juliet?*" Killeen gave me a sideways glance. "Doesn't sound like anyone from our department."

"Yes, well, who knows what drives a killer. If I'm right, and Geoff's behind this, then the tragedy is a metaphor for his feelings of betrayal. The play has murder, revenge, ill-fated lovers—and a double suicide at the end."

"Let's avoid re-creating that ending, okay?" Killeen said. "So what were the quotes you found at the house?"

"I saw only one of them. I made educated guesses about the others. I didn't see them, but they were found outside in places linked to the play." I made a note. "I'll have to ask La Joie for the whole list."

"Now that you've described Sarah's attack, I see another similarity." Killeen sped up to pass a car. "La Joie may have noticed it," he continued, when he was back in the right lane. "Might have been looking for it, in fact—a little plastic rock on the counter next to Rhys-Evans's tape case. It didn't mean anything to me. I thought one of his kids must have left it."

"Did it beep? It's supposed to be a motion sensor from a kid's spy kit."

"Is that what it was? No, it didn't beep when I opened the door—or when La Joie went in later. But I saw him glance at it just before he went over and opened the ammo box."

"It was important," I said. "Did the killer—" It was hard to ask the question, but I needed to know. "Did he . . . mutilate Dai's body? He ran over Sarah's legs after he hit her the first time. I think he ran over her legs because running was her only passion—outside of geology."

"No, unless you count multiple blows to the head. He made very sure Rhys-Evans was dead."

I saw the unsuspecting Dai, sitting on a stool, just as I'd done so often when grinding thin sections or polishing rock slabs. He was wearing headphones, listening to *The Little Prince*. Was Dai picturing Antoine de Saint-Exupéry's drawing of a boa constrictor? Was there an elephant inside?

"Frankie?" Killeen's voice pulled me back with a jolt. "Did La Joie make any other notes?"

The words on the computer screen swam into focus, and I read them to Killeen. La Joie was able to add details about Bernie Venable and Geoff Travers. Bernie's dental records had been faxed by his childhood dentist in Pasadena. They showed a likely match to the remains from the ravine. La Joie was waiting for a baby tooth and hair sample from Venable's parents for DNA confirmation.

Ohio State's geology department had faxed photos of Geoff Travers as an undergraduate. They weren't very good. So Mulroney had scanned the driver's license photo from the Mexican citation and the group photo I'd taken of Geoff with the others in Nevada. The department replied that the man in those photos had been an undergraduate there at the same time as Geoff Travers. He'd been expelled for cheating on a final exam. His name was Perry Edwards, from Milwaukee. They gave his last known address and phone number. No one in the department knew what had happened to Perry—and no one had heard from Geoff Travers since he left for UC–Del Rio.

So the real Geoff Travers, La Joie wrote, was now missing and presumed dead, murdered by Perry Edwards of Milwaukee. But Milwaukee had no record of a Perry Edwards.

I stopped reading aloud, overwhelmed by the proof that it had all been a lie—the fabricated past, the adopted English accent and family. Smoke and mirrors. No wonder "Geoff" hadn't wanted to take me home to meet his parents.

In Pair-a-Dice, Nevada, last summer, a woman had tried to warn me about Geoff. She'd said he was manipulative. I hadn't understood, hadn't read the subtext. I'd felt betrayed by Geoff and distrustful of men in general, but I couldn't have imagined how profound that deception was. And it was nothing compared to what Geoff had done in the past twenty-four hours.

"Why didn't I see Geoff for what he was, Killeen?"

"You mean, how could you have fallen in love with a serial killer?"

"That's pretty brutal."

"Just getting to the bottom line."

"I could use a little empathy here, Killeen. Finding out your lover plagiarized your work is one thing—planning a future with a serial killer's something else entirely. I'm pretty damned observant. How could I have been so blind?"

"And stupid."

"Okay, blind *and* stupid."

Killeen relented. "Remember the BTK killer in Wichita—the one they finally caught last year? For thirty years he flew under the radar. He raised a family, went to work, had friends, was active in his church. His family didn't guess; his friends trusted him. He was two people—one public, one private. The BTK killer hid in plain sight, Frankie."

"Like 'The Purloined Letter.'"

"Like your Geoff. Was he charming?"

"Until we became engaged." I looked down at my left hand. Geoff and I had been engaged for five months. The pale circle where the ring had been disappeared last summer, but I could still picture the Hopi-crafted silver band, etched with symbols of clouds and rain. A nontraditional ring. I hadn't thought, at the time Geoff gave it to me, that the rain might, just as easily, symbolize tears.

"What happened to the ring?" Killeen asked.

"He wouldn't take it back, so I tied it to one of his running shoes and added it to his pile of stuff."

"No fires of Mount Doom handy?" Killeen was a Tolkien fan.

"At the time, I didn't think it was necessary."

"Frankie, Ted Bundy was charming. He was handsome, engaging, intelligent. Even after he was convicted and sentenced, women still wanted to meet him. The attraction of the dark side, I guess."

I thought back. "Geoff had a dark side, too—a buried hurt that lent him a subtle vulnerability. I couldn't fit him into any category, any pigeonhole. He was a bit unpredictable, with an offbeat sense of humor . . . He didn't bore me. He intrigued me."

"I suspect that you glimpsed his dark side peeking through the charming veneer. No wonder he intrigued you."

We both were silent for a time, following the separate paths of our thoughts. While we weren't looking, the day had become overcast. Clouds piled on top of each other in the south, with only the occasional patch of sky showing deep blue as sunset neared.

Traffic was light on the road. We climbed toward the pass between the San Gabriel and San Bernardino Mountains on one of the oldest routes to and from California and the Pacific Ocean. Innumerable fault zones cut through these ranges, including the granddaddy of them all, the San Andreas. The rocks are shattered by the scraping and gouging of two tectonic plates, jockeying for dominance. We were about to cross from the Pacific Plate to the North American Plate. The driving forces that locked these blocks into perpetual tension and conflict lay miles below our asphalt ribbon of road . . . just as the driving forces behind Geoff's violent acts lay buried so deep in his psyche that none of us had seen the danger. We'd accepted the facade Geoff presented and never looked below the surface. Well, he had our attention now.

"It's so crazy, Killeen. *He's* crazy—killing Sarah and Dai and Bernie . . . and the real Geoff Travers." My skin prickled, remembering Geoff's touch. "I need a shower."

"They'll catch him, Frankie. His luck's run out." He downshifted on the grade, reached over, and held my hand. "Trust me on this. It's only a matter of time."

"I hope you're right," I said.

The San Bernardinos showed burnt umber and orange slashes where the wildfires of last autumn had seared the slopes. The coming rains would trigger flash floods and debris flows. I had the awful feeling it would happen soon.

Killeen read my mind. "Rain's forecast for Barstow tomorrow."

I welcomed the change of subject. "Meaning it could rain or snow in the Cadys. I don't suppose you brought along spare rain gear?"

"A poncho. Thought you might need it. And if you're gonna call La Joie, you better be quick about it," Killeen said. "I'm betting we'll lose reception in the pass. Won't get it again till the descent to Victorville."

La Joie picked up on the first ring.

"No wonder you wanted us out of Dodge," I said. "The man you're hunting is a very proficient killer."

"And good at covering his tracks," said La Joie. "So what did you want to know?"

"Was the plastic rock on the table in the lab the same kind as the smashed one last night?"

"Your friend Killeen's observant. But this one didn't have a battery."

"What was on the note you found in the ammo box?"

"Another quote."

"Would you read me all the ones you have so far?"

It took a few minutes for me to write them down. "Got it," I said. "They're all from *Romeo and Juliet.* But you already knew that. And before you ask, no, Geoff didn't quote *Romeo and Juliet* to me—at least not that I can remember."

"I'll trust your memory, Dr. MacFarlane. Anyway, the symbolism's obvious."

"Don't tell me you skimmed the Cliffs Notes over breakfast?"

La Joie gave what sounded like a laugh. "Nothing quite so

drastic. I talked with the profiler." He covered the mouthpiece for a moment, then said, "Her name's Debbie Adams. She wants to know what Geoff was like. She's listening in on an extension."

"Good. Killeen and I were just talking about that." I gave them a recap.

"What did he do in his free time?" asked Debbie. She had a strong, assured voice.

"Grad students don't have much free time."

"Still, he must have done something to relax," said Debbie.

"You mean, besides sex," I said. "And I'm not going there on a cell phone, Detective La Joie."

"Understood," he said. But he sounded amused. "What else?"

"He bagged peaks."

"What's that?" Debbie said.

"Climbing the tallest peaks in a state," La Joie answered for me.

"By the time I met him," I said, "Geoff had done ten or twelve states."

"How old was he?" said Debbie.

La Joie answered for me. "According to his driver's license, he was twenty-seven."

"But he seemed older," I said. "Maybe because his hair was thinning."

Debbie asked something, but the transmission was garbled.

"Could you repeat that?" I asked.

"How did he act toward you?"

"He became possessive. I didn't notice it at first because I wanted to spend my free time with him, too. But after we were engaged, he wanted all my time. It was over long before it was over, if you know what I mean."

La Joie's next question was broken. "I'm losing you," I said. "I'll call from Barstow."

"Stop thinking about it," Killeen said when I hung up. "Give yourself a break. Think about geology. Think about nothing. Meditate."

I shut down the computer and put it away. We crossed the San Andreas fault zone and entered a landscape dominated by steeply dipping ridges of coarse-grained sedimentary rock. The entire area had been sculpted by running water over the last six hundred thousand years.

Soon we were crossing the inface bluffs at Cajon Summit. Below us lay Victorville and the Mojave Desert. The broad-shouldered San Gabriel Mountains behind us blocked the setting sun. A huge alluvial fan dotted with juniper and Joshua trees dipped down toward the desert. We paralleled Oro Grande Wash as we descended, crossing the entrenched Mojave River just north of Victorville. The Mojave Narrows held railroad tracks, and cottonwoods full of mistletoe. Around us, the granite hills glowed ghostly white. I could smell rain in the distance—not what the Apache call male rain, accompanied by the Sturm und Drang of thunder, lightning, and hail, but female rain—steady, constant, life-giving, renewing. Yet even female rain can lead to flooding.

Faced with the immensity that was the Mojave Desert, I worried about Dora. Was she frightened and alone? Was she wandering the arroyos? Was she alive?

# 27

## Barstow, California

Tuesday, December 14, 6:00 p.m.

It was dark by the time Killeen and I reached Barstow, a railroad town on the Mojave River, not far from the Old Spanish Trail. Barstow had been a fort and a stop along Hi Jolly's camel route in the nineteenth century, when the army experimented with using camels to move supplies across the desert. Now, businesses from different eras rubbed shoulders on Barstow's Main Street, the fabled Route 66. A palmist offered a five-dollar special. At the Bun Boy, a peeling landmark across from the Holiday Inn Express, tumbleweeds clustered at the edges of the rutted parking lot. The lot held only one car—from Alberta, Canada.

We took rooms at the Super 8 on Coolwater Lane. Killeen called Crank at the Sheriff's office to see if there was any word on Dora. The garages in town hadn't heard from her, Crank said. The search dogs had found nothing at the Afton Canyon campground. It was as if she'd flown away from the site. Or been carried. They'd mount a full search in the morning.

Killeen told him we were grabbing dinner before we checked out Dora's vehicle—if that was okay with him. It was. Killeen asked him to join us. He declined. He'd see us in an hour.

"Looks like your shower's gonna have to wait," Killeen said.

We found dinner at Los Gueros, a Mexican restaurant on Route 66. Neon beer signs in the window advertised Corona, Pacifico, and Cerveza Sol. Inside, rust brown carpet underlay five brown-leather booths with fake flowers on the tables. Four faux-marble tables hugged the interior walls. The salt and pepper shakers were Coronita Extra bottles. But it's never about the décor. Or the music, though the toe-tapping, intrusive polka jarred with my mood. What mattered was that the place served homemade *salsa fresca* and handmade tortillas.

The other patrons spoke Spanish. So, I found out, did Killeen. We ordered guacamole, made fresh at the table. The server mashed avocadoes in a vesicular basalt mortar, added spices, and set the mortar on the table with a flourish before delivering the rest of our order—a chili verde burrito with tomatillo sauce for me, the burrito special combination for Killeen. He polished off his dinner and part of mine, then looked longingly at the deep-fried ice cream. He passed. I swear I could hear his arteries rejoicing.

The sheriff's office was clustered with the police and highway patrol in old-town Barstow. The car-impound lot was on the west side of their white single-story building on a bluff overlooking the valley. At this hour, all we could see to the north was a field of lights, diminishing into the distance.

Inside the glass doors, the simply furnished foyer held a Toys for Tots box in one corner, a pine wreath hanging above it. We were the only customers. Déjà vu. Was it just yesterday afternoon that I'd been sitting in the Del Rio PD reception room, reading a vandalized copy of National Geographic while I waited for La Joie? It seemed as if I'd known him since preschool.

The receptionist sat behind a window on the left. She had thick, neatly coiffed, honey blonde hair, fingernails so long she couldn't possibly type accurately, and a nobody-gets-by-me set to her jaw. We introduced ourselves. She told us Crank would be right out.

Conway Crank had one blue eye and one brown, pale hair, a ruddy complexion, and no expression whatsoever. "Thanks for coming," he said. He didn't sound thankful. "La Joie said you'd know if there's anything missing from the truck." His tone implied that otherwise we wouldn't get beyond the foyer.

Crank took us back through the offices. Without breaking stride, he grabbed a heavy brown jacket from the back of a chair and shrugged into it. He stopped at a door leading to the fenced impound lot. The Ford F-150 was parked under a spotlight near the door.

"Half the geology department's fingerprints and hair will be inside that truck," I said. "We all used it."

"So we discovered," said Crank. "Eudora Simpson's were the only fresh ones."

"Eudora?" I asked.

"She *really* doesn't like it if you call her that," Killeen said to me.

"The truck started right up," Crank said.

"So it didn't break down." Killeen sounded relieved. He was responsible for keeping the departmental vehicles running. "Anything unusual about the emergency call?"

"One thing. She called Afton Canyon by its old name—Cave Canyon," Crank said. "We had to look it up."

"Then the caller wasn't Dora. She only knew it as Afton," Killeen said. "But whoever the caller was, she knows her history."

"Somebody local?" I said.

"Maybe," Crank said. He handed us latex gloves and a copy of the inventory, then leaned against the wall.

The wind was cold as an Arctic ice core. I pulled my knit hat more snugly over my ears, wrapped my knit scarf more tightly around my throat, and pulled close-fitting leather gloves from my pocket. Killeen was wearing only a windbreaker. He didn't seem to feel the chill.

"It'll be down below freezing tonight," Crank said. "I hope she found shelter and can build a fire. Her sleeping bag's still in the truck."

I struggled to pull the latex gloves over my leather ones. I'd worry about removing the talcum powder later.

In back of the truck were two empty water barrels, a five-gallon gas can, and an assortment of cooking and camping gear. While Killeen ran down the list and checked it against his memory, I zeroed in on her personal belongings and geologic tools. The only clothes that appeared to be missing were her outerwear—hat, gloves, and boots—and whatever clothes she must have been wearing yesterday. Her backpack had a field notebook, poncho, dusty sweatshirt, and webbed belt with Brunton, canteen holder, penknife in its sheath, binoculars, and Estwing rock pick.

"Did she wear a field vest, Killeen?"

"No, she kept everything in her pockets, on her belt, in her backpack, or in her bucket. I checked through the collecting tools in the plastic bucket—everything's there."

"What about a purse?" Some women brought them to the field, some didn't.

He looked up from his list and thought for a second. "Yeah, a leather one. Light brown."

"It isn't here. Nor are her house keys, watch, and diabetic testing equipment."

"There's emergency glucose in the ice chest, and there's still ice left," he said. "A few fruits and vegetables, too. The trash has a used syringe and test strips—only a week's worth. She must have brought her garbage in when she made the last supply run."

"So her purse is gone—with her test strips, I assume—and her outerwear, watch, and the clothes on her body. Her computer's here, but no GPS or camera."

"She was using them when I left her," Killeen said. "The digital camera was small enough to fit in her pocket. She clipped the GPS to her belt, along with her cell phone."

"Someone could have come by and stolen the camera, phone, and GPS off the truck," Crank said. "It wasn't locked."

"Then why not take the computer?" I asked. "It's even more valuable."

"A lot of the people wandering around out there have more use for cameras, phones, and GPS units than computers," said Crank.

"Or they might still be with her," Killeen said.

I unearthed her maps, mapboard, and a couple of relevant theses on the area. In cardboard boxes I found the fossils she'd collected, some in plaster-of-paris jackets, some in sample bags. All were labeled with her field number, which matched the entries in her notebook. The field notebook had sketches of the position of the bones in the bed, along with detailed measurements of each bone, tentative identifications, and field numbers. The list included horse, camel, rhino, beaver, rodent, dog, and antelope. The days and field numbers were linked to digital photos and GPS coordinates. She'd also noted the weather. It had been windy yesterday morning—windy and cold.

I skimmed the earlier entries. "She's made a note here about having dinner with an anthropologist named Jed Strong from the San Diego Museum of Man," I said to Crank. "Ten days ago."

"We checked," Crank said. "No Jed Strong in their anthropology department, or working at the museum."

"Somebody illegally digging for artifacts?" Killeen asked.

"Big business, even out here," said Crank.

"She might have caught him prospecting for bones or collecting a site," Killeen said. "If Strong felt threatened, he might have killed her so she wouldn't talk."

I put Dora's notebook on the seat of the truck and looked at Killeen. "Then why was her truck at the Afton Canyon campground when she was working farther south in the range?"

"As good a dumping ground as any—better than most," Crank

said. "It'll take days to explore every crevice and side canyon. Meanwhile, he'll be hundreds of miles away."

"A group of us from the department will be heading out to Afton Canyon in the morning to help with the search."

"Just don't get in our way," Crank said. "You finished here?"

"Could we take her computer inside and copy the information onto a thumb drive?" I asked.

"I'll have to do it for you."

"Fine. Would it also be possible to photocopy the pages in her field notebook? Good. We'd like to backtrack her, reconstruct her movements . . . that is—Killeen did you bring a GPS unit, by any chance?"

Killeen just grinned. "I think we've done all we can here," he said. "You ready to go back inside, Frankie?"

I was through the door before he finished the question. The office was blissfully warm and inviting after the impound lot. I took off the gloves, found my USB drive in my pocket, and handed it to Crank. "It's got plenty of memory."

We pointed out the relevant files and watched over his shoulders as he copied them to the portable storage device. Dora had taken pictures of the outcrop and the section surrounding the bone bed. The GPS coordinates were already plotted on a topographic base map saved as a file. Dora was thorough.

While Crank copied the pages of the field notebook for us, Killeen and I sat shoulder to shoulder, absorbing the warmth and quiet. "Tuesday nights must be slow in Barstow," I whispered.

He winked, which I took to mean, "Every night's slow in Barstow."

I thought about what we'd seen on her computer. No, it was what *wasn't* there that bothered me. "The pattern makes no sense," I said. "There are pictures of Afton Canyon from the day you and Dora arrived in the Cadys, but none from yesterday. Nor are there any entries in the computer of the data she collected yesterday at the fossil quarry—data that's in her field notebook."

"Maybe she didn't have time to enter the data into the computer. Maybe she was running late and decided to wait until she got home," Killeen said.

"If she was running late, why did she detour to Afton Canyon? We keep coming back to that question."

"Insulin imbalance, maybe? It can happen quickly," Crank said, handing me the pages. "It's a place to start. But whatever the reason she's missing, we need to find her soon."

Back at the motel, I realized I'd run out of energy. I handed Killeen my notebook, opened to the page on which I'd copied La Joie's quotations. "The words are swimming before my eyes," I said.

Killeen followed me into my room, took the only chair, and read over the quotations silently. "I'll see if I can get the gist of what they're trying to tell us," he said. "Want me to check in with La Joie?"

"Would you? I promised Philo I'd call. I'm going to do that and then sleep."

"After your shower?"

"Maybe I'll sleep in the shower. It'll save time."

"Don't drown," said Killeen.

Later, I'd remember that advice.

# 28

## Barstow, California

Wednesday, December 15, 6:00 a.m.

"You're lookin' more lively," Killeen said, as we tossed our overnight bags into the Jeep.

"No police knocking on the door at midnight," I said. "Where do you want to eat?" We had a choice of breakfast places—Carrows, Bun Boy, IHOP.

"IHOP," he said. "It's close."

We sat at a table near the front. The only other customer was a man in a booth, talking to the server as Killeen and I reviewed the menu. They made no effort to keep their voices down.

"Didn't Loretta used to work here?" the customer asked.

"Where hasn't she worked? Last I heard she was at Bun Boy. But the gift shop sells some of her jewelry, if that's what you're looking for."

"You might want to put 'em on eBay," he said. "Collector's items, you know."

"What's she done this time—slept with the mayor?"

"You didn't hear? They found her body . . . at her house. It was on the radio this morning."

"Loretta was murdered?" The server stopped wiping the tables. "They're not sayin'."

"Oh, geez," she said, twisting the cloth in her hands. Drops of water rained on the floor. "Poor Loretta."

Even quiet towns like Barstow aren't immune from tragedy, I thought, as the server retreated into the kitchen. I heard her relating the news to the cook. A minute later she was at my elbow, ready to take our orders. Killeen ordered a full stack of buttermilk pancakes, eggs, and ham. I went with the Southwestern omelet, stoking up on protein. But I couldn't resist a side order of biscuits and honey.

"What were you saying about a slow night in Barstow?" Killeen asked me.

"Placid waters hide lethal currents." I drained my coffee cup and signaled for more. She filled our cups and left the carafe. By the time I'd finished the second cup I was feeling more human.

"I reached Mulroney last night. He said he'd pass the info along to La Joie," Killeen said. "And I called Nakata. She'll meet us out at Afton Canyon this morning. They planned to leave around four. She's bringing Rudinsky, Marsh, and four grad students."

"Let me guess . . . Cassie, Dee, Ryan, and Zev?"

"Yup. Rizzo can't make it—there's a problem on the drill rig. He'll come out later if we need him."

"We won't. And as long as he's out of Del Rio, he should be okay."

Breakfast arrived as the sky was beginning to lighten. But there would be no sunrise this morning. The rain that had been forecast for Barstow was already falling.

"Nasty day for a search," I said. "Any tracks will be long gone by the time we get there." I smothered my omelet with the side of salsa I'd requested. Spice boosted endorphins and made even a gray day seem warmer. "Any luck with the quotes?"

Killeen slid my notebook across the table. He'd numbered the quotations. "Just a suggestion," he said.

I read them aloud, in the order he'd chosen: "'*One, two, and the third in your bosom,*' . . . He's speaking first to me, and then to everyone else in the department."

"And to the police," said Killeen. "How many attacks are you attributing to Geoff?"

"Peter Snavely went off a mountain road last spring. He'd be one. Sarah's two. And Dai makes three. He was killed in 'the bosom' of the department."

"You're forgetting Bernie Venable and the real Geoff Travers. Weren't they the first two victims?"

Killeen was right. "Then Peter—if his death wasn't an accident—or Sarah would be three," I said. "And since I'm close to Sarah, the quote would easily apply to her. After all, she was killed by her home, in the bosom of her family, which includes me."

I spread boysenberry jam on my wheat toast, and munched while I studied the rest of the quotations. *Lady, by yonder blessèd moon I sweare / That tips with silver all these fruit-tree tops . . .*

*Stony limits cannot hold love out . . . Where care lodges, sleep will never lie,* was found under the lemon tree. *One fire burns out another's burning, / One pain is lessened by another's anguish . . . I'll prove more true than those that have more cunning to be strange,* was collected from the stone barbecue pit.

"He still loves you, Frankie, and he's not going to rest until he's punished—or 'burned'—everyone in the department who hurt him."

"Which is what he's been doing," I said.

"Until we prove otherwise—which doesn't seem likely. The real Geoff Travers is missing and presumed dead. Your fiancé assumed his identity—and killed Bernie Venable."

I looked down at the list. "When he wrote, '*Ask for me tomorrow, and you shall find me a grave man . . . [But] what's in a name? That which we call a rose / By any other name would smell as sweet,*' he seems to be admitting that he's used different names in the past. He wants us to ask for him 'tomorrow'—which was yesterday—and we'd find him 'a grave man.' He knew the police would discover, when they went back far enough, that Geoff and Bernie were dead, and that Perry Edwards was a student at Ohio State. I think he's telling us that Perry Edwards wasn't his real name either—that if we keep going back we'll find a trail of Perrys, Geoffs, and Bernies."

"His original name and identity is dead and buried. We'll never find it," Killeen said. "But the scariest note is the fifth: '*The time and my intents are savage and wild . . . [Go] wisely and slow; they stumble that run fast.*' They found it with Rhys-Evans's body. Your Geoff's turned 'savage and wild,' like a government operative who's gone off the grid."

"And he's warning the police that they'd better track him with great care, or they won't have a prayer of catching him."

"That's not what he means by 'stumbling,' Frankie. He means he'll take out anyone who tries to follow him."

"So they'll have to stay alert . . . You told this to Mulroney?"

"No, I wanted to talk with you first."

I picked up the check and headed for the cashier. "You drive. I'll call."

# 29

Killeen and I filled the gas tank and merged with the truck traffic on I-15. We followed the Mojave River, as so many travelers had before us, toward Afton Canyon—the old Cave Canyon of Jedediah Smith and John C. Frémont. When the Mojave River leaves that cut in the Cady Mountains, it disappears for good beneath the sands and alkali crust of the Mojave Sink. Beyond, in the desert reaches, water holes are scarce.

To the north of the highway the Calico Mountains, source of rich silver and colemanite deposits more than a century ago, were shades of blue gray, red, yellow, and black—colors associated with the four directions in Navajo sandpaintings. The roadbed was half red, half gray, becoming all red as we drove east. Blue call boxes marked the miles along the highway. The off-ramps lacked exit numbers. We were in Wonderland.

Mary Austin called this southeastern corner of the Great Basin the "Land of Little Rain." The intrepid Padre Garcés, the same cleric who helped select the town site for Tucson, crossed the Mojave Desert to and from the mission of San Gabriel in Alta, California, in the winter of 1779—the first white man to do so. He rejoiced when he reached the perennial water in Cave Canyon. I'd rejoice when we found Dora.

Only jeep roads lead into the Cadys. There are no springs, no water sources except in Afton Canyon, on the northern edge of the mountains, and in tanks holding rainwater after rare storms pass through. Dora Simpson had brought in her water. The barrels were empty by the time she left.

The call to La Joie was short. He didn't have much time to spare. "Anything new?" Killeen asked when I'd signed off.

I slid Fauré's *Requiem* into the CD player, and let the melodies begin to work their magic before I spoke. "The victim in the ravine was Bernie Venable." Killeen reached over and held my hand. I was grateful he was there. "There's more. The hair sample I gave

La Joie didn't match the one Geoff's parents sent. So we still don't know where the real Geoff Travers is. But they traced Perry Edwards to Montana—not Wisconsin. He disappeared ten years ago. His missing persons photo didn't match our Geoff, either. But Perry's grandparents said Geoff's photo looked like a boy Perry met in their church youth group. A nice boy, they said. He disappeared the same time as Perry."

"None of this is unexpected," Killeen said.

"No, it's not. But I wonder if Geoff even remembers what his real name is."

"Somewhere, deep down, he remembers."

Off to the south, the Newberry Mountains showed a strip of clean blue sky framed by cumulus. Just beyond Yermo, past the inspection station for westbound traffic, a car kicked up dust along the dirt track leading to the Calico Early Man site. Dr. Louis Leakey, of Olduvai Gorge fame, believed that man had lived near the shores of Pleistocene Lake Manix two hundred thousand years ago. Leakey and his fellow excavators unearthed what they believed were primitive stone tools and hearths. Though Leakey died more than thirty years ago, the excavation continues. So does the controversy.

"Jedediah Smith made two trips across the Mojave Desert," Killeen said, as if I'd asked him a question.

"I don't suppose there's any way to stop you," I said.

"It'll take your mind off other things."

"Your presumption is that I have a mind, Killeen."

"On the first trip, in 1826, his Mohave Indian guide showed him the water holes and springs, until they reached what he called the 'Inconstant River'—"

"So named because it refused to stay above ground," I said. "Like a lover with a secret life." But that train of thought led back to Geoff. I didn't want to go there. "Are we done yet?"

"In your dreams. Smith followed the Mojave to its headwaters and crossed the San Bernardino Mountains to reach the San Gabriel Mission. He was only twenty-seven—not much younger than you, Frankie. He went again the next summer. The Mohaves killed ten men and two women in his crew. Fell on them while they waited for the first group to cross the Colorado River. Smith was caught in the middle of the river with three men. They managed to escape into the Mojave Desert during the night."

"I bet you know the names of the men who were killed, but not the women," I said.

"Don't start with me," he said. "I'm not responsible for historical bias."

"Granted. So if I tell you I know about Kit Carson, John Frémont, Beale's Road, the topographical surveys, and the celestite and magnesite mining in the Cadys, will you let me listen to the music in peace?"

"Spoilsport."

I looked out the window at the morning shadows spilling across the creosote flats. The rain had stopped—for now. Coalescing alluvial fans half-buried the near hills. We continued to follow the trace of the Mojave, a topsy-turvy river, larger at its source than where it finally disappears in the Sink. It flows north, like the Nile, then east, but its waters don't find the sea or empty into a larger river. And only for the first seventy miles or so does it carry snowmelt and runoff at the surface. For the next forty miles it plays hide-and-seek with the atmosphere . . . until old Cave Canyon, with its crenulated, pastel cliffs, its caves, and its history. In the desert, it's all about water.

When we stopped at the rest area so I could use the facilities, the wind was raw, whipping sand against the Cady Mountains to the southeast. The mountains, caught in the Mojave Shear Zone, had a long history of faulting. In 1947, an earthquake struck the Manix Fault on the north side of the range. The epicenter of one in 1999 was near the southern edge of the Cadys. Today the mountains sat, placid and quiet, awaiting the next jolt.

"Ready?" Killeen asked, handing me the keys.

"We'll have a devil of a time finding Dora if she wandered back into the mountains," I said, getting behind the wheel.

"We'll find her."

The washboard dirt surface of the Afton Road held standing water that mirrored a gray sky. Rain was falling to the north and east, but here the gods had smiled—we'd have a breather from the storm.

We came down off the pediment surface into the canyon carved by the river. Old Camp Cady, a fortification along the Old Government Road, was several miles upstream. The cliffs paralleled the railroad tracks that crossed and recrossed the river, which was flowing with runoff from the storm. The campground, consisting of a few open campsites and chemical toilets, occupied an old river terrace north of the road. The graded road petered out at the river, turning into a four-wheel-drive trail beside the railroad tracks. We parked behind a UCDR Suburban and Nakata's Blazer. The gang from school had beaten us here. Perhaps twenty other vehicles were scattered throughout the campground. The search for Dora was already under way.

Nakata and Cassie were speaking to Crank. Dee Marsland and Ryan Fitzpatrick stood off to one side, involved in an intense discussion. I doubted they were debating geology. Raised voices—one angry, one controlled—came from the other side of the privy. Zev's gutteral tones interrupted the argument.

"Marsh and Rudinsky," I said. "My money's on Marsh. He's the volatile one."

"What's wrong?" Killeen asked Cassie, who walked over to meet us.

"It started with Dee and Zev," Cassie said.

Dee Marsland, a grad student studying igneous and metamorphic petrology, was waifish and fine-boned, with pale skin, close-cropped mousy brown hair, wire-rimmed glasses, and a chip on her shoulder the size of Mount Whitney. Zev was an intense, husky geophysicist, who'd served in the Israeli army. He'd seen and done things there he couldn't bear to think about—or so he'd told me once.

"Dee is fed up with the muddle in the Middle East," Cassie continued. Her German accent was thick this morning. "She thinks the United States should pull out completely and let the Israelis duel with the Arabs, winner take all." She twisted her thick curly brown hair into a topknot and secured it with a clip. "Zev disagrees."

"Naturally," I said.

"They were about to come to blows, so we stopped in Victorville to avert an international incident. We gave Dee to Nakata in exchange for Ryan."

Ryan Fitzpatrick, a blond stolid geochemist from Minnesota, had measured speech and a perfect memory of where he'd met other scientists, what was said, and when. Dee was on scholarship, so she looked down her nose at Ryan. That hadn't stopped the two from hooking up last spring, but it hadn't lasted more than a month.

"I'm missing something here, Cassie. How's the fight between Dee and Zev connected with Marsh and Rudinsky?"

Cassie sighed. "Ryan mentioned the abstract."

"What abstract?" I asked her, as the argument behind the privy rose in volume.

"Marsh identified some fossil bones Rudinsky and Rhys-Evans brought back from the Alvord Mountains last year."

"I helped collect those bones—a horse and a camel."

"Yes, well, Rudinsky submitted an abstract to GSA, but didn't include Marsh as an author. Ryan let the cat out of the purse—"

"Bag," I said.

"Bag?" Cassie repeated. I nodded.

"Ryan let the cat out of the bag as we were unloading our gear. Marsh erupted. He slammed a thermos into Rudinsky's chest. Zev had to separate them."

Rudinsky was a subtle backstabber. Marsh was as unpredictable as a pit bull. Rhys-Evans or Sarah had managed to maintain an uneasy equilibrium—until now. Rhys-Evans was dead. Sarah was down for the count. Nakata had her own issues with Rudinsky. The department was fragmenting, imploding. Geoff's plan was working, but in ways he hadn't anticipated . . . or had he? Had this infighting and disaggregation been part of his master plan?

"I think I'll go investigate," Killeen said. "Maybe calm things down."

Nakata glanced over at the ruckus, then shrugged, as if to say, *There's only so much I can do.* She nodded to Crank and walked briskly toward us, meeting Killeen, Zev, Marsh, and Rudinsky midway. Ryan and Dee came from the opposite direction. An uneasy, four-part truce had been declared.

"Any news?" I asked Nakata.

"No. The official search party's concentrating on this side of the river. They've given us the south side."

Both sides were steep, with innumerable gullies leading off the meandering river bottom. Each geologist held a mapboard—an aluminum or fiberboard folder, commercial or homemade. A few carried GPS units. The first assignment for any geologist is locating himself—a scientifically sanctioned version of "finding yourself," but with more rules.

Nakata held her map so that everyone could see it. "We'll pair up—professors and students. Don't want to complicate the search by losing one of the searchers. Dee and I will take the first tributary. I'll climb up to the rim and stay on top. I'll have better reception there. Dee will take the low ground. Marsh and Cassie, you're searching the next wash to the east." Nakata circled a section of map. "Then Rudy and Ryan. Frankie, Zev, and Killeen, you're the farthest out. Cover the river bottom first. Then check the branch washes. Be careful, these cliffs are extremely unstable." She tucked her topographic map in her mapboard, on top of a geologic map of the area. "Report to me each time you reach the end of a wash. We'll rendezvous back here at noon. And don't forget—this is a protected area for the desert tortoise. Please tread carefully."

Killeen, Zev, and I drove the Jeep as far along the track as we could, crossing under a railroad bridge before parking in a wide space just before the trail climbed up again to parallel the track. We forded the stream at a narrow spot and, spaced twenty feet apart, combed the south side of the riverbed. A helicopter was flying parallel to the canyon walls, dividing the sky into strips. We checked out the caves, large enough to have sheltered man and beast over the millennia. Shelter and water, the magical combination that spelled survival in the desert. It was odd to stand where a host of travelers—some famous, most anonymous—had slept and eaten. Now the only residents were bats. I could find no sign that Dora had been here.

Killeen picked up a handful of sand from the floor and let it dribble through his fingers. "In 1854, the army left a Mexican—unnamed, of course, Frankie—guarding a couple of tired mules here while the rest of the troops went on."

"Let me guess," I said. "The Mohaves moved in?"

"The Paiutes. The Mohaves tended to stay close to their corn and squash and bean fields along the banks of the Colorado. Anyway, when the herder didn't catch up with the rest of the pack train, soldiers went back for him. Found his bloody clothes shot full of arrows, but no body."

"And the Paiutes were feasting on mule meat?"

"Yup. Later on, a Captain Blake camped here and left troops to guard it for a while. So they called it Blake's Camp for a few years."

"But the herder never turned up?"

"Nope. It's a mystery."

"Well, let's not say the same about Dora."

"No," said Zev. "We search till we find her."

Killeen picked a spindly plant from near the entrance to the cave and handed it to me.

"Desert trumpet," I said.

Killeen smiled. "*Eriogonum inflatum.* Frémont named it."

"Since when did you add botany to your list of accomplishments, Killeen?"

"When in Rome," he said.

Zev looked at me questioningly from gold-flecked hazel eyes. His wild black hair was tucked under a maroon ski hat. He carried a shovel like a rifle, suspended by a strap over one shoulder. The shovel was for dispatching snakes and scorpions. He'd been bitten by a scorpion as a child and almost died. It was against school policy to carry a gun. Just as well. Otherwise, he might have dispatched Dee on the road.

"But we are not in Rome," Zev said.

I looked at Killeen. "You explain it."

Killeen said something in a foreign language. I'd forgotten he'd worked in the Middle East. Zev replied. They both laughed.

"Do I want to know?" I said. They shook their heads. "It seems like a waste of manpower to have all three of us covering the same route. How about splitting up?" Killeen just looked at me.

"I agree." Zev slid the shovel strap from his shoulder, jabbed the spade under a small cobble, and flicked it into the air. We all tracked the arc until the rock landed with a small splash in the water. A raven flew up, squawking. Zev grinned. "Let's split up."

"I promise to be careful," I said to Killeen.

Killeen looked at his watch. "Call me every half hour—or, if the reception's no good in the canyons, every time you top out."

Zev and I both nodded. "I'll meet you both back at the Jeep at eleven forty-five," I said.

Zev slipped the shovel over his shoulder and said something to Killeen, again in that foreign language. They were laughing as they left me there without a backward glance.

# 30

## Northeastern Cady Mountains
Mojave Desert, California
Wednesday, December 15, 8:00 a.m.

Seth had left the cave as soon as the narrow band between clouds and earth began to lighten. No sunrise followed, only weak light through the tan tarp he'd stretched under the camouflage net to keep the front half of the room dry. The result was a kind of gloomy twilight.

Seth had said he'd kill her if she took down the tarp and the net he'd repaired the previous night. He'd put out the fire before he left. She prodded the coals. No heat. If she succeeded in making a fire, the smoke would quickly fill up the room, unless she built it near the opening. But it would be difficult there with the wind funneling through.

Dora's hands shook with cold as she checked her blood sugar and injected insulin. She crawled back into her sleeping bag, thinking about her options while eating a cold breakfast of trail mix, apple, and jerky. Her options were limited. She looked at the used needle—too fine and small to be a weapon. But it could put out Seth's eye, maybe give her an advantage—if she were free of the shackle . . . or if the shackle were free of the ground. The pin was set in concrete. But concrete was an aggregate. What she wouldn't give for her hammer and a chisel right now, or even metal nails or pegs. She went through Seth's gym bag. Found nothing except women's clothes, socks and shoes, a wig, a lipstick. Another disguise?

The metal base of the lipstick wasn't strong enough to serve as a chisel. She'd have to make her own hammer and chisel from the tuff core and flakes she'd hidden yesterday. Dora used the socks to cover her hands. In ancient times, jade had been carved into beads with only the laborious twirling of stick or stone and sand. She'd grind her way to freedom. All she needed was time. Time and patience. She already had plenty of grit.

Dora found the rocks where she'd hidden them and began to grind away at the cement, millimeter by millimeter . . .

# 31

## Afton Canyon

Across the river, Dora's name echoed from the cliffs, overlapping like plainchants in disparate minor keys: *Dora, Dora, Dora . . . Adoro te devote . . . O memoriale mortis Domini . . .*

I waited until Killeen and Zev were out of sight around the bend in the river before I left the cave. I wanted to let my ears attune themselves to the natural sounds of the area. And the foreign ones.

Adjusting the shoulder straps of my daypack as I walked, I searched the bottomland and, finding nothing but some old tire tracks, started up the closest side canyon. The rocks here were steeply tilted gravels. Alone with the rocks and relative white noise of the whistling wind, I began to relax. The last time I'd been alone for any length of time had been on the drive from Tucson to Del Rio. The sensory assault from all that had happened in the past thirty-six hours had overloaded my system. I craved this solitude, even as I broke it occasionally to call Dora's name.

Yet I sensed something out of kilter here. I didn't believe Dora was in this twisting gorge, lying—alive or dead—in a pastel side canyon. She'd have left some trace of her visit. It made no sense. I remembered the pictures Killeen had taken when he and Dora arrived in the Cadys two weeks ago. The woman was slightly built. Her hands, holding a rock hammer and cold chisel, were fine-boned but capable. Olive skin, almond-shaped brown eyes, graying brown hair caught back in a ponytail. The sunlight had touched the gray she wasn't vain enough to color. She wore the determined look of a woman to whom life hasn't come easily. Her eyes held no illusions. But they were smiling. She'd chosen this work. It satisfied her.

Dora was steel wire wrapped with woven cotton. She was

careful. She wanted to live a long, full, interesting life. She wouldn't have allowed herself to become disoriented because of a metabolic imbalance. Something unexpected had happened. She was caught unawares. But it didn't happen here. The dogs would have picked up the scent. Killeen and I would have sensed it.

Using my rock pick for added purchase I scrambled up the final hundred feet to the top of the canyon wall. The view down was stunning, but the wind here was blowing so strongly that it pushed me back toward the edge. I had to bend double to counteract the force. I couldn't see anyone else among the outcrops and ridges, could hear nothing but that roar. So I walked east to the next ravine and climbed carefully down so that the roar was lessened but my phone's antenna was level with the rim. Nakata answered on the first ring.

I gave her my position—township, range, and quarter-quarter section. No one else had seen anything. Rudinsky and Ryan had split up to cover more ground. Cassie and Marsh had argued. He preferred to work alone.

"Getting you guys to stick to a plan is like herding emus," Nakata said.

"That's putting it mildly," I said.

Everyone but Marsh, Killeen, and Zev had reported in, Nakata told me. She wasn't worried about the last two—they'd had farther to go before turning upstream. But if Marsh didn't call in soon, she, Dee, and Cassie would have to go looking for him.

I offered to help, but Nakata wanted me to finish with my section. "I know Theo's miffed," Nakata said. "I just wish he wouldn't take it out on the rest of us."

I called Killeen. Zev was with him. They'd come up empty.

"I don't believe she was ever here," I said. "And by the way, Marsh hasn't called in."

"I'm not surprised." In the background, I could hear Zev agreeing.

"You'll have to hustle to make it to the Jeep on time," I said. "Don't break a leg."

Killeen laughed. "I'm not the one who trips over cracks in the sidewalk," he said, and signed off.

The next ravine was a straight shot down. I could see the entire watercourse, except for a segment near the bottom. The gully was empty. I decided to descend farther east and then check that dogleg from the bottom. I climbed out carefully, bracing myself against the wind that pelted my face with silt and sand. I saw searchers across the river congregate on the north rim. They were looking at the map. They hadn't found anything, either.

Afton Canyon campground now was hidden around a bend in the canyon. Water gleamed like pewter. Reeds and grasses in the riverbed rippled in the wind as they had for thousands of years. The only imprints of civilization were the railroad tracks. I wondered if that anonymous Mexican mule herder who'd left his bloody clothes in the canyon had escaped into the Cadys with his life. Maybe. There was water there, if one knew where to look.

I thought, for a moment, I heard a donkey bray. But the wind snatched it away. Or was it my imagination?

I walked east along the rim until I came to the next canyon—a larger, more sinuous cut down to a tributary wash. I tried calling Nakata, but she didn't answer. She must be down in a cleft looking for Marsh. I tried Killeen—same result. I saw a figure way off to the west, and waved. The figure dropped out of sight. Rudinsky? Cassie? I didn't know if they saw me.

I dropped down off the rimrock and entered the shadow and relative silence of the ravine. But I sensed something was wrong. So I hurried now, anxious to get to the bottom, to finish my search, to rendezvous with Killeen and Zev and head back to camp.

They were waiting for me at the Jeep. "Do you smell sulfur, Zev?" Killeen said.

Zev sniffed the air. "I don't—"

"That's Killeen's way of saying 'the last one in's a rotten egg,'" I said, unlocking the doors and throwing my pack in the back. "An old American expression."

Zev thought about it while we buckled up. A smile lit his face and he thwapped Killeen on the shoulder. "Ah, the rotten egg smells of sulfur, yes? And Frankie is the last one to arrive."

"Zev will go back to Israel with a skewed version of Amerispeak," I said to Killeen.

"Just doing my bit to further foreign relations."

Back at the campground we compared notes with Nakata, Cassie, Ryan, and Dee. Rudinsky strolled up twenty minutes later, as if he'd just returned from a walk on the beach.

No Marsh.

# 32

## Northeastern Cady Mountains
Wednesday, December 15, 11:30 a.m.

Dora's arms were exhausted from boring into the cement holding the pin. It was all she could do not to give in to the emotional storm hanging over her head. So much time had passed. Were her colleagues from the department even looking for her? Or had she been such a bitch, such a loner, that they'd written her off?

There was nothing she could do about that now. She wrapped herself up in the blanket, had a snack, and distracted herself by reading Seth's journal, beginning with the pages she'd skimmed before. He'd written most of it at his family's homestead, sitting at an old pine table by the window:

*I can see Quick sitting across from me, eating stew made from venison he killed this morning down at the salt lick.*

*Quick and I were born at home, so we didn't have birth certificates or Social Security numbers. Pa didn't want us in any damn computer. We were taught to keep the world at bay, to put on a pleasant face before strangers, but to answer no questions. We were taught to lie, which was not against Biblical law. Only bearing false witness against neighbors was wrong. We had no neighbors.*

*Quick and I didn't go to school. Ma taught us to read from the Bible. She taught us math from an old textbook she traded for at a craft fair in Sandpoint. That was my favorite craft fair. One bookseller would let me read all day for free. He told me about libraries, too, and always gave me a book or two in trade for fetching and carrying. That's how I learned about science and history and literature. Once he gave me a copy of Shakespeare's plays and sonnets. I still have it. I carry it with me everywhere, though I've memorized every word. It's a comfort—my one link with the old days, before things went bad.*

In winter we were snowed in. But I liked that. I had Quick to play with and studying to do. And there was always work—gathering and cutting wood for the stoves, feeding the animals, mucking out the barn. Come spring, I was in charge of the kitchen garden. Quick took the animals. He needed to be moving around all the time. He liked to hunt. I liked to grow things. I was good with a bow, but not as good as Quick. Pa wouldn't let us use any of the guns he had stored in hideouts all over the mountain—for when the enemy came. The enemy was the Government, of course. They were after him. He figured it was only a matter of time before they'd come take away his guns and put him in jail. That's why we lived in the mountains where nobody'd take us without a fight. That's why we didn't go to school, or mix with folks, or have friends. And that's why we hunted with a bow. Bows are silent. They don't give away your position.

That's the way it was till the summer I was fifteen. One day Quick and I went elk hunting. We split up, like always, to cover more ground. But this time Quick circled back around. I shot at the noise. I knew better, but I shot at something I couldn't see. The arrow took him in the neck. He bled out by the time I got down to him. And my life changed forever.

I brought Quick home, and we buried him in a little clearing above the house. Then there was only that name written in the Bible to say he'd ever existed. Even that's gone, now, and my name with it. I'm a ghost, wandering the land in other people's skins because Ma sent me away that day. Told me never to come back. I stayed away till yesterday.

I was crying. That's all I remember. I was crying by Quick's grave when Ma pointed her finger and said she'd put the mark on me. "What mark?" I asked her, not understanding. "The mark of Cain," she said. "Don't you never come back, boy." And she turned her back on me. Pa never said a word. He didn't even look at me.

So I took one of the motorcycles and left. I worked as a day laborer, where I didn't need ID. One of my employers taught me to drive a truck. I slept in shelters when it was very cold—though I rarely felt the cold. I didn't make friends, at least at first. I didn't know how. I spent my free time alone, reading whatever caught my eye in the library, visiting museums, exploring the backroads. I moved on every few days, but I stayed in the northern half of the country, where there were

*trees to hide among and rivers to drink from. I camped. Camp-*
*grounds were a luxury, with showers and toilets and fireplaces*
*for cooking. I bought a used pup tent and clothes at second-*
*hand stores. I needed little. That's the only gift Ma ever gave*
*me, besides Quick . . . and teaching me how to throw pots on*
*a wheel and fire them in a kiln.*

*Sometimes other campers would invite me to share a meal.*
*I made up stories to explain why I was alone. Said I was an*
*orphan. My stories touched their hearts. They gave me leftover*
*food, even spare change, just to tide me over. They gave*
*because I never asked. They said they wished their own sons*
*were as motivated and hardworking. They asked if I was*
*lonely. I told them no, which was the truth. I was reconciled to*
*being alone because I'd killed my brother. But I didn't tell them*
*that.*

*I had my first girl in a cathouse in Nevada—no strings, no*
*expectations, no declarations of love. It was a business*
*arrangement, pure and simple. I preferred it that way.*
*Romantic love's just a myth anyway, pushed by novels and*
*movies and Hallmark cards. Or maybe it's just that my parents*
*didn't teach me about love. Maybe that's something you have*
*to learn when you're young.*

*In Missoula, a runaway named Johnny showed me that*
*belonging to a church gave you access to people who shared. I*
*knew the Bible backwards and forwards. When the church-*
*goers asked what church I'd belonged to before, I said I'd been*
*taught at home, but hadn't been allowed to attend a regular*
*church. Poor boy, they said, as they welcomed me into their*
*youth circle, into their homes and lives. I was a young man on*
*my own; therefore, I must need rescuing. They were good at*
*rescuing.*

*I watched and learned the different buzzwords, the dif-*
*ferent rites. A Biblical quote was all that was ever needed by*
*way of response in any conversation. Silence, punctuated by*
*Biblical quotes, and maybe a line or two from Shakespeare,*
*with a "Praise the Lord," "Hallelujah!" or "Amen" thrown in*
*for good measure. The words were just words. I didn't believe*
*them anymore. I'm not sure I ever did. I believed in the earth,*
*in its secrets and mysteries, in its history and promise of rebirth*
*each spring.*

*I learned to manipulate people, to get what I wanted*
*without asking for it, making others think it was their idea. I*

*watched Johnny charm waitresses and shelter workers and*
*shopgirls. I mimicked him, adopting his style as I would a*
*wool shirt in winter. I found I had a talent for imitation.*

*When I was 18, I tried to register for a community college,*
*but with no birth certificate or Social Security number they*
*wouldn't let me in. So I killed Johnny and used his ID to reg-*
*ister in another state. As Johnny, I took class after class, like a*
*hungry man at an all-you-can-eat buffet. Only I couldn't bring*
*myself to take the finals. I'd register for classes, learn the mate-*
*rial, then move on without finishing. I just enjoyed the process*
*of learning.*

*I kept moving from state to state, adopting the identities of*
*homeless young men I met along the way. I burned their bodies*
*in desolate areas and boxed up the ashes. And I always took a*
*pottery course so I could mix the ashes with clay and make*
*them into large pots. I carved each boy's name—the name I*
*stole from him—on the base of his pot. It was my way of*
*remembering those boys—my way of thanking them. I sold*
*those pots at local craft fairs to make a little extra money . . .*

Dora looked at the bottom of her drinking mug. A name was
carved in the bottom. It wasn't Seth's. She almost vomited.

One burro called to another from the arroyo below. Dora
dropped the notebook, pushed sand into the holes she'd drilled in
the cement, and brushed dirt over them. If Seth noticed her work,
he'd stop her somehow. He'd tie her hands so she couldn't escape.

Or he'd kill her.

# 33

## Afton Canyon, Cady Mountains
Wednesday, December 15, 1:00 p.m.

Theo Marsh was missing. We looked at the map. Dee circled the draws she'd searched. Cassie did the same, then pointed to the draw Marsh had entered. If he'd stayed in his quadrant we'd find him quickly.

He might have decided not to report in. Theo was like that—contrary and cantankerous. He was still smarting from his run-in with Rudinsky. He might just be licking his wounds.

We started where Cassie had left him. The sand was damp from the rain. It was easy to track his progress. Footprints going in, none coming out.

"At this rate, it will be dark before we find him," Zev complained.

Nakata knew what was coming next, and intercepted him at the pass. "You can't go alone, Zev."

"I'll run with you," said Ryan. They removed their field belts and put them in their backpacks. Zev had to strip the tools off the belt and put it back on when his baggy pants began to slip. He couldn't hitch them as he ran.

They took off at a steady jog, Zev looking down to check Marsh's tracks, Ryan looking up to scan the area and choose the best route. Within seconds they'd disappeared around a bend in the wash.

We followed more slowly, walking in silence, listening for stray sounds above the wind. I called Dora's name, then Theo's. No answer.

The air smelled damp and clean, scented with creosote from the bajada. The narrowing canyon walls consisted of old alluvial fan deposits, disrupted by activity on the nearby Manix Fault. As we approached the fault plane itself, the rock layers became more fractured. I wondered what it would have felt like to be standing in this canyon when the ground shook and one fault block moved several inches west relative to the other. No doubt I would have been eating sand.

Nakata and Rudy glanced at the canyon walls as we passed through the fault zone, but didn't stop. Killeen watched everyone without seeming to watch them. Something was up.

Nakata's phone rang. It was Ryan. The reception was broken, but a few words came through. She turned up the volume so we all could hear. They'd found Marsh—alive but unconscious. Looked like he'd fallen while climbing out of the southern end of the canyon. He'd need to be stabilized and carried out by a rescue team. Ryan gave the coordinates.

We split up. Nakata, Rudy, Dee, and Cassie went back to organize the rescue and redistribute the gear in the vehicles. Someone would have to follow Marsh into Barstow to supply information to the hospital. Killeen and I went on to find a good landing site for the helicopter—or clear a site if necessary.

"You want to have a look at Marsh's wound, don't you," I said. A statement, not a question.

"Accidents happen, even to experienced climbers. But Rudinsky was late getting back to the campground."

"You think Rudinsky pushed Marsh off a cliff?"

"Or dropped a rock on his head. Wouldn't be the first time a scientist tried to settle a score."

"Rudy?" I couldn't envision it. "He prefers verbal and written combat. Marsh might attack Rudinsky, but not the other way around."

"Rudinsky was a soldier who fought in Afghanistan—a hopeless war. Soldiers can snap, even twenty years later."

"We'll know soon enough," I said.

We hurried, following the narrowing arroyo to the point where Marsh had left the sandy floor and climbed a steep gully to the ridge crest. Rocks trickled down on us from the rim. I looked up. The sky was a strip of gray. Ryan's disembodied head peered down, like the Cheshire cat in the tree. But Ryan's stolid face wasn't grinning. It was grim. Though I knew he must be lying on his stomach, it was an odd, unsettling sight.

"Sorry about that," Ryan said. "Marsh and Zev are around the next bend."

Cobbles and gravel eroded from the fanglomerate of the cliff littered the narrow gully. There was a channel deposit cut into the gravel. The waterlain rocks were imbricated, showing that the flow had been from the south. The sediments were volcanic, eroded from the heart of the mountains or from the older sedimentary units. When we got to Zev, he was guarding Marsh the way a soldier guards a fallen comrade. His face was fierce.

"I think he slipped and hit his head," Zev said. "There is swelling. I did not move him in case he injured his neck or spine."

"Let me take a look," Killeen said. "Why don't you go up and help Ryan pick out a landing site and direct the rescue team here." It was an order, though gently given.

Marsh lay facedown. He hadn't fallen and hit his head. Something had hit him on the back of his crown, probably a rock from above. He'd been looking down, picking his way carefully as he climbed. He hadn't seen it coming. Hadn't heard anything. Hadn't looked up. He was lucky to be alive . . . I looked at the felt field hat, lying by his foot. Lucky, and hardheaded.

"Killeen," I said, crouching beside him while he examined Marsh. I was reassured to see that Marsh's color was good and his breathing regular.

"I know. It wasn't an accident."

"We'll need to check the rim," I said. "And I want to take pictures of the site. Can you leave him?" I heard a helicopter approach. "Quickly."

Killeen moved up the gully, careful not to roll rocks down on Marsh or disturb the surroundings. I took scene shots and close-ups, checking Marsh's pulse every few shots to make sure he was still with us. When I looked up, Killeen shook his head.

"Other side?" I called.

He couldn't hear me, but he could read my lips. He navigated to the south rim of the gully. I tossed the camera up to him and moved out of the way. He shot down on the scene, then disappeared. In a couple of minutes he was back at the edge. He gave me a thumbs-up. He'd found the place—probably a scar in the desert pavement from which a rock was plucked.

I looked down at my feet, then around me until I spotted a small boulder, about the size of a bowling ball. Unlike the other rocks in the gully, this one was black with desert varnish. But there was a pale patch, crusted with caliche and fine dust.

"Killeen!" I called over the roar of the wind and helicopter blades. I pointed.

He tossed down the digital camera. I clicked three shots and then signaled to him to circle around. Killeen was strong enough to lug this rock up to the ridge.

Killeen arrived from the bottom just as the rescue team descended from the top. Killeen snatched up the boulder as if it were a soccer ball, and left me. I was in the way, now.

I backed down to the stream channel, found a parallel gully, and climbed to the ridge. I was breathing hard by the time I reached Killeen. He extended his arm, palm up, and swung it in an arc, as if to say, "Find it."

On that ridge, plants were few and far between, each needing space for its roots to gather moisture from the infrequent rain. Already they were responding to the storm, turning green, sending out shoots. Another few days, plus a change to warmer weather, and wildflowers would spring up almost overnight.

I'd seen the base of the rock and knew its general dimensions, but still it took me five minutes to locate it in the desert pavement. A fresh chip off one edge showed crisp, white feldspar laths in a gray groundmass. Andesite. Because Marsh had been wearing a hat, the surface wasn't bloody.

Killeen joined me beside the boulder. The rock was ten feet from the lip of the gully.

"Definitely not an accident," I said in Killeen's ear. The wind and helicopter noise were so strong that otherwise he wouldn't have heard me. He nodded.

I took the digital camera from my vest pocket and snapped a few more pictures, using my Brunton both for scale and to show the direction to the gully. Killeen scoured the ridgetop, looking for any clue to who the assailant had been and from which direction he'd come. I made an arrow of rocks to duplicate the path from rock to the gully. When investigators came back to work the scene, I wanted them to find it easily.

"Anything?" I mouthed when Killeen came back.

Killeen shook his head. Together we watched Marsh, strapped on a stretcher, being maneuvered up the gully to the rim and into the waiting helicopter. It took off moments later, heading west to Barstow.

I put the camera away. Killeen motioned me to follow him. We climbed down the gully into the side wash and began trudging toward the campground.

I came across the carapace of a desert tortoise. Three bullet holes had shattered the shell. A slow-moving target, defenseless, unthreatening, harmless. Killers kill. No explanation. No justification.

Whoever had dropped a rock on Marsh's head was a killer. I'd discovered in the last six months that I couldn't identify a killer on sight. No universal characteristics give him—or her—away. Motives vary. Revenge, anger, lust, and desperation are just a few of the keys to the padlocked door allowing us to justify taking a life . . . And some killers practice their marksmanship—or test their nerve—on other animals first. The desert hides innumerable proving grounds.

Killeen touched the shell gently with his broad hand. It was like a caress.

"Senseless," I said as he stood up.

"Worse," he said. "Premeditated."

We continued on in silence for a minute. I didn't know what Killeen was thinking about, but my mind was trying to link Marsh's attack with the ones in Del Rio. Could I have been wrong about who killed Dai? I'd been so sure about Geoff. Everything seemed to fit the old pattern. Now I had an extra piece or two, like screws left over after you assemble a computer. Something was wrong. Were there common threads?

I shared my doubts with Killeen, ending with, "Rudinsky?" Even as I said it, my mind protested that there wasn't a motive. And Rudinsky was too cold and calculating to flip out.

"It's possible," Killeen said. "He could have attacked Marsh. And he was at school Monday night. When Nakata called him from the hospital, he said Dai wasn't in the lab."

"Then he'd also have had to hit Sarah. Those two cases are linked."

"You know them both better than I do—what motive would he have?"

"I don't know." I tucked strands of hair back under my hat. "The whole *Romeo and Juliet* thing could be a red herring. It might not be a crime of passion. Dai was struck on the head—like Marsh. Sarah was struck with a vehicle. Not so different."

"But there was no note with Marsh. It could just be a crime of opportunity. Only you, Zev, and I are in the clear. We were too far away."

"Not Nakata. She's straightforward. No artifice . . . Cassie will take you on in an open fight. Ryan's too unimaginative. Dee? . . . I don't know. There's a lot of subliminal anger and resentment supporting that chip on her shoulder. But I'd have expected her to go after Zev, not Marsh."

"Marsh gave her a B in Vertebrate Paleontology this quarter. The first one she's ever gotten, she said. I heard her arguing with him about it when the grades were posted Monday morning."

"How heavy was that boulder?" I asked him.

"Maybe twenty pounds. Not much heavier than a large bowling ball. Dee could carry it to the gully and drop it, no problem."

"But did she also have a beef with Sarah and Dai?"

"Sarah's insisting she take two quarters of a second language. Dee's pissed. Thought she'd finished her basic requirements."

"But what about Dai?"

"Motive, you mean?" Killeen scratched his head. "They had an affair a few months—"

"No kidding!"

"It happened after I arrived in September," Killeen said. "Rhys-Evans was thinking of leaving Tara for her. So your crime-of-passion scenario might be right after all."

"Anybody else on Dee's shit list?"

"Not that I know of."

"So what do we do now, Killeen? Everyone sees this as an accidental fall, not attempted murder."

"When Marsh wakes up—"

"*If* Marsh wakes up."

"The glass is half-full, Frankie. Anyway, Marsh might have heard or seen something suspicious before he was konked on the head. Maybe he can set the record straight."

"Unless Dee or Rudinsky gets to him first."

"Then let's make sure they don't have the opportunity."

"You want to camp out in the Cadys?" I said.

"Yup. It would keep Dee and Rudinsky with us. We're not ready to give up searching for Dora anyway. If we camp out, we can begin again at first light. You came prepared. I saw your sleeping bag in the Jeep."

"Sarah had planned a field trip to the Marble Mountains after my defense," I said. "I was going to help her measure and collect a section on my way home."

"And I figured we might have to spend a night out here to maximize search time since the days are so short."

"What about food?" I said.

"I went to the market last night, while you were sleeping. And I talked to Nakata earlier. They brought camping gear, too. And firewood."

"I could use a good fire right now. Is it my imagination, or is it getting colder?"

Killeen pointed off to the south, where the tops of the Cadys were wreathed in cloud. "It's snowing up there."

"I'll take snow over rain."

"We'll get both before we're through. So we'd better choose our campsite carefully."

"But not in Afton Canyon," I said. "Dora wasn't here."

"No. Dora's campsite's near the quarry," Killeen said. "Might as well start backtracking at the last known spot. It's isolated. If someone balks at the idea or finds an excuse to go to Barstow—"

"Presumably to take care of Marsh—"

"We'll have our suspect. And the advantage of surprise. He or she won't know we suspect them."

"I hope you're right, Killeen."

"The pieces fit, Sherlock."

"They fit just fine before, Watson. That's what bothers me."

We reached the confluence of the wash with the Mojave channel. Across the river, the troops were waiting.

"Ever played Go?" said Killeen.

"No." I followed him into the shallowest part of the river. It had more water now. The rain in the south and west was swelling the flow.

"The main objective is to control the most territory by surrounding and capturing your opponent's men."

"Backing him into a corner from which he can't escape, and then moving in for the kill?"

"Pretty much."

"Does your opponent smack you with big rocks?"

"Nope—little black or white pebbles."

"I'm not afraid of pebbles."

"It's not the size of the projectile, Frankie, it's the force behind it." Killeen looked at the group waiting by the Suburban. "Now the game gets interesting."

# 34

Cassie had departed in Nakata's Blazer by the time Killeen and I reached Afton Canyon campground. Though he was voted down, Rudy continued to object to the necessity of camping out and continuing the search again at first light. The official search team had found no trace of Dora in Afton Canyon. They were packing it in for the day. But they offered to help us tomorrow if we found some sign of her farther south.

I called Philo before we got on the road. He'd just reached the motel in Del Rio.

"There's been a change of plans," I said, and explained the situation. Philo was slow to respond. I sensed something was wrong. "What is it?"

"I have news," he said. "But it's . . . but not on the cell phone. We'll talk when I see you."

That didn't sound good. "I'll be in Del Rio by dark tomorrow," I said. "Or I'll call. Did you bring work with you?"

"I'm connected. And I'll visit Sarah after dinner—if they'll let me in."

"Call La Joie before you leave. He'll put you on the list."

"He already knows my name?"

"Just like the song," I said. I was about to sign off when the full ramifications of the day's events hit me. "Philo, wait."

"Hmmm?"

"There's no way I'll be able to defend my dissertation on Friday—not with Marsh out of commission. He's the third member of the committee. He was drafted after Dai was killed."

"Jesus, Frankie. It's like the Fates are conspiring against you. What are you going to do now?"

"I haven't the slightest idea. Nakata and I haven't talked about it. But the ranks are pretty thin."

"That's understating it a bit."

"Anyway, if something's come up—if you need to be somewhere else—well, you don't have to stick around till Sunday. I'll apologize to Killeen about his loss of a best man."

"No, Saturday's still on. But I won't be able to drive back to Tucson with you. I have to fly out on Sunday. And no, I can't tell you where, or why."

"You'll be gone for a while?"

"Yes," Philo said. "But we'll have Friday."

"Then it'll have to be enough."

Killeen closed his own cell phone as I finished. "Sylvie?" I asked.

"Oh, yeah."

"How'd she take it?"

"She's gonna invite Philo over for dinner."

I had to laugh. "Well, they'll have lots to talk about . . . Did she visit Sarah?"

"She called. Sarah's still in a coma. But her vitals are improving. It's wait and see."

*Wait and see. Wait and see.* As I got behind the wheel, the words played over and over in my brain like a song on a scratched, old LP. But, Jesus, I was tired of waiting.

The mesa holds very level here, cut across at intervals
by the deep washes of dwindling streams.

—Mary Austin, *The Land of Little Rain*, 1903

I would fain die a dry death.

—William Shakespeare, *The Tempest*

# 35

## Northern Cady Mountains
Wednesday, December 15, 2:30 p.m.

Killeen and I followed the Suburban back to the highway and drove a few miles east to the turnoff giving access to the northeastern Cadys. Thirty minutes later we reached the main wash leading south into the range. A high flat-topped hill brooded over the lower mesas and ridges. Someone sitting up there would have an unobstructed view of our movements.

The canyon walls were a rainbow of pale green and buff sandstone beds interleaved with marker beds of weathered basalt, white airfall tuff, and one salmon pink ignimbrite—the Peach Springs Tuff. Eighteen and a half million years ago the fiery cloud of ash and gas exploded from a volcanic center near the point where Nevada, Arizona, and California come together. The Colorado River canyon didn't exist then. The tuff flowed west into the Mojave Basin, filling channels, rolling over ridges, ponding in basins. It lapped the flanks of mountains and destroyed everything in its path.

Dora had camped at the mouth of a tributary wash separated from the main wash by a low finger of the tuff. In the late afternoon the campsite was in shadow. Wind funneled down the wash, cooled further as it swept over damp sand.

We were the only creatures abroad. As the winter solstice approaches, life in the Mojave goes underground. Most cold-blooded reptiles and warm-blooded small mammals hibernate, waiting for longer days and new forage.

Rudinsky parked the heavy, less maneuverable Suburban on a spit of sandstone above the main wash—just in case it rained tonight. I parked the smaller Cherokee on a shelf of welded tuff. I was taking no chances with flash floods.

The sandy bed of the tributary wash was a perfect campsite,

sheltered on two sides from the wind. Killeen helped unload the Suburban. I dealt with the Cherokee, setting the ice chest near the broken circle of rocks marking Dora's campfire pit. The usual banter was absent. Everyone seemed absorbed in his or her thoughts. Maybe it was because we were here, at Dora's campsite, while she was still missing. It would be another bitterly cold night. I hoped she was somewhere warm.

With only one stove, we'd have to eat in shifts. With few words we divided the cooking duties. Killeen heated the refried beans and tortillas and started cooking the chuck steak. Dee and Nakata cut up tomatoes and lettuce. Rudy opened a bottle of zinfandel, poured himself a cup, and climbed atop the ridge to watch the sunset—and to get away from us. Zev shrugged and helped me gather rocks to enlarge the fire ring. When I scraped out the pit to lay the fire, I exposed the remains of Dora's last meal.

"Killeen," I called. Dee reacted as if I'd shouted during a silent retreat.

"Not like Dora to leave trash behind," said Killeen. He took a pencil from his pocket, inserted it into the neck of a wine bottle, and lifted it from the sand. "Someone was here with her."

I found a paper grocery sack and held it open to receive the bottle. Killeen took the bag from me, labeled it, and put it in the Jeep. He brought back a shovel and dug around in the pit. All he found were old ashes and charred sticks. I'd never seen him look that somber.

"It's something, Killeen. It's the reason we came."

"I just wish we'd started here this morning," he said, and threw another steak on the stove.

I went back to the fire pit, smoothed the surface into a bowl. Zev added three rocks in the center to support the tinder and kindling off the damp sand. Focusing on the basics—building a fire, cooking food, making coffee, eating, doing dishes—quiets me. Life goes on, even in the rough times.

I got the fire going and put on a pot of water for boiled coffee. Killeen had remembered cream for my coffee and salsa for tonight's burritos and tomorrow's eggs. The necessities of life. If we wanted, we could live out here for a week.

I left Zev tending the fire, and walked around the finger of tuff. Upstream a short way was an inlet designated as the women's room. The sun chose that moment to slip under the clouds, turning the tuff rose red. On a shelf at eye level, under an overhang, something reflected light . . . a digital camera. And beside it were a GPS unit, a small cell phone, and a used insulin pen. Dora had left us a message.

I carried them back to camp, holding them as if they were Fabergé eggs. Killeen handed his cooking fork to Nakata and intercepted me. He took the camera first, turning it on and reviewing the last pictures Dora had taken. Only one wasn't of rock or bones: a bald man hunkered down by a campfire, his back toward the camera. Sunlight reflected off his skull. The rocks in the background were of this small wash. And the date was Monday, December 13 . . .

"Dora knew she was in trouble," I said. "She left this for you to find, Killeen. She knew you'd come."

"And she may still be here," said Rudinsky. I hadn't heard his footsteps in the soft sand.

Killeen tried to phone out. No luck. We all tried. Same result. Massing clouds and the canyon walls interfered with the signals.

"I need the Cherokee, Frankie." Killeen caught the keys I tossed him.

"Check on Marsh, will you?" said Nakata. "And Sarah?"

Killeen nodded. "I'll be back before midnight."

"I won't wait up," I said.

After dinner and cleanup the six of us sat sipping our drinks and staring at the flames, each absorbed in his or her own thoughts. Rudy had a liter of vodka, which he drank straight from the bottle. He seemed intent on saving nothing for tomorrow. Nakata drank coffee laced with Yukon Jack. Dee sipped tequila. Ryan nursed a beer. And Zev drank wine from an old leather wineskin, shooting a stream into his mouth every minute or so. There would be no rock talk tonight, no singing in four-part harmony, no storytelling.

The fire exploded—one shot, then a second. Rock shards and embers struck our faces and bodies. We danced a frenzied macarena, brushing at our clothes and hair. Someone was screaming. Zev. His hair was smoking. He ran frantic hands over his chest, then tackled Dee, covering her with his body. He yelled at the rest of us in Hebrew, signaling *Down, down.*

Rudy got to him first. "It was sanidine," he said, putting his hand on Zev's shoulder. "Just sanidine." It sounded like "sanity."

"Get down," Zev yelled in English. "They'll get you, too."

"Let me up." Dee's voice was muffled.

"No one's shooting at us, Zev," I said. "The heat of the fire caused the sanidine crystals in the tuff to explode."

"Get *off* me," Dee said again.

I watched the intensity drain from Zev's eyes. Rudy and I helped him up. Ryan checked on Dee while Zev stripped off his jacket, shirt, and pants to look for bullet wounds. He didn't find any. "What the fuck," he said, looking at the fire. "Sanidine? Really?"

Everyone nodded. "The water in the crystal structure turned to gas," said Nakata.

"That is awesome," said Zev, stepping back into his pants. "Fucking awesome."

"You said it," Dee said under her breath, watching him button his shirt. "I suppose I should thank you," she said to Zev.

Zev grinned. "Any time. Any place." He took his time with the buttons on his shirt.

"That wasn't what she meant, idiot," Ryan said.

I picked up Zev's shovel and lifted the rocks, one by one, from the center of the fire. I deposited them in a depression by my sleeping bag, and covered them with a layer of sand. They'd help warm my feet while I slept.

By eight o'clock, aided by alcohol, the adrenaline had worn off. I rolled up in my sleeping bag, toes toward the fire. But I had a tough time corralling my thoughts and putting them to bed. When the camp was quiet, I heard the whispering of Zev's sleeping bag being dragged next to Dee's. The rustlings that followed kept me awake for a time. I thought of Philo, alone in his motel room, and wished I was there, curled into his warm body. I wondered what his news was. A case, no doubt. Something clandestine. I just hoped nothing happened tomorrow that would change his plans. I hoped we'd still have our Friday.

I got up and added fuel to the fire. Dragging my sleeping bag closer to the flames, I watched them till I drifted off . . .


Killeen returned at eleven. I'd unrolled his sleeping bag and pad next to mine. He shifted around, molding the sand to his body. When he'd finished, I whispered, "How's Marsh?"

"Concussion. Under observation for a night or two. He'll be fine. And no, he didn't see who tried to kill him. Didn't hear anything, either—except a donkey braying."

"That's odd. I thought I heard one, too."

Killeen didn't follow that up. Maybe he hadn't heard me. Carrying on a conversation in whispers is difficult when you're competing with the wind and the rustle of sleeping bags. Dee and Zev were at it again. The wind has that effect on some people.

"Marsh said to tell you that your defense is still on for Friday," Killeen said. "He'll finish reading your dissertation tomorrow. He brought it with him."

"Damn."

"I thought you wanted it over and done with?"

"I do. But there went my Friday with Philo." The Fates, I decided, were conspiring not only against me, but against us. I'd have to call him in the morning.

Killeen was quiet. I sensed something was on his mind. "Did you talk to Sylvie?"

"She approves of Philo. He brought flowers—and a book for Tommy."

"I'm glad you're not the jealous type, Killeen."

"Speak for yourself."

His attempt at humor seemed forced. "What's wrong?" I said.

"I talked to Crank. The bumper of Dora's truck was dented. There was blood on it. And under it. I didn't notice it last night."

"I didn't either. But why didn't Crank say anything?"

"He was being territorial. He decided it wasn't our concern. We were there to look at the contents, not examine the truck for trace evidence. He said he wanted to get the DNA results first."

"And?"

"The DNA didn't match Dora's. On a hunch he faxed the results to La Joie. It's Sarah's."

"Jesus H. Christ, Killeen. He thinks Dora drove back to Del Rio Monday night, hit Sarah, killed Dai, got her insulin and food from her apartment, and drove back out to Afton Canyon to dump the truck?"

"You can't blame him, I suppose. Someone did—except for the insulin. That's a bit of a leap."

"The dogs didn't pick up her scent in the canyon," I said.

"Okay, then who did this, Frankie? Dora had the truck. She was due back Monday evening. Monday night that truck struck Sarah. It was parked up the street for a couple of hours beforehand, and notes were planted around Sarah's house. Monday night that same person killed Dai in the rock lab. Dora had a key to the building and the lab. And for all I know, she had bones to pick with Dai and Sarah."

"A paleontologist with bones to pick. That's a new low, even for you, Killeen." The attempt at humor fell flat. "You really believe Dora could do all those things?" He was silent for so long I thought he'd fallen asleep. "Killeen?"

"I have to at least consider the possibility. That's what the police are doing right now." He paused for a fraction of a second, then said, "They found Dora's purse this afternoon, Frankie."

"But that's great news. We finally have a lead. Where was it?"

"In Loretta Stanton's car."

"Loretta Stanton?" I repeated, wondering why that name sounded familiar.

"Remember the guy in the restaurant this morning?"

I felt as if fifty years had passed since our IHOP breakfast. "He'd just heard on the radio that they'd found Loretta's body."

"Yes. Crank said that when they processed Loretta's house, her purse and car were missing. An anonymous caller—a friend of Loretta's, Crank thinks—reported seeing Loretta's car parked behind a convenience store not far from her house. Dora's purse was under the driver's seat."

"Excuse me?"

"It gets worse. The car matches Dora's neighbor's description of the one she saw parked outside her apartment yesterday morning."

"And a woman was driving . . . Loretta?"

"Or Dora. Crank's speculating that Loretta and Dora knew each other, that Loretta rendezvoused with Dora along the highway—maybe at the Afton Canyon turnoff. They switched vehicles and drove to the campground, ditched the truck, and drove back to Loretta's house in Barstow. If Dora never left the car, the dogs wouldn't have picked up her scent in the canyon."

"She was there, but not there." I mulled over the police theory. This Dora wasn't the woman Killeen had described to me. How had she met Loretta? "Did Dora ever mention knowing anyone in Barstow? Did she have relatives there?"

"Not that she said. She was new to the Mojave. She'd been out once with Marsh, but that was a quick weekend trip to check out a few old quarry sites—Mud Hills, Daggett, the Cadys. I was with them. So was Cassie. Dora said it was her first time in Barstow."

"So she had to have met Loretta when she went into town for supplies?"

"I just don't know, Frankie. But I think we've been chasing our tails out here."

"Was Loretta murdered?"

"Yup. Broken neck—though someone made it look like an accident, like she'd slipped and hit her head. But here's the odd part—Dora's prints weren't in the house or in Loretta's car. The car had been wiped clean. The only evidence she was there was her purse and ID."

"You said Loretta's purse was missing?"

He sighed. "With ID and credit cards. Crank thinks Dora left the car because it would be too easy to spot and hitchhiked out of town."

"Then she couldn't have dropped a boulder on Marsh's head."

"Not necessarily. The police didn't find the car till this afternoon. The owner of the convenience store wasn't sure how long it had been there—maybe a couple of hours, no more than a day."

"The jigsaw pieces may fit together, Killeen, but I can't see the picture-postcard scene. Dora suddenly becomes a serial killer. She tries for Sarah, succeeds with Dai, kills Loretta, then attacks Marsh? You think that's possible?"

"Anything's possible. I've had buddies I knew a whole lot better than Dora put their lives on the line for me, then go home and murder their families. I've known rational, grounded types who flipped out when they were turned down for promotion. I met Dora only three months ago, when I joined the department. She's prickly, like I said before—a loner with a chip on her shoulder even bigger than Dee's. An abuse survivor, I think, but I'm just guessing. Anyway, I didn't get to know her till we spent a weekend working out here in the Cadys. She opened up some, but not much. She has trust issues. Abuse survivors can keep a lot bottled up inside."

"Then it's possible Crank's right. So let's try to poke some holes in his theory . . . I don't know what happened to Loretta, but the other attack styles seem awfully random for a serial killer."

Killeen grunted softly. "One way or another, they all were struck. No guns or knives. That's not random."

"Okay, so why would she leave her camera, GPS, phone, and insulin pen for us to find out here?"

"Maybe she didn't leave them for us. Maybe she abandoned them. Maybe she didn't want to keep anything that would connect her to UC–Del Rio. Remember, she left them here before she went into town to kill Sarah and Dai."

"This throws off my entire theory of what happened and why, Killeen."

"Welcome to the club. Looks like we've got two killers—your

**Quarry** 179

Geoff and Dora. If Crank's theory is correct, Geoff went underground after he claimed Venable's remains. Everything after that belongs to Dora."

"But what about those quotes from *Romeo and Juliet*—especially the first one?"

"Sarah would have been the first death, Dai the second, and Marsh the 'third in your bosom,'" Killeen said. "Marsh was out here searching with all of us when he was struck."

"Then why didn't she finish the job?"

"Maybe she saw one of us—or one of the searchers across the canyon. We weren't the only ones out here."

"Damn. We've a bucketful of maybes, but no answers, Killeen. It's as if you just upended the table with a nearly completed puzzle. Now we have to start over."

"Crank's team is delving into Dora's and Loretta's backgrounds. And they're checking Loretta's tires to see if there's any evidence she was at Afton. They'll know more in the morning."

"Meanwhile, Dora has no car, no gear, and no reason to hang around the Cadys. She can't use Loretta's credit cards out here." My tone was wry. I stoked the fire, using the time to think. "That first note said she was after three people. She got them. The danger now is to Marsh in Barstow. She may want to finish the job."

"Crank's already there."

Something about that note still bothered me. "If Dora was after three people, then why kill Loretta?"

"It might have been an accident." Killeen's tone said he was grasping at something a lot less substantial than straw.

"Or Dora wanted to cover her tracks."

He sighed. "Well, the only thing I'm sure of right now is that we should leave the search for Dora in Crank's hands."

"So we might as well go home first thing in the morning?"

Right then it began to rain.

"Shit," said Zev and Dee in unison. The sentiment was repeated as everyone scrambled out of their sleeping bags, tugged on boots, grabbed gear, and headed for higher ground. Ryan stretched a tarp from the Suburban doors, holding down the ends of the lean-to with tent pegs. Zev, Dee, Nakata, and Rudinsky climbed into the Suburban. Killeen and I sprinted for the Cherokee.

"Take the back," Killeen said, no longer needing to whisper. "I can sleep sitting up."

I pushed everything to one side, flopped my mat and sleeping bag on the other. The Jeep bed wasn't level or long enough for my body, but it was dry.

"Dee and Zev?" said Killeen, when we were settled.

I told him the story of the exploding mineral, adding, "Having two professors in the SUV might cramp Zev's style."

"I doubt it," Killeen said. "Sanidine's a mineral?"

"A lovely opalescent blue feldspar. I'll show you in the morning." I repeated my earlier question about a departure time and waited for his rain-delayed answer. But his breathing was deep and regular. He was asleep.

I wasn't as lucky. My mind refused to shut down. Try as I might, I couldn't fit the new information into a pattern. Perhaps we had pieces to more than one puzzle.

I decided to let my subconscious sort through the myriad facts and clues. My last semicoherent thought was an image of a three-dimensional puzzle—the Tower of London. Dora was chained in the dungeon, along with the Crown Jewels.

The cessation of rain on the windows and roof woke me around four. Wind gusts buffeted the Jeep. Clouds streamed across the sky, exposing, here and there, ragged patches of star-studded black velvet. A few feet below us, water flowed in the wash. I heard the clash of rocks driven by the flood. Killeen and I were marooned.

# 36

Killeen was up at first light, checking on our situation. He was wearing a coat this morning. "We'll leave after breakfast," he said, picking up the thread of our midnight conversation.

Though tempted to snooze after my night of broken sleep, I rolled up my sleeping bag and mat, laced my boots, and crawled out of the Jeep.

It had to be in the thirties. My breath hung like white smoke before my face. The water bottles and jugs were blocks of ice. Luckily, I'd had the foresight to line the inside of my sleeping bag with water bottles so my body heat would keep them from freezing. I wasn't being heroic. I wanted water for brushing teeth, washing hands and face, and most important of all, making coffee—and tea, of course, for Nakata.

The floodwaters had receded, at least for now, but the wash needed to dry out a bit before we could leave. I opened the back hatch, took the Coleman stove from under the Jeep, and started the coffee. Below, in the side canyon, Killeen was starting a fire with the wood Ryan had stowed under the Suburban. The surface was damp, but not saturated. Killeen pulled yesterday's newspaper from the Jeep to use as fuel. Ryan helped him rebuild the fire pit, telling him last night's story. Their laughter echoed off the rocks.

I had chorizo going in the frying pan, the percolator on the other burner. Killeen took over the cooking while I stumbled down to the main wash and baptized a new privy.

As I climbed back up the ridge of tuff, I heard cursing from the opposite hillside. Four figures stood on the far side of the Suburban. It was canted at an odd angle, as if the ground had slumped under one side. Killeen handed me back the spatula and started down the ridge. I hoped we'd still be able to leave after breakfast. I was tired of the goose chase. I was ready to see Philo.

I drained the sausage, tossed in two dozen eggs, scrambled them together with the leftover tomato, onion, salsa, and cheese from last night, and sprinkled cumin over the top. Killeen arrived as I finished eating my burrito.

"What happened?" I said.

"The Suburban's out of commission. Two flat tires. Looks like rocks punctured the sidewalls, maybe when Nakata drove up onto the shelf. Unfortunately, there's only one spare. And yours won't fit the Suburban." He stopped to catch his breath. "Nakata called a repair service to bring a new tire," he continued. "Figured it was faster than having us make the round trip to Barstow in the Jeep. But they won't get here for hours. The Mojave River's flooding. The road's closed. They'll have to wait for the water to recede."

If the truck couldn't get in, we couldn't get out, even in the Jeep. And I wasn't about to ford a flash flood. We were stuck here for a while. The Fates were working overtime. Time to call Philo.

I found my cell phone. I'd inadvertently left it on all night. The battery was low. But Philo answered on the first ring. I brought him up to date about Dora, the flooding river, and my on-again Friday morning dissertation defense. So much for spending the entire day together. "Three nights, no days," I said, remembering the wedding on Saturday.

"Then the nights will have to do," he said. "How's Killeen taking the news? Sylvie told me he'd gotten to know Dora better than anyone."

I looked over at Killeen, who'd stepped away to place his own call. "He looks like somebody kicked the chair out from under him."

"I know how he feels." Philo clearly wasn't thrilled about our lost hours together.

"Me, too."

"Frankie? Why don't I meet you in Barstow. Killeen can take your Jeep home, and you and I can have a meal and drive back together."

I put the suggestion to Killeen. He gave me a thumbs-up.

"All systems go," I said to Philo. "Would you do me a favor and call La Joie and give him our new schedule—such as it is? Now that his murders are linked to Dora's disappearance, he'll want to talk to Killeen and me when we get back to Del Rio."

"Will do. Where shall I meet—"

My phone died. "Shit," I said.

Killeen walked back, tucking his phone in his breast pocket. "What's up?"

"Dead battery. Philo won't know where to meet us."

I spooned eggs into a warm tortilla for Killeen and passed him the salsa bottle. One can never have too much salsa.

"Don't worry, he'll find you," Killeen said between bites.

"Right—unless the Fates are still on the warpath."

Killeen grinned. "Have faith, Frankie. They have to rest sometime."

I wrinkled my nose at him. "Breakfast," I called down to Ryan, who was dumping coffee into the pot on the fire. He moved the pot to the edge of the coals and went to get the others. They filed up, filled their plates, and took them down to the campfire. I sipped my coffee and watched Killeen polish off his burrito. He spooned eggs and salsa into a second tortilla and rolled it up.

"Who'd you call?" I asked him.

Leaning against the bumper of the Jeep, he said, "Crank. He'd already spoken to La Joie. No sign of Dora or Geoff in either Barstow or Del Rio, but a couple of people thought they spotted Dora at a truck stop near Las Vegas."

I shook my head. The situation seemed surreal. "So she's on the run. Have you told the others about the evidence?"

"There hasn't been time."

I looked down at the group around the fire. Judging by their faces, they were not happy campers. Ryan stood a little apart from the others, watching and listening. He must have felt my eyes because he glanced up.

"Need help with the cleanup?" Ryan called.

"Hot water," I called back.

Ryan lifted a pail of steaming water from the fire, circled the end of the ridge, and stumped it up the gentler slope. He poured some into the frying pan and set the pail down on the ground. "You two cooked. I'll wash up. Great eggs, by the way."

"Thanks." I watched Ryan empty coffee grounds into a plastic garbage bag and rinse out the pot.

"Bummer about the tires," Ryan said. "Rudinsky's pissed at Nakata. She drove the thing up there."

I dried the percolator and handed it to Killeen. "I'm surprised no one saw the flat tires last night."

"We were parked on a slant anyway," Ryan said. "What with the dark and the rain and all, I just don't think we noticed." Ryan tossed out the last of the dishwater and handed me the frying pan. "There's a powwow in ten minutes. See you down there."

Ryan collected the damp paper towels we'd used, trotted down off the ridge, and tossed the towels into the fire. Black smoke rose and was shredded by the wind.

Killeen and I packed away the stove and dishes. "Would you mind telling the others about Dora?" he asked.

"You'd rather watch the fireworks from a distance?"

He smiled, but it was bleak. "I've got some thinking to do."

"No problem. I'll shout if I need rescuing."


The bedraggled group around the campfire was studying the overcast sky when I joined them. They weren't ready for more bad news.

I told them what Killeen had learned from Crank last night and this morning—that Sarah's DNA was on the dented front fender of Dora's truck, that Dora's purse was in Loretta Stanton's car, that the search for a missing person had morphed into a manhunt, that she'd reportedly been spotted near Las Vegas. The news was met with silence, followed by everyone talking at once. Their world had shifted on its axis. No one could believe Dora was a murderer.

But faced with convincing evidence linking Dora with three crimes, the group conceded the possibility she was guilty. It was only a small step from that concession to several conclusions: If Dora was guilty, she wasn't in need of rescue. The Nevada sightings tended to support Crank's theory that Dora had hitchhiked out of town. She was long gone from the Cadys. It was time to get back to Del Rio—as soon as the floodwaters subsided and the repair truck arrived.

"We've got a few hours to kill," Nakata said. "How do you want to spend them?"

I wished she'd phrased it differently.

"I'm going to go take a look at the basalt outcrops farther down the wash," Rudinsky said. "There's a discrepancy in the dating. I'd like to collect fresh samples and try again. I'll ride back up with the repair truck."

"I'll go with you," said Ryan.

"Good. You can carry the samples," said Rudinsky, as if bestowing knighthood on a squire.

Zev and Dee followed the main wash upstream, ostensibly prospecting for fossils. Zev wouldn't know a fossil if one bit him on the foot. They wanted privacy—a sandy cove out of the wind, preferably not too damp. Nakata opted to walk northeast, to see how far she could trace the Peach Springs Tuff. I decided to check out the quarry.

"Then I'll circle south to meet you," said Nakata, pointing to a place on the map. "We can walk back together. Rendezvous in ninety minutes?"

"Ninety minutes." Smiling, I added, "Don't be late, Nono."

For a heartbeat she must have thought I was serious. Then she picked up her daypack and mapboard and smiled back. "You know me, Frankie. I'll be early to my own funeral."

*God, I hope not,* I thought, watching her climb up the steep canyon wall and disappear over the ridge.

# 37

I took a few minutes to upload Dora's digital photographs into my computer. Sitting in the passenger seat of the Jeep, I scrolled through them quickly. Most were of the quarry. A few were panorama shots in different directions. They showed gravel-topped ridges in the foreground, stretching out toward mountains or valleys. We were in a corner of the Basin and Range Province. No matter which way Dora had looked, there were mountains in the background.

Behind me, Killeen rooted around in the ice chest. "Mustard, mayo, or sandwich spread?" he said.

"What?"

"On your ham sandwich."

"Mayo," I said. "But you don't have to fix me lunch, Killeen. I'm not going to be gone that long."

"I've double-bagged it in plastic," he said, a minute later. "Just in case it rains again."

He zipped the lunch into my daypack, opened my door, and pointed to the computer screen. The photo had been taken from a ridge west of Dora's quarry. "You think visiting the quarry will help solve the puzzle?"

"I'm curious. Maybe if I can see where Dora worked and read through her field notes, I can get into her head, maybe figure out what set her off. I'm still having a tough time picturing her as a killer—picturing her at all, really."

Killeen shrugged. He was subdued, a mood I hadn't seen before. He was rarely wrong about people. But the evidence against Dora was too strong to ignore. It had thrown him.

"Worth a try," he said finally, and pointed to the bottom of the screen. "The quarry will be above your head. Look for debris in the wash from when I cleared off the overburden. You can't miss it."

I transferred Dora's GPS site location from the computer topographic map to my paper copy and shut down.

"Watch your step up there," he said, handing me the daypack.

I knew he was talking about more than my footing. "Even if those Nevada sightings are wrong and Dora's still out here, she's no threat to me, Killeen. We've never met."

Out of habit, I put my wallet in the outside pocket, first removing a stiletto-thin tinker's knife in a worn leather sheath. The sheath dangled from a leather cord. I wore it around my neck whenever I was in the field. It had saved my life.

"When did you start carrying a concealed weapon?" Killeen said.

"Last month." I took the knife from the sheath and passed it to him, haft first. "A neighbor gave it to me."

"Beautiful, balanced, and very, very lethal," he said, handing it back. "Do you have a permit for a concealed weapon?"

"Even if I did, it wouldn't be good in California."

"I'd get one anyway," he said. "Just to be safe."

"I will if you will." I smiled, and gave him my cell phone and the keys to the Jeep. "Would you mind charging my phone while I'm gone?"

"No problem. Want to take mine?"

I knew Killeen hadn't had a chance to call Sylvie and Tommy this morning. My leaving would give them time to talk privately. "I won't need it. I'm not going far," I said. "Just honk the horn if the repair truck gets through. I'll be at the quarry until it's time to meet Nakata."

I followed the wash south, climbing steadily. Surrounded by rock and sand and sky, a landscape nearly devoid of vegetation, I was aware of the low angle of the sun behind the clouds. The fallow time was upon us, the dormant season when plants and animals recover their energy. I was looking forward to having my own fallow time—at least on weekends—once I finished my degree.

The canyon narrowed quickly as I moved upstream. The rocks here, freshwater limestone and tuffaceous sandstone, dipped gently east. An old fault separated the white sedimentary beds on my left from the welded tuff on my right. I collected a tuff sample to show Killeen the sanidine crystals.

The wind quieted a bit, but still chafed my skin. My hip ached. I'd injured it back in my volleyball days, and now it reacted to changes in atmospheric pressure. Another front was moving in. The barometric pressure was falling. More rain would follow. Soon. I hoped the Suburban was fixed before the storm hit.

I scrambled up a damp waterfall. The rock walls closed in.

Blocks of rubble, the overburden Killeen had cleared off to expose the quarry, dotted the streambed. I climbed straight up to a ledge of sandstone dipping into the ridge. I could see the chisel marks where the blocks with fossil bones had been removed. Otherwise, the site was clean. Dora had packed up her tools and prepared to go home. She was finished here. But something had happened when she left. A man was at the campsite. Someone she knew. Someone who wasn't a threat: Jed Strong, the archaeologist or site robber, the only man mentioned in Dora's notes, the only one with whom she'd have shared a last meal. Perhaps they'd shared many meals in the two weeks she worked here. I thought of the old movie, based on a true story, *The Sugarland Express*. Sometimes people with no history of violence digress into murder sprees. Could Jed have triggered such a change in Dora?

I thought back to that last photo in her camera: white sandstone, bald man, back turned, sitting on his heels by the campfire. What else was in that photo?

The wine bottle by his right boot. He'd cooked Dora a meal. They'd shared a bottle of wine. But faced with a long drive home, Dora wouldn't have had more than a few sips, if that much. Insulin-dependent diabetics limited their alcohol intake, though tolerance varied from person to person. In any case, I hoped Crank could lift Jed's fingerprints from the bottle. Even a partial fingerprint would help. One more piece of the puzzle.

I took off my backpack and sat, cross-legged, on the cold rock of the quarry. Beside me, caught in a crevice, were two strands of silver hair. Dora's? The photos she'd taken on the day she and Killeen had checked out Afton Canyon showed a slight woman turning prematurely gray. The strands made her seem more real somehow.

Besides the color of her hair, what did I know about Dora? She used leverage and perseverance to compensate for small physical stature and limited strength. She'd lived successfully with diabetes and raised a child on her own. She was a survivor . . . And she'd made friends with Killeen. That was important. Killeen was perceptive. How had she fooled him? How had she fooled them all?

I pulled the photocopy of Dora's field notes from my pack, searching for clues to a bizarre change in personality. The notes revealed nothing. She was neat, thorough, capable, methodical. What was I missing?

Dora was lonely. She'd welcomed a stranger's companionship, trusted him enough to accept food and wine. Jed must have seemed normal—whatever that meant. Her red flags hadn't gone up. Had there been a physical attraction between them? Had Jed charmed Dora into letting down her guard? I knew all about charm, about letting down your guard. That's what I'd done with Geoff. We all make mistakes.

I thumbed through her notes to the day she met Jed. Later, on December 4, he'd taken her to see where he was working. Dora described the place as "a low, narrow mesa jutting east into the basin." Underneath were the words "Crucero (the crossing)." But did she mean a road crossed by the interstate? A crossing of the Mojave River? A railroad siding? A water depot? A ghost town?

On my topographic map, I traced the railroad line east along the Mojave River, starting at the northwest edge of the Cadys: Dunn, Afton . . . Crucero. The siding was a collection of buildings sitting in the middle of the Mojave Sink. Any mesa striking east into that basin would be a ridge coming off the Cady Mountains. I turned the page in her notes to find a sketch—circles and parallel lines spaced, seemingly at random, within the outline of the mesa. No scale, but she'd included a North arrow. A serpentine line ran along the southern edge of the ridge.

The next page contained notes made after she'd returned to camp. They were for future reference, background to explain the photographs she'd taken. She listed the photo numbers. They must be included with the photos I'd scrolled through on her computer, dismissing them as location shots near the quarry.

> No one knows who built the rock alignments, her notes read. Or when. Paleo-Indians? Man settled the Great Basin >13,000 years b.p. So made when the Mojave River flowed into Soda Lake? When Crucero basin held water?
>
> Jed's theory: Rock alignments represent celestial chart. Rock corridor (>400 ft.) crossing northeast end of mesa will line up with the Milky Way during winter solstice. Corridor that long required organization and manpower. Would mark event of major importance (solstice sunrise or sunset, movements of planets or constellations, moon's path).
>
> Jed's research into aboriginal belief systems: the winter solstice is major. Sun seems to stand still. Beginning of the longest night of the year, the battle between darkness and light. Sunrise of the first day of winter reassures that light has won the battle. Days will grow longer. Storytelling time begins with story of creation—when light was born.

*Meanings (according to Jed):*
*Circles = Sacred places/spaces/representations—e.g., camp-*
*fire, dancing circles, chanting circles, sleeping circles (tipi,*
*wikiup, hogan), the four directions, whirlwind, Medicine*
*Wheel, sun, moon, stars, bowl of sky. Circles have power.*
*Snakelike alignment: Snakes = important symbols of*
*ancient cultures. Great Serpent Mound, Ohio. Quetzlcóatl,*
*(sp? Feathered Serpent), MesoAmerica. Ngalijod (sp? Rainbow*
*Serpent), and Ungud (sp? Great Serpent), Australia. Constella-*
*tions Draco (Dragon), Hydrus (Water Serpent), Eriadnus (the*
*River).*
*Why build on that mesa? Nothing there but sky and rocks.*
*Place of vulnerability. No place to hide.*
*Jed's theory: Mesa's east-west orientation and isolation*
*made it special, sacred, and worth the time and effort needed*
*to construct alignments. No outcrops for petroglyphs or pic-*
*tographs, but plentiful supply of rocks for alignments. Rela-*
*tively flat (to gather on, build on). Great expanse of sky for*
*viewing celestial events. At sunset on winter solstice, Milky*
*Way will line up with longest parallel rock corridor. Path ends*
*at a large circle (= Auriga, the Charioteer?). The line heading*
*southeast from the circle = rising path of Perseus, the Pleiades,*
*Taurus the Bull, Orion the Hunter. Also the path of the sunrise*
*the following morning.*

I wondered if Jed had asked her to stay and witness the show on the solstice. She didn't say. Nor did she say she planned to come back for the event. But her interest was piqued enough to record her visit to the site and to write one final note: "Check Rogers, Campbell (myth), Fagan, etc. (summary of archaeo.), recent arti-cles, star charts, etc." Dora had planned to review the literature, to prove or disprove Jed's theory. Two weeks ago, then, she'd planned to return to Del Rio and continue her schooling. I thumbed through the rest of her notes again. They were straightforward, routine. More importantly, *Dora mentioned no recent contact with Sarah or Dai, no motivating event.*

To a scientist, negative evidence can be as powerful as positive evidence. I posed the question again: *What had angered Dora enough to want to kill Dai and Sarah on Monday night?*

Answer: *Nothing. Dora Simpson was not a killer.*

Killeen's instincts had been dead-on. So where did that leave us?

Only one other person had had access to Dora's truck on Monday—the enigmatic Jed Strong. I let my mind play with the evidence. The wine bottle had been buried in the fire pit. Killeen assured me Dora wouldn't have left it behind. Her field notes revealed no radical personality change on that final morning. Ergo, Jed must have buried the bottle. Had he hurt or killed Dora and stolen her purse and truck? If so, it followed that Jed had attacked Sarah and Dai. And Loretta Stanton.

I should have trusted my own instincts—or at least my problem-solving skills. The only person with a deep-seated, driving motive for harming the geology faculty was my former fiancé, Geoff Travers. Which meant that Geoff was Jed Strong—just one more in a long line of assumed identities. Dora had let him into her safe zone, just as I'd welcomed him into mine. Dora and I both had blind sides; we both were more proficient at dealing with rocks than with people.

I thought back to my time with Geoff, trying to match him to what I knew of Jed Strong. Had Geoff ever talked about archaeoastronomy or spent time watching the constellations? Not really. In the desolate reaches of the Great Basin, where there is no light pollution, the night sky is so black, the stars so bright and close, that one can't ignore them. Like the length of the day, the constellations help confirm the progress of a field season. But my father, an archaeologist who'd worked at Chaco Canyon, knew more about archaeoastronomy than Geoff did—and I'd never heard them discuss it. So was this a recent passion, something Geoff picked up from a man named Jed Strong? When the police found him, maybe I'd have my answer.

I had a *motive*. The *means* had been established. I let my mind play with *opportunity* . . . Geoff must have been hiding out in Barstow and the Cadys since last summer. He could have met Loretta Stanton in Barstow. He could have killed her and left Dora's purse in her car. But had he also killed Dora?

Geoff—I had trouble calling him Jed—had taken her to see his mesa. She hadn't felt threatened when he'd shared his theories, his excitement. He seemed to want a witness to his discovery, perhaps a witness to his life. Would that be enough to protect her? Not necessarily. He was unpredictable. But someone—Loretta Stanton, Geoff, or Dora—had picked up Dora's insulin from her apartment on Tuesday. Dead diabetics don't need insulin.

Sitting on that outcrop, I became convinced Dora was alive. She'd do everything in her power to stay that way, to escape if she could. And her powers were considerable. I bet Geoff had underestimated her. And if it meant postponing my defense again in order to keep searching, I decided as I put away Dora's field notes, then I'd do it. Killeen and Sylvie could get married without me.

I wished I'd had my cell phone so I could call Crank and La Joie. No matter. I'd be in Barstow soon enough. In the meantime, I wanted to check out Jed Strong's mesa.

I marked several likely targets on the map, then folded it and stuffed it in my daypack. It was time to circle around to meet Nakata. From higher ground I might be able to pick out Jed's mesa.

Turning my back on the quarry, I started climbing. My brain was multitasking as I walked, noting details like fossil root casts in the sandstone, limestone marker beds, faults that truncated units. But I was asking and answering questions, too. Why was Dora's truck left at Afton Canyon and not in Barstow?

There was only one answer: Because Geoff wanted it found there. Because he knew we'd join the search for Dora. He wanted to maneuver us into position, to split us up and pick us off. Was that what he was doing right now? Had Geoff punctured the tires of the Suburban to keep us here?

If Geoff was still here, so was Dora. And it was just possible he'd be holding her within sight of the mesa.

# 38

I hurried now, wanting to reach a place with a view. The desert pavement, punctuated by sparse vegetation, made easy walking. I climbed high enough so that I could circle around on the ridgetops, meet Nakata, and come back to the campsite from the east.

Kneeling, I took out my binoculars and looked for Rudinsky and Ryan in the main wash. The ridges below me were shaped like fingers, pointing north. Basalt, welded ashflow tuff, and old alluvial fan deposits capped the mesas, proving more resistant to erosion than the soft, friable Miocene sedimentary beds. I should have been able to see Rudinsky pounding on a basalt flow. Nothing.

Back at camp, Killeen was looking into the engine of the Jeep. He'd repacked everything in the back. Off to my left, I caught Dee and Zev, arms gesticulating. They were arguing, whether over politics or geology, I couldn't tell—until Dee stopped to pluck a piece of basalt from the outcrop. Geology, then.

I made another sweep with the glasses, found two figures, not far from our campsite, examining the brick-red bake zone under a basalt flow. Rudinsky and Ryan. As they moved on and rounded an outcrop, Rudinsky stumbled and fell. Ryan was at his side, helping him up. Rudy seemed to be okay. I climbed farther, looked back. They were out of sight.

Where was Nakata? She'd planned to come up this ridge. We should have crossed paths by now. Maybe she'd followed the tuff farther east than she'd planned, losing track of time, absorbed by the geology. I'd done that. We'd all done that. The fact that I couldn't see her didn't mean she was in trouble.

In another five minutes I was on the south end of a ridge leading out into the Mojave Sink. Crucero was in the distance. For two hundred years, Spanish and American explorers searched for a link between the Mojave River and the Colorado. Like the legendary Northwest Passage, it didn't exist. The Mojave River disappeared forever into the sands out there in front of me. This morning, water stood in the basin. The wind was blowing at least fifty miles an hour, buffeting me, lifting—

I dropped belly-down on the ridge, elbows bracing the binoculars against the wind, and scanned the lower slopes. A slight movement. Graying black hair lifted by the wind. Dora's? No, too short. Nakata's, then.

The rest of her was obscured by a shelf of rock at the edge of a draw. Was she checking an outcrop? Taking a bathroom break? A snack break? I kept watching. No. She should have moved by now.

Why hadn't I taken Killeen's cell phone when he offered? I'd have to improvise. I located Zev and Dee again and signaled them with my compass mirror. I hoped they'd realize I wanted them to rendezvous—or at least turn back.

Nakata still hadn't moved. I flashed the reflected light onto Killeen's face. He set down his coffee cup and pulled out binoculars. I signaled him again. He nodded and signed back. He'd keep me in sight till we could holler at each other—or that's what I thought his gestures meant.

I located myself on the topo map and took a compass bearing on Nakata. Still no movement.

Dee and Zev had started back. Good. I ran north down the slope, keeping an eye on Nakata's position in relation to two landmarks. I knew they'd look different as I changed altitude and angle.

I took another bearing just before I lost sight of Nakata's hair. The intersection of two points isn't as accurate as triangulation, but it narrows the scope. I started running again and stopped abruptly. Shit. I'd set down my binoculars while I triangulated. I went back up the slope. As I bent down to retrieve the glasses, I felt something whiff by me. It struck an outcrop on the next ridge over and bounced. An arrow.

I grabbed the binoculars, dropped off the skyline, and flattened myself against the rounded cobbles of an old channel deposit. My heart hammered. Blood pounded against my eardrums.

I was being hunted. We all were being hunted.

# 39

I peeked over the ridge crest but could see nothing. No arrows followed.

The arrow had come from somewhere behind and southeast of me. Was the archer working around for a better shot? Was it Geoff? Was this what had happened to Nakata?

Turning over onto my back, I located the spot where the arrow had hit the far bank. Same elevation. I wanted that arrow. Maybe it would provide some answers.

I stuffed the binoculars in my backpack, crouched, and ran to the V where the two ridges came together. The bulk of the first ridge hid me till I reached the far slope. I held my breath, dashed along the slope, grabbed the arrow, and retraced my steps. I needed to intercept and warn Killeen and the students. But I also needed to reach Nakata.

I slipped and slid into the tributary wash and headed downstream, stopping only to zip the arrow into my daypack. I didn't want to lose it.

The canyon wound around, changing direction. When I'd gone a quarter of a mile, I saw a knob above me on the ridge. Good. Something to screen me. I climbed the hundred feet to the crest, crawling the last ten yards. I put the finger of rock between me and the mountain massif, making myself as small a target as possible while I caught my breath.

It was just nine o'clock. The sun, buried in a mass of clouds streaming from the southeast, gave no warmth. The wind chill was turning my hands blue. I tugged on my gloves and pulled the wool knit cap more firmly over my ears, tucking up my hair underneath it. Despite the fleece vest under my parka, I was shivering. But the temperature was only one reason. The other was fear. The wind took one of my senses away—two, really. I wouldn't be able to smell anything unusual. And I wouldn't hear an archer—or an arrow.

I had to get to Nakata. If she weren't already dead, she'd be losing heat and blood. I had to find out if Rudinsky and Ryan were okay. And I had to tell the others there was a wacko with a bow running around the hills.

I needed help. Killeen first. Looking down, I saw the Jeep was gone. Where was he?

I drew a line on the map from my spot to where Nakata lay, then tucked the compass and map away. Dropping off the ridge into the next ravine to the west, I ran toward where I'd last seen Killeen. The students would be headed there, too. He'd have left us a note or a sign. Or I could just follow his tire tracks.

Why had Killeen moved the Jeep? Had he seen something that put the Jeep—our only transportation—in jeopardy? Had he left the Jeep to rendezvous with me, only to have someone steal it?

Nearing the camp, I paused in the shelter of the welded tuff to check the area. It seemed undisturbed. No sign of the archer. But Killeen, Dee, and Zev weren't back yet. I couldn't waste time tracking them down. I'd have to deal with Nakata alone. I made a cairn and a rock arrow, pointing the way for the others. I tucked an explanatory note under the top stone. I'd have to trust they'd find me.

I struck due east across the landscape, perpendicular to the drainage pattern—which meant trudging up one ridge and loping down the far side, crossing wash after wash. Anyone up on the mountain would see me, would know where I was headed. Couldn't be helped. Nakata needed me. I had to get to her first.

I shoved fear aside and ploughed ahead. I marked each mesa with a cairn and rock arrow. Why had Nakata come this way? What had she seen that piqued her curiosity? It wasn't the Peach Springs Tuff. That trended more to the northeast.

The sky was growing darker. It was raining to the east. No sun for signaling. I was mute—we all were cut off, as if on a desert island. *Damn,* I thought, as I looked south. Rain obscured the peaks. In minutes the rain would reach me. These dry channels would be flooded.

That was why Killeen moved the Jeep. He'd anticipated more flooding and thought the low ridge of tuff might not be high enough. I just hoped he'd hidden the Jeep so well that the archer wouldn't find it. Of course, neither would I or the others, especially if floodwaters wiped out the tire tracks.

And then I saw what Nakata must have seen—a faint trail coming in from the northwest. It was no more than a disturbance of the desert pavement, rocks overturned, desert trumpet trampled. And on the gently sloping banks of the wash, burro tracks. Unshod. The wild burros of the Mojave? I'd never heard of them being in the Cadys. But here were two sets of tracks. The rain last night had washed away most of them, but a few deep ones remained.

As I stood up, the rain started. I pulled Killeen's spare poncho from my backpack. The rain on the plastic further reduced my sense of hearing and increased my sense of isolation. I missed Nakata by ten yards and had to backtrack. She was half hidden by a ledge of conglomerate. She'd taken an arrow just under her right collarbone, inches from the neck. There was a swelling on her temple. But she was breathing.

The arrow shaft, identical to the one in my backpack, was too short for a longbow. Was the bastard using a crossbow? It'd be more accurate in this wind. Nakata was lucky to be alive. Why hadn't the archer finished her off?

I couldn't carry her by myself. I had to go back for help.

I elevated Nakata's feet and covered her with my parka, then with her poncho. She groaned slightly, but didn't open her eyes.

Right above her on the ridge, I built a cairn and scraped an arrow into the desert pavement, then started back to the campsite, retracing my steps from cairn to cairn. My body itched the whole time, wondering when an arrow would find me.

Water flowed in the sixth tributary. I debated entering, but it was shallow and only twenty feet across—a slot canyon, deep and curving and narrow. I listened for a roar that would signal a flash flood. Heard the rain on my poncho and the sound of the wind, blowing so hard now I had to lean over just to stay upright. I sensed someone behind me. Turning sharply, I instinctively stepped back.

The cliff edge gave way. I slid and rolled into the wash, knocking the wind from my lungs. I saw him above me, a man in camouflage-pattern fatigues. Geoff. He held a crossbow aimed at my heart. He was smiling.

"Hello, Frankie, my love," he said. The wind whipped away the words. I read his lips.

I felt the earth beneath me vibrate as I opened my mouth. An icy wall of muddy water swept around the corner and over me.

# 40

The debris-laden water carried me downstream until my poncho caught on a submerged outcrop. I clung there as boulders tumbled past like marbles, narrowly missing my head. The poncho strained against my neck, cutting off my air supply. I clawed at it with my left hand, ripped it over my head, watched it disappear downstream.

I tried to climb the outcrop, get above the flood, but the force of the water was too great. Like a trolling lure I clung there, ducking and twisting, until a cobble hit my fingers. Swept free again, I was thrown against one curve in the bank, another, and another, until I bounced onto a sandy bench inches above the water. I curled up into a ball, sucked in air like a fish, gingerly tested my fingers—bloody, but unbroken.

A clicking sound announced that I wasn't alone. A rattlesnake, swept from hibernation by the flood, lay coiled five feet away. By all rights, the chilly conditions should have rendered him lethargic, at best. I wasn't that lucky. He clearly wasn't happy about being so rudely awakened from his winter nap, and hostile about sharing his space. So I stayed still, knowing he could sense my body heat, hoping he'd decide I wasn't a threat. No dice. The dry clicking became more insistent.

I inched backward, met a vertical wall. On one side was the flood, which seemed to be rising, instead of falling, as if a dam upstream had broken. On the other, a semicircular wall of crumbly tuff about twelve feet high. No handholds that I could see. No driftwood to push the snake into the water. I reached for my trusty rock hammer . . . gone. Carried God knows where by the flash flood. And Geoff was somewhere above me on the ridge. Did he know I'd washed up? Did he know where? Was he waiting?

I pulled out the knife I wore around my neck and inched my way to a standing position, avoiding sudden movements. Fear wouldn't let me turn my back on the snake. Holding my arm out to the side, I gouged out finger- and toeholds in the soft tuff, grateful that here, at least, the rock wasn't welded. The lowest toehold was at thigh level; the highest, about seven feet up. I worked as quickly as my shaking fingers would allow. And then I heard a soft sound above me. A pebble rolled past my ear. I pressed against the concave surface of the bank and held my breath.

The snake had stopped rattling, but was still coiled. He would be visible from above. As I watched, a pebble landed in the center of his coils. The rattling started again, though sluggishly. He was feeling the cold—needed warmth to survive. He began to uncoil, began to move . . . toward me. I froze with my ear pressed against the rock wall. Apparently reassured, Geoff continued down the ridge. I saw pebbles trickle down to the water as he passed.

I waited several minutes, watching the snake start and stop, inching ever closer. I knew he could strike from a laid-out position—he didn't have to be coiled. I had to choose between the devil above, the flood below, and the snake beside me. All were lethal.

He was close enough to strike. I fitted my right foot slowly into the first pocket, my right hand at shoulder level. So far, so good.

The snake struck when I swung my body to face the cliff, catching the side of my left boot. The force of the blow knocked me off balance. The snake's fangs lodged in the leather. Screaming silently, I slipped back to the shelf, dragging the snake with me. I jumped and kicked, trying to dislodge it.

The snake arced through the air, slapped the water. I prayed Geoff hadn't been close enough to hear it. I looked down. The fangs had broken off. They stuck out of my boot. My foot was numb. I was going to die.

But I wasn't going to die on that damn bench.

# 41

I punched and scrambled and pulled my way up the wall of tuff. Heaving myself over the top, I lay sobbing on the cold, rain-slick desert pavement. I must have swallowed enough water to float the Spanish Armada. I couldn't take a breath that didn't catch in my throat. I was afraid to check my foot. Afraid not to.

I don't know how long I'd spent in the water, waiting, climbing out. Not even a ghost of a number showed on the face of my watch. When I stretched, my body reacted as if I'd been used as a punching bag. Every muscle screamed when I rolled to a position where I could scan the ridge, looking for Geoff. He was running, eyes focused on the roiling water. His back was to me, but his head was turned at an angle. His peripheral vision would pick up any quick movement. The only thing in my favor was that the rain would wash away any sign of my passing.

Using small flat rocks as tweezers, I plucked the fangs from my boot. Two perfect holes were left, a half-inch apart. Inside the water-logged leather were three layers of soggy sock. I peeled them off, one at a time, exposing a foot decorated with a darkening bruise. No puncture wounds. I wasn't going to die after all. At least, not from snakebite. Maybe from hypothermia. Or Geoff's arrows.

My poncho was one with the Mojave River by now. The rain poured down, rinsing mud from my face. I'd lost my gloves and hat. My muddy hair had come loose from its braid and now hung lankly against my neck and shoulders. I felt miserable.

I took off my other boot and squeezed out as much water from my socks as I could before dragging them back over cold feet. My body wanted to assume the fetal position and rest for a couple of hours. Overcoming inertia seemed impossible. I argued with my feet, my legs. They rebutted. I continued to lie there, in the rain, regrouping. I still had to get help for Nakata. But which direction to choose? Where did safety lie?

I was on the same side of the stream as Geoff. If he realized I'd fetched up behind him, would he expect me to go upstream, down, or across? He'd expect me to head for the Jeep.

Where was *he* staying out here? He had to be holding Dora somewhere close—if she was still alive. I hoped she was. But would he kill her now that he thought he'd finished me?

If I got to higher ground, I could figure out where the others were while watching Geoff's movements. Then maybe, after we rescued Nakata, we could track him back to his lair, reversing the tables.

I needed Killeen to get Nakata out or call for a helicopter. But could a helicopter fly in this weather?

I saw Geoff's body turn so that he was looking directly away from me. I bolted, running uphill till I reached an outcrop to screen me. I dropped flat. Moving slowly, I peered around the side of the conglomerate, my head just another cobble. Geoff was facing uphill, scanning this ridge and those nearby. Had he heard me? Seen me?

He turned to look west. Sunlight leaked through the clouds for a moment, reflecting off his shaved head. I didn't move. Peripheral vision is better at catching movement than direct vision. He turned his back, then snapped his body around, bow at the ready. He must have sensed my movement, not seen it, or he'd already be moving upstream.

He lowered the bow. I waited until he was fifty yards farther away, focused again on the floodwater, before I moved my head. Another storm cell was sweeping downhill. Soon it would help obscure any movement. But the sun wasn't far behind.

Geoff kept moving, increasing the distance between us, increasing my little edge of security. I scoured the ridge, looking for a good position to monitor him. The fingerlike ridges coalesced into a flat-topped hill, one of many similar resistant mesas. The crown was about four hundred feet above me. Could I make it to the top undetected? Not unless I went up a streambed or clambered along the wall of a channel. Both were dangerous.

My teeth were chattering. Hypothermia would be next. And the cold of the low-pressure system couldn't be far behind the storm. I watched Geoff stop, raise his bow again, and fire at something down in the streambed. It couldn't be one of the geologists—they'd gone in different directions . . . My poncho? He might have found my poncho and thought I was inside it. He'd discover soon enough that I wasn't, and then he'd continue looking.

He lowered his bow, took one last 360-degree view of the terrain, and dropped down off the ridge. He wanted a closer look at that poncho—or whatever he'd found.

I scrambled for the next ravine over. It was shallower, leading only to the mesa, so it carried local runoff, nothing from the interior of the range. I diagonaled down to the floor and ran upstream until my breath heaved in my chest. The water was just deep enough to wash away my tracks. I climbed up small waterfalls. The rough matrix of the conglomerate scratched and tore my hands, already abraded by my trip down the flooded wash.

It bothered me that I couldn't see Geoff, didn't know where he and his arrows were. He could be notching one right now, aiming for that space between my shoulder blades. My body tensed, waiting for the impact . . .

It didn't come. The gully petered out a good fifty feet below the crest. Now what?

Once I started climbing the mesa I'd be exposed—unless I could get around to the back side.

I was warm now from the exercise. I crawled out on the far ridge, lay prone, scanning for movement just as Geoff had done. I found the place he'd gone off the ridge. The storm cell was directly over it. If I couldn't see him, I hoped he couldn't see me.

Binoculars. I had them in my backpack. I'd forgotten all about them. But if I wasted any more time here, I'd lose the advantage of the rain screen. So I turned my back again and sprinted around the steep, talus-strewn side of the mesa, keeping as low to the ground as possible. I reached the saddle behind the mesa just as the sunbeam struck the hill, turning it to bronze. I scrambled up the back side and inched onto the desert pavement of the hilltop. The buffeting gusts tore at me. If I stayed here long, exposing my wet body to the wind, hypothermia would definitely set in.

I opened my backpack. Killeen's carefully packed sandwich was a sodden mess, compliments of the flood. I tossed out the sandwich, folded up the plastic bag, and tucked it back in the pack. I found the binoculars, and washed them off with bottled water. The binoculars weren't powerful—only 8 x 23—but enough, enough. I was using that word a lot lately—the word Dora had posted in bright red letters on her office door.

I could see miles in the clear spaces between the squalls. I looked back toward the tuff by Dora's campsite. The Suburban was a white Lego. Where was the Jeep? Had a flood taken it, too?

It was a hell of a long walk to the highway, but doable. I'd gone the distance before. But how long could Nakata survive without help? And what about Dora?

Then I saw them—Killeen and Geoff—on ridges a mile apart. Killeen was at my elevation, sitting atop another mesa to the west. Geoff was moving east-northeast at a good clip. I took my Brunton from its leather case. The case had a hole in the bottom of it, so the floodwater had drained straight out. Though the compass was gritty with silt, the metal casing had held against the water pressure. The needle moved freely.

I took a bearing on Geoff's course, noted it on the waterproof paper of my notebook. Pulling out a plastic protractor and the soggy topographic map, I plotted Geoff's course, projecting it to the east. He was headed toward a low hill overlooking one of the mesas I'd marked after reading Dora's notes.

Geoff dipped into a wash, and I used that breather to flash my compass mirror at Killeen. The sun didn't cooperate. I remembered my penlight. I dug it out and flashed the first two letters of an SOS. Would Killeen understand? SO . . . as in *I'm here. I see you. The situation's all fucked up. So what do we do now?* I was at a disadvantage. I didn't know any more Morse code than that.

Killeen blinked just once in return, left his basalt-capped perch, and started circling south. Relief swept over me. I hoped to hell he'd brought some dry clothes in his backpack. My body felt like a block of ice. But if I went to intercept Killeen, I'd lose sight of Geoff.

So I stayed where I was, watching, tracking Geoff's course. He was aiming for the basin east of the mountains. Why had he chosen that area? Because it was close, yet outside the search perimeter for Dora. Because there was nothing there to draw our attention. Because it was unexpected. He'd planned well.

Geoff seemed to be making no effort to deviate from his path, a line as straight as a phone-line road. He must believe I was dead, buried under the sand brought down by the flash flood. I couldn't help wondering what he felt—satisfaction? triumph? emptiness? What would he do next?

He'd left Nakata for dead, just as he had left Marsh yesterday. I didn't know what had happened to Rudinsky, but he wasn't back at camp. Had Geoff found him, too? Was that why Rudinsky had stumbled? I knew only that Geoff would keep hunting till he'd killed us all—or believed he had. And then he'd disappear again.

I couldn't let that happen. He'd find out soon enough that I was alive, and I'd be looking over my shoulder every minute of every day. I refused to live that way. I had to stop him. I also had to find Dora. In my gut, I knew he had her.

It would take Killeen another ten minutes to reach me, though he was moving faster than I thought possible for such a big man. He charged the ravines and hillsides like a tackle keying on the quarterback, his poncho blending with the rocks. The rain slowed to a drizzle and ceased just as he dropped down beside me, sucking air. Sweat ran in rivulets down his cheeks. I saw concern in his eyes. "What happened to you?" he said.

"Flash flood." My teeth were chattering so hard I stuttered over the words. "Geoff's down there with a crossbow. He shot Nakata." I took the arrow from my daypack and handed it to him.

"Ah," he said. A world of comprehension lay in that one brief word.

"Geoff is Jed Strong, Killeen—the man in Dora's photograph. I think he's been holding her nearby."

He put the arrow back in my pack, took off his poncho, and put it over my head. It did wonders as a windbreak. "Where's Nakata?" he said.

I pointed to where she lay, then quickly filled in the rest of the story. "Have you heard from Ryan or Rudinsky?"

"Nope." He saw my expression. "Don't worry, we'll find them, Frankie. But first things first." Killeen's face was unreadable, but his body radiated anger as he switched to military mode. He pulled out his phone, reached Barstow emergency. They'd alert Crank. The net would be lowered around Geoff—if Crank could get across the river.

Dee and Zev were much closer to Nakata than we were. They could reach her more quickly. He wasn't able to raise Zev, but Dee answered. Killeen relayed Nakata's situation and position, and explained that Geoff, not Dora, was the archer.

Below us, Geoff paused on the edge of a wash, looked east for a moment, as if considering. He turned, trotted west over the ridge, and dropped out of sight. Had the first wash been flooded? Was he taking an alternate route? Would we be able to beat him to Dora?

Killeen was dialing Rudinsky's number. When that didn't go through, he tried Ryan's. Got through on the second try. Ryan had climbed to higher ground. We saw him wave to us from the top of a black-capped mesa not more than half a mile from Nakata's spot.

So Geoff must have shot Nakata, left her for dead, gone after

Rudinsky, then circled around behind me as I ran down the ridge toward Nakata. Perhaps Nakata and Rudinsky—and maybe even Ryan—were alive right now because Geoff had been anxious to go after me. But how had he slipped by Killeen, Dee, and Zev? And would Geoff try to finish what he'd started? The answers would have to wait till I was warm and dry—relatively speaking, anyway.

Killeen's conversation with Ryan was short. Rudinsky had taken an arrow in the back. He'd lost a lot of blood. But he was breathing. He was holding his own. Killeen explained Geoff was the killer. Though I couldn't hear Ryan's words, his relief about Dora's innocence was mirrored in Killeen's replies to his questions. Killeen jotted down the GPS coordinates, relayed the information to Barstow, and called Ryan back to tell him help was on the way.

Killeen was smiling when he ended the call. "Ryan has things under control—for now. He said to tell you Rudinsky muttered that if his rescue is in our hands, he doesn't hold out much hope."

*Screw Rudinsky,* I thought. Aloud I said, "I'm freezing. Do you have any dry clothes with you?"

"Sweats." He pulled a black sweatshirt, pants, and a stainless steel thermos from his backpack. He handed me the clothes.

The sweatpants and shirt were XXXL. Luckily the pants had a drawstring waist that I could cinch so they wouldn't fall down.

I stripped off Killeen's poncho, my vest and turtleneck, and slipped into the sweatshirt. Killeen twisted my vest to wring as much water from it as possible. It still felt clammy when I put it back on.

He handed me a steaming cup of coffee. "Sorry—no cream."

"It doesn't matter. It's hot. If you weren't already spoken for, I'd marry you myself."

"For my coffee?" he asked, as I removed my boots and socks for the second time in an hour. This time my nylon field pants followed. Killeen wrung them out as well.

"For your coffee and the sweats," I said, wriggling into pants that were four inches too short. "I'm shallow. What can I say?"

Killeen fished a pair of socks and a knit cap from his backpack. "What about that Philo fellow?"

"Alliteration, too? Be still my beating heart." I quickly braided my lank hair, pulled on the cap, dragged on the dry socks, and laced up my boots. The socks covered the bare parts of my legs. Heaven was hot coffee and dry socks.

Killeen rinsed off my hands, covered them with antibiotic ointment, and bandaged them. His touch was gentle, but the process hurt like hell. "You seem to have a lot of bruises, and your right knee's swollen."

"Is it?"

"You're lucky your body wasn't deposited in the Mojave Sink."

*And shot full of arrows*, I thought, stuffing the wet clothes into my soggy backpack. "If you're finished, Dr. Killjoy—"

"I thought I was Watson?"

"Not today."

Killeen was staring at my rainwashed boots. "Well, Dr. Killjoy wants to know how you came by those little holes in your boot."

I looked down at the fang marks. "The flood woke up a Mojave green. He was a tad bit irritable."

"Rattlers can be testy." His tone was light; his expression wasn't.

"I'm okay, Killeen."

Movement far below us distracted Killeen. Dee and Zev crossed one ridge after another, heading east. Dee, I was surprised to see, was keeping pace with Zev. They reached the last cairn and rock arrow. I held Killeen's arm tightly with one hand, the binoculars with the other, as Zev bent down to examine Nakata. He was upright in seconds, giving a thumbs-up as he called Killeen on his cell phone. Nakata was alive. It hardly seemed possible.

"Have Dee stay with her," Killeen said. "You'll need to get my sleeping bag from the Jeep. Get Nakata warm and guide the helicopter." Killeen went on to ask the same questions he'd put to Ryan. "Can you handle it without us? You're sure? Okay. We're going to look for Dora. We think Travers has her . . . Yeah. I know. It's crazy . . . Don't worry, we'll find her."

"Speaking of the Jeep," I said, when Killeen finished, "what did you do with it?"

It was the first time I'd ever seen Killeen disconcerted. He hunted around for the right words. I waited.

"I thought you were going to stay where you were—"

"Damn."

"Thought I'd reach you faster if I drove upstream and then cut across the ridges."

"And . . ." I prompted.

"I got stuck in the sand. Dee, Zev, and I had the devil of a time getting her out."

So that was how Geoff had gotten behind me without being seen. All three of them had been busily digging out the Jeep. "Idiot. Is the Jeep okay?"

"She's fine—no thanks to me."

"Don't worry about it," I said, watching him put away his thermos and check around us to see if we'd forgotten anything. "Your pride will heal . . . Have you got your gun?"

He patted his side, hidden by his Windbreaker. "Have you got a plan to find Dora?"

"Geoff will lead us to her." I showed him Geoff's azimuth, plotted on the map. It led toward a hill due west of one of the mesas I'd marked earlier—one that closely resembled Dora's drawing. Killeen copied the line onto his own map. "If we circle around to the east, instead of using his route, we can follow this ridge straight to the hill without crossing a lot of washes."

"Washes that slow us down—and are hard on a bum knee."

"And carry flash floods. Geoff had to turn west. If we hustle, we can reach Dora before he does."

"Can you walk?" Killeen held out a hand.

"Of course. Well enough to find Dora. And then I'm going after Geoff. I'm not letting him disappear again." But when I stood, my knee gave way. "Just give me a minute."

"Don't worry, Travers won't get away."

Killeen took a couple of painkillers from his first-aid kit and handed them to me with his canteen. I washed down the capsules and returned the canteen, taking a long last look at the sites where Nakata and Rudinsky lay.

"There's nothing more we can do for them right now," he said. "They're in good hands. They'll be in Barstow before us."

But I couldn't shake the feeling I was abandoning them in favor of Dora.

Killeen's phone rang. Crank was calling from Barstow. "It's for you," Killeen said, handing me the phone.

"Did I get the story from the dispatcher correct?" Crank said. "Were Drs. Nakata and Rudinsky shot with a crossbow?"

I described what had happened. "Would you please call Detective La Joie—"

"He's standing right here, Dr. MacFarlane. With Philo Dain. We're about ready to leave. Hold on."

And then I was talking to La Joie. "You've seen the last picture Dora took—the bald man by the fire?"

"Yes. Jed Strong?"

"And Geoff Travers." The following pause was one long ah-hah.

"You saw him?" said La Joie.

"Too close for comfort. I was lucky. Would you fill Crank in on Geoff's story?"

"Of course."

The next voice on the line was Crank's. "Sit tight. We'll get you after we get Drs. Nakata and Rudinsky."

"By then, it might be too late for Dora Simpson." Killeen handed me his topo maps. I gave Crank the coordinates of the target area.

"We'll meet you there. Is Killeen armed?"

"Yes."

"Then locate Dora Simpson if you can, but don't engage Strong. Can you see him right now?"

"I lost him—maybe twenty minutes ago."

"Then be careful. We'll be there as soon as we can."

Killeen and I started down the hill, heading northeast. "You didn't answer the question about your relationship with Philo," he reminded me. Killeen's spirits had risen with the news that Geoff, not Dora, had attacked the Del Rio faculty. It was nice to have the old Killeen back.

"You're right," I said.

He tugged my braid, a short version of the one I'd worn last summer—the one that had almost gotten me killed. This braid barely touched the top of my shoulder blades when I turned my head.

"He makes a mean cup of coffee," I said, "and killer chiles rellenos."

"No doubt he has other fine qualities, as well."

"No doubt."

# 42

The ridge we traversed became broader and flatter as we descended. Killeen's phone rang after we'd gone a mile. It was Philo. Killeen again passed me the phone, and I talked as we walked.

"La Joie gave me Killeen's number," Philo said. "I kept getting voice mail with yours." I heard the worry in his tone. Despite my conversations with Crank and La Joie, Philo wasn't convinced I was okay.

"The battery died. It's recharging back at the Jeep." Beside me, Killeen stopped abruptly and shrugged out of his backpack. "It's just as well, though. If I'd been carrying the phone, it'd be water-logged," I said, as Killeen unzipped the pack, rummaged around, pulled out my phone, and passed it to me. "Check that," I said to Philo. "Killeen brought my phone."

Killeen and I started walking again, but even faster now to make up the time. Philo, meanwhile, was lagging behind.

"Waterlogged? You fell in the drink?" There was an unspoken "again" tacked on at the end. Philo knew my propensity for slipping into lakes or creeks. It was a source of great amusement for my family.

"Well, Geoff was trying to kill me at the time." I didn't stop to think what effect this casual statement would have on my lover, miles away.

"You're sure you're okay? Let me talk to Killeen."

"I'm okay, Philo. Really. Bruised, but mobile. Better than Nakata and Rudinsky. Where are you?"

"Near Yermo. With La Joie. The posse's ahead of us."

"How'd you hook up with La Joie?"

"When I called him this morning about your new schedule—"

"Which quickly went awry."

"No kidding. Anyway, La Joie and Crank had concluded independently that the Dora evidence was a little too pat—especially those anonymous phone calls. All the principal actors in La Joie's case—with the exception of Sarah—were in the Mojave. So La Joie was coming out to talk to Crank—and Marsh. La Joie let me tag along." I heard La Joie's voice in the background. "He says he hopes you'll stay put till the cavalry gets there. I second the motion."

"As I told Crank, I think Geoff's heading back to where he's been holed up—where I think he's keeping Dora. We're going to try to beat him—"

"God damn it, Frankie. Don't give him a second chance at you."

"We have the advantage, Philo. Geoff thinks I'm dead."

Philo didn't say anything for a long time. "Crank gave us the coordinates. Let me double-check them with you."

As Philo read back the coordinates, I looked at Killeen's map, praying I was right about the location, checking out the trails closest to the mesa. We had a problem. The same flooding that might prevent Philo from moving south would prevent an escaping Geoff from heading north.

"Wait a minute, Philo. Geoff's got to have a vehicle stashed somewhere. Because of the flooding, I think Geoff will try to escape by driving south to I-40 . . . or maybe retreat west though Cady Wash."

"I'll call Crank. He'll plug the escape routes. We'll get there as fast as we can."

"Tell him Geoff won't want to be taken alive." I didn't know how I knew this, but I did. Geoff had lived on his own terms. He'd rather die than relinquish his freedom.

"Suicide by cop?" Philo said.

"I'm afraid so."

"Killeen's armed?"

"Yes."

"I should have insisted you take one of my guns."

"For my dissertation defense? That would have gone over well." I heard La Joie laugh. He must be able to hear my side of the conversation.

"I forgot for a moment why you came to California," Philo said.

"For a moment, so did I . . . Philo, you never told me why you have to leave so soon."

Philo was silent. I thought I'd lost the connection, but he was only weighing his answer—probably considering security-clearance issues, cell phone vulnerability, and the witness driving the car. "I've been called up," he said at last.

I couldn't have heard right. "You're thirty-four, Philo—"

"And I limp, I know. But it doesn't affect what I do, Frankie."

"And you report on Sunday?"

"Yes."

"Then ford the damn Mojave. We're wasting time."

Philo was laughing as I punched the end button and handed the phone back to Killeen. "Easy there," Killeen said. The phone rang again. He handed it back.

"What," I said.

"I love you," said Philo. But he ruined the moment by adding, "Don't do anything stupid." The line went dead before I could respond.

"He's been called up?" asked Killeen, as he holstered the phone.

"Yes."

"You upset?"

I stopped and faced him. "What do you think?"

"Good. Use it. We've a long way to go yet."

"You missed your calling, Killeen."

"There's a lot of psychology in making war, Frankie."

"And strategy, too, Sun Tzu."

We broke into a jog—though my gait was more of a lopsided hobble. Anger, adrenaline, and the pain in my knee pushed me on. Even so, I was breathing hard by the time we came within sight of the hill I'd marked on my map. By unspoken agreement, we stopped to catch our breath and make a plan.

We dropped off the ridge into a shallow gully, pulled out our binoculars, crossed the wash, and climbed up until just my head showed. "There," I said, pointing to a low hill, innocuous, not more than a blip on the landscape. The crown was perhaps a hundred feet above us.

"I see it."

At the rate he was traveling, Geoff should reach the hill within the next few minutes—unless he'd stopped or detoured for some reason.

I thought about that for a minute. Geoff was sure I was dead. He must think Nakata was, too—or so close to death that rescuers wouldn't find her in time. But he couldn't be sure about Rudy. Geoff had hit the target, seen Rudy fall, then watched Ryan help him into the shelter of an outcrop. But would Geoff be satisfied with that? Or would he have detoured to make sure of Rudinsky?

I'd tracked him with the glasses till he descended into a gully. I

pulled out my sodden topographic maps once more, thankful the
USGS used sturdy paper. I found the wash where Geoff had disappeared, traced it northwest to where it joined the main wash. The
point was just north of where I'd seen Rudinsky go down.

"Do you see him?" I asked Killeen, who'd kept his more powerful binoculars trained on the hill.

"Nope."

"Damn. Do you think he cut his losses?"

Killeen lowered the glasses and looked at me. "Do you?"

"No. I think he might have gone back to make sure of
Rudinsky. Can you reach Ryan?"

Killeen and I switched places. I watched for signs of movement
on the hill. Nothing. Had I been wrong about Geoff's destination?
Had he doglegged behind us?

Ryan answered. "Is Rudinsky still alive?" said Killeen. "Good.
Conscious? Okay. Have you seen or heard anything? Did you try
to call? I see. Are you hidden? Good. Stay there. Keep him quiet.
Don't come out till the helicopter lands near you. They may get
Nakata first. I don't know. And don't forget to turn your phone to
silent mode. Just hang in there. It'll all be over soon."

I hoped Killeen was right. I noticed he took his own advice, setting his cell to silent mode after signing off. I did the same. Was he
worried, or just being careful? I could never tell with Killeen.

"Well?" I prompted.

"Ryan saw Geoff go up the main wash, then come back
down—maybe forty minutes ago. To reach me by phone, Ryan
would have had to climb to the top of the mesa, like he did last
time. Too risky, with Geoff around."

"Do you suppose Geoff was trying to steal my Jeep?"

Killeen grinned. "He'd be shit outta luck—unless he's got spare
spark plugs in his pocket."

"You are a man to ride the river with, Killeen."

"If you don't mind, I'll skip the pleasures of surfing flash floods
with you."

"I don't mind. My surfing days are over anyway."

I searched the map for the most likely route between the main
wash and the hill, one that would keep Geoff out of sight the entire
way.

"Son of a bitch," Killeen whispered, handing me the glasses.
"Frankie MacFarlane, meet Dora Simpson."

**PART VI**

Violent delights have violent ends.

—Shakespeare, *Romeo and Juliet*

Whatever their original intention, the long-dead artists and hunters confront us across the centuries with the poignant sign of their humanity. I was here, says the artist. We were here, say the hunters.

—Edward Abbey, *Desert Solitaire*, 1968

The heavenly bodies look so much more remote from the bottom of a deep canyon than they do from the level. The climb of the walls helps out the eye, somehow. I lay down on a solitary rock that was like an island in the bottom of the valley, and looked up . . . and presently stars shivered . . . like crystals dropped into perfectly clear water.

—Willa Cather, *The Professor's House*, 1925

# 43

Through the binoculars I saw a petite woman in a knit hat, wearing olive cargo pants and a red jacket. Dora stood on a ledge perhaps fifteen feet below the crest of the hill. Focusing the glasses more carefully, I saw that the rock behind her looked odd. Camouflage netting covered a form too straight and even to be the old alluvial unit that capped the hill. It was a wall. This was Geoff's hideout, all but invisible to the naked eye.

If Dora had been free to leave all this time, why hadn't she? Was she Geoff's partner?

Killeen took a small flashlight from his backpack. He was about to signal her, when I put a hand on his arm. "Wait."

Dora scanned the countryside for a few seconds. I couldn't tell if she was waiting anxiously for Geoff's return or was hesitant to leave until she knew where Geoff was—or wasn't. She held something in her hand, something dark, like a belt . . . It was the end of a chain, attached to her ankle.

"Oh, God, Killeen. He kept her chained up." I handed him the glasses, and took out my own.

Killeen's face revealed nothing, but I could feel the anger flowing from him in waves. On the hill, Dora dropped flat and shifted along the ledge. She couldn't see the back side of the hill, the country due west, but she had perhaps a 300-degree arc. Killeen blinked the flashlight—on, off, on, off . . . But Dora was looking northwest, not south. She eased off the ledge, jumped to her feet, and took off down the hill, carrying the chain. She hadn't seen the light.

I was kicking myself for having doubted my instincts yet again, for having asked Killeen to wait. "I'm so sorry," I said. "If I hadn't—"

"Don't go there, Frankie. At least we know she's alive."

He called Crank with Dora's last position and ours. She was mobile, Killeen assured him. We'd find Dora and stay with her until help arrived.

"We haven't spotted Travers," Killeen told Crank, "but we think Dora did. He should be heading toward his hideout—that position I gave you . . . No, we don't know which way she's heading." He listened for a few moments. "Okay . . . Got it." He was smiling when he ended the call.

"They're taking Rudinsky out first, coming back for Nakata. And Geoff's escape routes are being monitored by air."

As if on cue, I heard the insistent beat of a helicopter to the west, the drone of a small plane to the south. They must be having a devil of a time with the wind.

"And that's why you're smiling?" I said.

"No." Killeen slipped his phone back into its case. "Dain and La Joie forded the river on foot. Love conquers all."

"I guess. Though that doesn't explain La Joie."

"Chalk it up to male bonding."

I'd had lots of experience with male bonding—both professionally and personally.

"You up for this?" said Killeen. He meant was I ready to find Geoff—to intercept him at the hideout or, at the very least, to get between him and Dora.

"Lead on, Watson."

Without another word, we were over the lip of the wash and running toward the hill. My knee had stiffened up. Each step was agony.

This direct route took us across shallow washes. I didn't know which was worse, the jarring downhill steps or the uphill ones. I knew I was slowing down Killeen. But when I suggested that he go ahead, he gave me one of those Killeen looks. "Not on your life," he said.

We took a breather in the relative shelter of a small wash. While Killeen kept his eye on the hilltop, I took out my topo maps. They were nearly dry. The dirt track south to Ludlow—Geoff's escape route, if I was right—ran down the center of the valley, paralleling the old railroad bed. Mesquite Springs wasn't far from the track. From the mountainside earlier, I thought I'd seen a faint trail connecting the springs to the Cadys. The trail wasn't on the map. I took out a mechanical pencil and plotted the route from memory. It ran by one of the mesas I'd flagged as a possible site for Geoff's rock alignments. If we missed Geoff at the hill, we might intercept him at this mesa. I put the maps away, and said, "Let's go."

"Hold it," said Killeen. "He's at the cave. If we move now, he'll see us."

"When he finds Dora gone, he'll cut his losses and head for his wheels," I said. "Want to see Plan X?" I pulled out the maps again.

"In a minute," said Killeen. "He's looking for Dora."

"Or checking his escape routes."

"He's back inside," said Killeen.

"We can't reach the hill in time to stop him," I said, and pointed to my penciled trail.

Killeen risked a quick glance at the map, then focused on the hill again. "He's out. Holding something—a gym bag, I think. And his crossbow. He's moving downhill." I stood up. "Wait, he stopped again. I can't see him . . . Got him. He's moving."

"Plan X?" I asked again.

But Killeen was ten steps ahead of me, talking on the phone to Crank, giving him the new coordinates. I followed as quickly as my leg would take me.

"So do we have a plan for when we get there?" I said when Killeen had finished.

"Too many variables. For one thing, we don't know where Dora is. We'll wing it."

"Do me a favor, Killeen? Just tell me when to duck and run."

# 44

Despite my injured knee, we reached the jeep trail at the foot of the mesa before Geoff did. Unfortunately, the wind aided the hunted. Geoff's vehicle could be around the corner and we wouldn't hear it.

There wasn't time to build a barricade across the trail. But where the road curved around a spur of the mesa, runoff had eroded a natural trench. The spot was hidden well enough that Geoff wouldn't see it till he was on top of it.

I helped Killeen pitch boulders from the wash onto the trail, creating an impromptu obstacle course. If Geoff was going slowly enough to see them before he hit them, he'd veer to the east. We had to remove that option. My job was to keep Geoff on the road or make him swing toward where Killeen would be standing with the gun.

I crossed the trail to stand by a hefty creosote. I had to trust that surprise and a driver's instincts would prevent Geoff from hitting me. Would my plan succeed? Damned if I knew. Geoff had used Dora's truck to strike Sarah. He might just do the same to me. But whereas Sarah had been caught unawares, I was prepared—more or less. I would have felt more confident with a weapon. I had the knife, but I wasn't accomplished at throwing it. I had to save it for self-defense—though it wouldn't do much good against a crossbow.

I looked around for something else to use as a weapon . . . Alluvial units covered ridges, floored washes, filled the basin, littered the margin. Rocks. Man's first weapons—and the one Geoff had used on Marsh.

I collected a pile of baseball-size rocks. I'd been a lousy pitcher but a pretty good fielder in high school. I still played softball when I had the chance. I might not be able to run or jump or slide at the moment, but I could throw accurately. And if I kept Geoff and the vehicle fighting flying rocks, he wouldn't be able to use his damn crossbow. I picked up a rock in each hand.

The wind quieted for a moment; I thought I heard something . . . an engine. I dropped flat behind the screen provided by the creosote. Killeen was kneeling, his gun held in both hands—angled away from where I lay, thank heavens.

Light reflected off metal. An ancient Land Rover, open to the sky, turned onto the trail from the wash north of the mesa. "He's coming," I yelled to Killeen.

The Land Rover accelerated. Geoff knew this road, knew where the potholes and rocks were. Closer, closer . . . I heard Geoff downshift. I stood up. Geoff saw me, veered away. He hit the first rock, bounced, swerved to avoid another. He was coming straight at me. I threw my first rock over the windshield, clipping the top of his head. The second stung his shoulder. He yanked the wheel toward Killeen, accelerated. I knelt and fired rocks as fast as I could pick them up. Two rapid shots found the windshield and one tire. Geoff sped up, glanced off another rock. He was going too fast when he hit the shallow trench. The Land Rover flipped, landing on the driver's side. Where was Geoff?

Pinned beneath the roll bar and side door.

Killeen crouched beside him, checking him out. I still knelt on the other side of the road, massaging my shoulder and waiting—for what, I didn't know. Killeen walked over and helped me up.

"I'm okay," I said. "You can put away the gun."

Killeen holstered his gun, took out his cell phone, and called Crank. When the short conversation ended, Killeen broke off a branch from the creosote behind me. He lit it with a match from his backpack. Sparks crackled and flew. Oily black smoke billowed up as he waved the torch back and forth over his head. The small plane, circling far down the valley, began a banking turn. Killeen doused the torch in the sand. Together we walked back to where Geoff lay.

"You look like hell, Frankie." Geoff closed his eyes for a second, then squinted up at me, as if to make sure I was real. "I came pretty close, huh?"

This wasn't Geoff's voice—or Geoff's face. This was a stranger.

"Go ahead. Finish it," Geoff said to Killeen.

"Fine by me," Dora Simpson said from the lip of the mesa above us.

# 45

Dora sat astride one burro and held the lead rope to another. She rode down to us and dismounted. The chain, attached to a shackle and a dangling metal pin, rattled as it struck the sand. She looked like a refugee from a Middle Eastern war. Her clothes and graying hair were full of silt and sand. But her eyes were a clear, arresting shade of blue. She didn't look at Geoff as she handed the ropes to Killeen. "I wondered if you'd come," she said.

"Are you okay?" he asked. "Do you need food? Water? Insulin?"

"I'm fine. I have my supplies." Dora patted the bulging pockets of her cargo pants. "He got them for me."

"Did he—" Killeen couldn't finish the question.

"No." Dora seemed to be in complete control of her emotions. "I was bait—and, in a way, his confidante, his witness."

Killeen tied the burros to the creosote bush across the road, then tried to call Crank. But his battery was low. I handed him my phone. "Set it back to ring mode when you're done?" I asked. He nodded.

"Dr. MacFarlane, I presume," Dora said to me.

I didn't offer to shake hands. Mine were bandaged, hers encased in dirty, shredded socks. "The title is still in doubt," I said.

"Good," Dora said, smiling as if she'd just won a fellowship. "Then I haven't missed your talk."

"It's been rescheduled."

An awkward pause followed. Her smile disappeared. I could see that she didn't know how to ask the question that bothered her most. "He killed Dai Rhys-Evans," I said. "The jury's still out on Sarah, Rudy, and Nono. Marsh will be fine."

Dora took a step toward Geoff. Killeen casually put his body between them. "Crank's on his way," Killeen said. And to Dora, "He's with the Barstow sheriff's office. But it'll be a while."

"I'm not going anywhere," Geoff said.

Dora finally looked at him. When she spoke, her tone was flat. "Yes, you are. One way or another."

Geoff lifted his left hand to shade his eyes from the sun and twisted his head to make eye contact with her. His chuckle sounded like the rustle of dry leaves. "Think so?" His right hand moved fractionally near his belt.

"I wouldn't." My voice was quiet. I stepped closer.

"Wouldn't what?" said Geoff.

His fingers moved and I kicked his hand. A hunting knife hit the wall of the wash, bounced off, and landed point down in the sand. My knee screamed silently.

"I didn't think you'd kick a man when he's down," Geoff said, cradling his hand.

"You don't know me. You never did." I stared at him, wondering how I could ever have felt love or even attraction for him. He seemed smaller than I remembered, though he'd always been shorter than I. The mysterious Geoff the Stalker, Geoff the Killer, had taken on a stature almost mythical. That was gone now.

"You have to admit it was a good plan," he said. "How many did I get?"

"Not as many as you wanted."

"Enough," he said.

"Frankie," called a voice behind me.

Killeen whirled, gun out and pointed. Philo and La Joie were hunkered down on the mesa where Dora had stood only minutes before.

"The cavalry has arrived," said Killeen.

"Infantry," I said. "We have the mounts."

Philo and La Joie came down off the mesa. "You took your sweet time," I said to Philo.

"Don't ever accuse me of not going the extra mile."

"Tell me about it."

Philo took in my odd garb and bandaged hands before putting his arms around me. "You okay?" he said in my ear.

"Marginally," I said. I turned to my companions. Dora was sitting against the bank of the wash. She had a black nylon case open in her lap. "Dora, this is Detective La Joie, Del Rio PD," I said. "Killeen, meet Philo Dain, your best man."

Dora nodded at La Joie and Philo, finished testing her blood-glucose level, and injected insulin. La Joie took a bottle of water from his pack and set it beside her. She stared at it for a moment, then burst into tears. It's funny how the kindness of strangers undoes us.

Killeen handed her a tissue, then helped her zip up the nylon case and stow everything in her pants pockets. "Do you have food?" he asked.

Dora took a deep breath and wiped the tears from her cheeks. From another pocket she took a stick of jerky and a bag of mixed nuts. "Any chance you can get this shackle off?" she asked Killeen.

He took a hammer and chisel from his backpack and attacked the padlock on the shackle. It gave way without much of a fight. Killeen put the pieces in his backpack.

"God, that feels good," she said, rubbing her ankle.

Geoff's face had a grayish tinge under the tan. His eyes were closed. La Joie hunkered down beside him. "So this is Travers," he said.

"Camber," Dora said.

"What?" La Joie and I said together.

Dora swallowed a bite of jerky and took a sip of water. "Seth Camber. That's Jed's real name." She carefully screwed the lid on the water bottle. Her tone was controlled as she added, "There's a notebook back at the cave with names in it—a lot of names. He cremated the bodies of the men he killed. He mixed the ashes with clay and made them into pots."

"Pots?" La Joie said.

"That's what he wrote. There's a mug in the cave with Geoff Travers's name scratched in the bottom. I about barfed. I'd drunk out of it."

"Dear God," I whispered. Geoff had given me a couple of coffee mugs for Christmas last year, part of a series he'd made and stored away. He'd given a couple to my parents, too.

"Yes, well, I think Seth lost sight of Him when he was fifteen. Seth accidentally killed his brother. That's when the whole identity thing started."

Seth's eyes fluttered open. "I think he's going into shock," said Philo. "If we don't get this vehicle off him, he'll die."

Killeen, Philo, and La Joie righted the Land Rover. Blood stained the sand, spreading out from under Seth's hips. "I can't move my legs," he whispered in Geoff's British accent. He was relaying facts, not asking for pity. "No more running."

"Good," said La Joie, standing over him.

"I wasn't going to kill you, Frankie." Seth's voice was raspy.

"Just Nakata and the others?"

"Yes."

"He's lying," said Dora. "It's in the notebook. He wanted the perfect plan."

The light seemed to go out of Seth's eyes. "What time is it?"

"Almost one," said Killeen.

"Perfect." Seth smiled. "The place, the time . . . But I'll have to be quick."

Some part of me recognized an old note in his voice. "What do you mean?"

"A man in his time plays many parts, Frankie." A spasm of pain crossed Seth's face like a shadow, then was gone. "I certainly have. Problem is, I got stuck in the fourth age." He was rambling now. "But all's well that ends—"

I jumped as a boom in the west cut off his words. "What the hell?" Philo said. He and La Joie scrambled up the face of the mesa. A plume of smoke rose from the direction of our campsite. Killeen looked at me. Either the Cherokee or the Suburban had gone up in smoke.

"My Jeep," I said. "Shit. That's what he was doing when Ryan saw him in the wash. That's why he wanted to know the time."

I turned back to look at the man on the ground. Seth. I'd have to get used to calling him that. He was fumbling, trying to open a small jackknife. "I don't think so," I said, prying it, none too gently, from his hand. "There'll be no double suicide at the end of this tragedy. Romeo pays the price for killing Tybalt. Juliet moves on with her life."

Seth smiled faintly. "You're just postponing the inevitable, you know."

"Are you sorry—for any of it?"

"Quick," he said. "I'm sorry for Quick."

He wasn't making sense. Behind me, someone's phone rang. Mine, still in Killeen's pocket. It was Dee.

"Ryan left with Rudinsky. Nakata was conscious when they picked her up," Killeen said, returning my phone. "Dee and Zev elected to stay with the Suburban. The repair truck got through, and the new tires are on. They're ready to go. They'll meet us in Barstow."

"What about my Jeep?" I asked. But I knew the answer from his face.

"Sorry," he said. "They got the fire out. The repair truck's bringing in what's left of it."

"Our stuff—oh, God, the laptop?"

Killeen shook his head. "Didn't make it. But they took pictures for your insurance."

I looked down at Seth. He was unconscious. Just as well. Then again, he might be playing 'possum. I'd feel a whole lot better when he was locked up somewhere.

# 46

Up the trail from Mesquite Springs came a convoy of vehicles led by Crank. He got out of the first vehicle, looked down at Seth, and said, "Jed Strong?"

I said nothing. Crank and LaJoie would have to sort out jurisdictional matters. Seth was wanted for murder and attempted murder in Riverside County, attempted murder and kidnapping in San Bernardino County. I figured the murder charge trumped the others.

Crank called the helicopter back for Seth. "Sorry, we have to airlift Camber out first," Crank said to Dora. "You can go back with one of us, or wait for the helicopter to return."

"I'm good for another few hours," Dora said. "If you'd just call my daughter—tell her I'm fine."

"She's waiting in town," he said.

"Annie's here?"

"She's at the hospital. The office told me she went into labor. But as far as I know, she's okay." Crank forestalled more questions by punching some numbers on his phone, speaking for a minute, then passing the phone to Dora. "Ask her yourself."

Dora was crying again when she ended the call. "It's a girl. They're doing fine."

Killeen hugged her; I shook her hand. "We'll get you there as soon as we can," Crank said. "Just tell me what happened and where he kept you. I need to check it out."

While a paramedic examined her, Crank took her statement. His team split up, some getting Seth ready for transport, others documenting and processing the scene, still others taking statements. I went first, Killeen second. La Joie listened, taking notes. Killeen handed Dora's shackle to Deputy Carmichael, our interviewer. She looked from the chain to Dora and then over at Seth. "Jesus, what a sick bastard," she said.

Crank's crew had brought sandwiches. I chose a sandy spot to sit, out of the wind. It felt good to ease the pressure on my knee.

Philo sat down on one side of me; Killeen, when he finished his statement, on the other. Together, in silence, we chewed our sandwiches. I couldn't get my mind around the fact that my Jeep was lost—clothes, laptop, gear, briefcase. Luckily, I had copies of my dissertation back in Tucson, and I'd tucked my wallet in my backpack. But I'd have to spend part of my Friday—my one day with Philo—calling my insurance agent and booking a flight home to Tucson. I looked down at the sweats I'd borrowed from Killeen. And buying clothes.

Dora came to say good-bye, then climbed into one of the vehicles. She didn't look back. Her mind, I suspected, was already on her new grandchild in Barstow.

La Joie brought over a thermos of coffee. "Any news on the faculty members?" I asked as he poured three cups and handed them round.

"Drs. Nakata and Rudinsky are in surgery. There's no change in Dr. Barstead's condition. Dr. Marsh has been released. One of the students—" he pulled out his notebook and looked up the name, "Cassandra Belman, drove him back to Del Rio."

I stared off at the Bristol Mountains to the east. There was snow on the top. Dune sand pushed up against the flank, an odd contrast. Clouds scudded like ships across a sky the color of bachelor's buttons. The world was clean and new. No shadows hovered. They danced instead.

I saw something dark under a bush across the jeep trail. La Joie followed my gaze. "We'll get it," he said, as I instinctively started to rise. I sank back.

La Joie called one of the investigators, the same one who'd interviewed me. She pulled on gloves and picked up the bulky item. She brought it to where we sat. Seth's gym bag. She handed a second pair of gloves to La Joie. Inside the bag were women's clothes and shoes, a wig, shaving supplies, and a copy of *The Complete Shakespeare, with the Temple Notes by Israel Gollancz,* 1911 edition. La Joie lifted out the book. Familiar phrases from *Romeo and Juliet* had been underlined; penciled notes filled the margins. Page 263, in the middle of *As You Like It,* was turned down:

> *Why should this a desert be?*
> *For it is unpeopled? No;*
> *Tongues I'll hang on every tree,*
> *That shall civil sayings show:*
> *Some, how brief the life of man*

*Runs his erring pilgrimage,*
*That the stretching of a span*
*Buckles in his sum of age;*
*Some of violated vows*
*'Twixt the souls of friend and friend . . .*

Words weren't necessary. La Joie closed the Shakespeare and put it back in the bag.

"These were in an outside pocket," Deputy Carmichael said, placing two objects in La Joie's gloved palm: a ring and a lipstick in a pale green case. La Joie opened the lipstick. It was worn down to the nub. He looked at me.

"I lost a couple of those—same shade—around the time Geoff left. I was packing up my stuff and heading for the field, so I didn't miss them till later. I don't wear lipstick in the field. God knows what he wanted with it."

"And the ring?" La Joie said.

I looked at the clouds-and-rain pattern, so apt it made me queasy. "My engagement ring."

"Will you want it back when this is over?"

He meant the trial. I gave him a look that said, *Would you?*

"Did you find Seth's crossbow?" I asked Deputy Carmichael.

She looked at me as if I'd lost my marbles. "He was carrying it when he left the cave," I said.

"I'll check," she said, and carried the gym bag back to the evidence cache. I watched her canvass the area near where she'd retrieved the bag. It took her less than a minute to find the weapon, hidden in a creosote. She smiled grimly and held it aloft. I just hoped she'd keep it well out of Seth's reach.

I started to shiver. Reaction finally set in. Philo found a blanket and wrapped it around my shoulders. Killeen draped another over my lap, borrowed my phone again, and went off to call Sylvie.

A helicopter beat its way toward us, landed a little ways away on the trail, the sound of its rotors drowning out everything else.

"We're heading for the cave as soon as Camber is away." La Joie had to shout to be heard. "I want that notebook. I'd like you to come, Dr. MacFarlane—if you're up to it."

"I don't think I can walk that far." I pulled up the leg of the sweatpants. My knee was swollen like a melon.

"Good God," said Philo.

"Why didn't you tell me?" said La Joie. "I would have sent you out with Ms. Simpson."

I didn't have an answer, at least that I could put into words. La Joie didn't expect one. He gave me a couple of ibuprofen, took an elastic bandage from his backpack, and handed it to Philo.

"What Camber said—that bit about the fourth age?" Philo said, as he wrapped my knee.

I leaned forward, putting my lips near his ear so he could hear me. "It's also from *As You Like It*. The fourth age is the soldier, 'quick to quarrel.' Seth may understand himself better than most people do."

"Maybe." Philo attached two clips to hold the bandage in place. "Then again, he might have been sending you another message. A quarrel is a crossbow."

Philo was right. Seth was still playing word games. When would it end?

"Nice work," I said, pulling down my pant leg. "Remind me to keep you around."

Philo grinned. "I'll remind you."

I looked past Philo and La Joie to where Seth was being strapped to a frame that would prevent further injury to his spine during transport. A deputy stood beside him. Seth's arms weren't yet restrained. I saw his eyelids flicker, then open just enough to allow him to scan the area. They zeroed in on me. His lips twitched. I swear he winked at me—as "Geoff" used to do.

One of the helicopter crew asked the deputy a question. He looked up to answer. Seth's right hand moved. "No!" I bellowed.

Philo jumped. La Joie stared at me, open mouthed. Crank turned, just as the gun slid out of the holster and into Seth's hand. He raised it, pointed it at me, then put it to his chin and pulled the trigger.

# 47

The burros broke loose from the creosote and ran back up the trail. La Joie, Philo, Killeen, and I followed them in a commandeered vehicle. We left Crank to deal with the aftermath.

There would be no trial now. I doubted there ever would have been. If Seth hadn't taken his life on Crank's watch, he would have found a way at some later time.

The burros had retreated to the safety of their stabling place. Seth had enclosed a tight bend in the wash and built a manger and water trough. They were there, with hay and water for the night. The Bureau of Land Management could send someone out to collect them tomorrow. We set the battered gate in place, found the trail, and climbed to the cave. Philo and Killeen half-carried me the last forty feet.

We reached the top just as the sun dipped below the clouds hovering over the southwestern Cadys. The remote and rugged terrain seemed to buttress the sky. The wind scurried across the drying playa. From the ledge outside the cave, we watched the helicopter lift off with Seth's body. The link between us was finally broken.

Below us, rays struck like a golden arrow across the surface of Seth's mesa, touching a rock-lined corridor. Long shadows curved like a serpent from rocks rimming the mesa's southern edge. In the fading light, my eyes picked out other lines and rock circles, spaced seemingly at random along the mesa. It was a gathering place for warriors, a place of trance and dreams and symbols of discovery— a place of magic and power, left for the ages.

Yet, overprinting the scene like a double exposure, I saw Seth's ghost of a smile and wink before he put a gun to his chin. Would I forever replay that scene in my dreams? And would I ever understand the emotional need that had led me to trust and embrace a killer?

Lacking answers, I followed the men into the cave, a semicircular hollow in the cliff face that Seth had enclosed by building two rock walls. He'd suspended a tarp and camouflage netting from a bolt in the cliff face above. A circle of cement in the floor marked the place where Dora's shackle had been attached to a pin. She'd bored her way to her freedom with shards of welded tuff.

The room's only furnishings were an old military footlocker, a mat, a sleeping bag, and a blanket. A rock hearth was near the entrance. Against one wall, a large earthenware bowl—a pot made from coils of clay—held water. A pottery mug sat beside it. I picked up the mug. The name Geoff Travers was etched into the bottom. I handed it to La Joie. He nodded, wrapped it carefully in a shirt from the footlocker, and placed it in his backpack. Then he picked up the cistern, tossed the water outside, and turned the pot over. "Bernie Venable," he said, his jaw tight. Killeen set the pot outside. I couldn't look at it.

Dora had told La Joie where she'd hidden Seth's notebook. He lifted the bottom of the footlocker off the floor, felt around underneath, and handed me the notebook. I took it out onto the ledge where there was more light. Philo sat with his back to the wall, I leaned against his body, and La Joie and Killeen read over my shoulders.

Inside the cover was Seth Camber's name. Geoff's writing. The notebook was dated July, five years before. Sitting with my back against the rock wall, I quickly skimmed the pages he'd written to his victims and potential victims—including me. The details of his early life—the time before I'd met him—explained much, but I concentrated on the Geoff Travers years.

> When I was 29 I was ready for a bigger challenge. I took the SATs and registered at Ohio State. I liked being on campus—liked the availability of girls and books and inexpensive entertainment. I still rode the motorcycle, but now I lived in a rented room. I was always polite to the landlady, a spinster woman I met at church. I took my time with school, working for six months, saving money, then going to school for a year. I focused on geology. The early classes were easy—I'd taken them all before. But for the first time, I took the finals. The upper division classes were harder, but I did well until I was accused of cheating on a final. I hadn't. Another student copied my test paper. But they blamed both of us. And they sent me away. That was when Geoff Travers took over my life.

*Geoff was heading off for graduate school in California. He was from England, and had no family in the States. I helped him move out, then hitched a ride, offering to pay half the gas. There was room for my motorcycle in the back of his truck. He'd planned his route so that he could climb the highest points of all the states we crossed . . . I cremated his body in a kiln I found in the Mojave Desert, and came home to Idaho. I left Geoff's truck in a campground, and took the old motorcycle up the track. I found my parents in the vegetable garden. My mother looked at me with a stony face. My father didn't meet my eyes. Seth Camber was dead to them. So I decided it was only right that they be dead, too.*

*I took my father's double-barreled shotgun from the cabin, shot them both, and cremated them in Ma's pottery kiln— along with the family Bible. I mixed the ashes with clay, pounding out the air bubbles and kneading them together. I formed two large, graceful urns on the wheel, wrote their names on the bases, fired them, glazed them, and fired them again. The pots line the shelves of the pantry alongside a box of little clay plaques I'd fashioned over the years, inscribed with the names of homeless men and boys . . . plaques of remembrance, with different glazes, different textures, different scripts and designs. Remembrance was more than my parents deserved—no one will miss them or recognize their names, even if they find this place—but they're there on that shelf, surrounded by the lost boys.*

*I'll stay here in the old homestead for a couple of weeks maybe—resting, thinking, writing, starting over. I'm exhausted from playing so many parts, adopting so many names and regional accents. But I can't go back now. Ma was right—Seth Camber is dead.*

*When I feel better, I'll close up the house with its pantry full of ghosts, turn the livestock loose, and begin my new life as Geoff Travers. I'll travel light, with just this notebook, my Shakespeare, a few clothes and tools, and my motorcycle in the back of the truck. I have two months before the fall term starts, so I'll drive slowly south, exploring the backroads as I go. I'll climb the highest points of each state I cross, because that's what Geoff would do. And I'm Geoff—at least for now.*

The next entries were written more than five years later—last October, the heading said, in Barstow. The entries were sporadic, and the pronouns varied from *I* to *he* to *we*. The handwriting was different, too—as if, when Seth became Geoff, his entire structure changed. It was spooky. Seth's psyche seemed to be shattering. He was losing himself. Maybe he'd lost himself more than twenty years ago.

La Joie made no comment when I went back and read the paragraphs more carefully.

*Who am I writing to now? Myself? Who's that? To Frankie? She'll never read this. Geoff's parents? Maybe. Yes. I'll send this to them when I let go of Geoff.*

*It hasn't been easy being Geoff. When I took his place at UCDR, I entered a landscape in which I couldn't hide—literally or figuratively—at least, not using the old ways. I felt open, vulnerable. The trees were sparse in my Nevada field area, too. Perhaps that's why I allowed Frankie into our life. She was camouflage. She was adapted to the desert. I asked her to marry me after we'd been together six months. I don't know why. It surprised me that she said yes. I became possessive— like Pa was with Ma. Only Frankie didn't react like Ma. Frankie couldn't be cowed. So I started looking for a way out. But at the same time, I was terrified that she'd leave me, terrified that she wouldn't, terrified that I'd have to finish Geoff's dissertation. I'd never finished anything in my life. And there was Frankie, moving along steadily, effortlessly. She made it look so easy. I couldn't let her finish first. She'd started a year after he did.*

*It made me crazy. I watched her, tried to learn how she did it. But I couldn't imitate her. It was Geoff who decided to borrow a few chapters of her work. I was going to reword it later—paraphrase it—but she caught me before I could. When she threw me out, her look was as cold and stony as Ma's. Geoff Travers was dead to her.*

*We'd been preparing for this moment for months, Geoff and I. We knew it would come. I'd killed Bernie Venable back in December. I helped him load his pickup, saw the medical and dental records I'd reminded Bernie to get before he left. I'd told him it was so much easier to start life in a new city if you've brought your records with you. I even drove to L.A. with him—just for a lark—and helped him move into his apartment. And then I killed him, brought him back to Del*

Rio in the U-Haul, and left his body in the ravine behind school—below the place where Frankie and I used to picnic—or where Geoff and Frankie used to picnic. Sometimes I have trouble knowing who's on stage.

Where was I? Lately, I find I'm losing track of my thoughts . . . Oh, yes. Bernie. Bless the coyotes and beetles, the flies and maggots, the vultures and crows. It was all so easy—easier than living as Geoff. After eight months, Bernie's bones were scattered all over the hillside. When someone found his body, I knew they'd think it was Geoff's. He was okay with it. He even put his ID in Bernie's pocket. All I had to do was wait. Geoff would be dead. Frankie, that bitch, might even mourn for him. And then we'd have breathing space to plan my revenge.

Revenge. Revenge isn't sweet. The planning is sweet. I planned to run Peter Snavely off the road to Crestline. He never saw me coming. The department lost its head. One down.

Then Geoff went to Mexico for a few days, just to think and plan. But Geoff, as usual, screwed up. He got in an accident and had his picture taken. So we followed Frankie to Nevada, camped for a few days in his old field area, and spied on her. To kill or not to kill, that was the question. Not yet. Not yet. I convinced Geoff to wait. There was plenty of time. I wanted to perfect the plan.

I took a job as a janitor in Barstow, close enough to Del Rio that I could be there in a few hours. Nobody knew me in Barstow. I bought an old Land Rover with Bernie's money, and explored the desert on my days off. I read the Del Rio newspaper. It took months for the body to be found, for the police to call my cell phone. I rather enjoyed being brother Harold. It was the first time I'd ever played a fictional character, though my whole life has been fiction—an elaborate lie. Maybe I'll try fiction next, become a writer. Write my life as fiction, using a pseudonym. I've had a lot of pseudonyms.

Anyway, we put Geoff's name on Bernie's dental charts and claimed the cremated remains. Later, I mixed Bernie's ashes with clay and made a large coil pot, scratched his name in the bottom, and fired it in one of the kilns I'd found in the desert east of the Cadys—where I cremated Geoff five years ago. I worked at night. No glaze this time. But it's a nice pot

*anyway . . . And then I hunkered down to wait in Barstow.*
*Frankie had to come back to Del Rio for her dissertation*
*defense. Geoff and I could be patient.*

*When the fall session started, we sometimes visited UCDR*
*late at night, using the old steam tunnels to come and go.*
*Sometimes I disguised myself as a woman to walk around*
*campus. Geoff says I move like a ghost. That's because I am a*
*ghost. Seth Camber is dead. Geoff Travers is dead. Only ghosts*
*are left.*

*We overheard conversations—learned which students were*
*working where, and when the professors were most vulner-*
*able. Dora Simpson had our old office, the one we shared with*
*Frankie. I overheard her tell the new guy, Killeen, about her*
*fieldwork in the Cadys. I heard them schedule the trip out.*
*And then Geoff and I planned exactly what form our revenge*
*will take. It's going to be perfect.*

The letter ended there. But two pages later was a list of names.
Abraham "Quick" Baca's name was at the top, followed by fifteen
or twenty male names. Jed Strong's was in the middle. Geoff's was
just before Daniel and Maeve Baca. Then there was a space, as
though he'd been on hiatus. The nine names below that space were
Venable, Snavely, Barstead, Rhys-Evans, Loretta Stanton, Marsh,
Nakata, Rudinsky, and MacFarlane. He must have entered those
nine names after he met Loretta—no earlier than last summer, no
later than this morning. Clearly, he was arrogant enough to think
he'd kill all of us before he was stopped, before the machine ran its
course. Hubris goes before the fall.

"He didn't include Dora's name," I said. "He'd planned to let
her go."

"One good act doesn't make up for all the others, Dr. MacFarlane."

"There were two acts. He made this list."

"Three," said La Joie. "He saved the state the expense and
hassle of trying and executing him. But the scales aren't balanced.
Look at that list." He rubbed the muscles at the back of his neck, a
familiar gesture. At least we'll be able to close a lot of missing persons cases."

I flipped through the remaining pages. Nothing. But inside the
back cover I found a list of places and elevations. The date was
from that summer, five years ago. I looked over at La Joie. They
were the peaks Seth climbed—first *with* Geoff, and then *as* Geoff.

They marked the route they took across country from Ohio. The ascents were like trinkets taken off a murder victim, I thought as I closed the notebook and handed it to La Joie. He slipped the book into a plastic bag he'd taken from his backpack.

"There's something odd about his parents' entry," I said.

"The Bacas? It's the only one with two names on the same line."

"No—I mean yes, but it's something else." I thought for a moment. "It's an anagram," I said.

"What?"

"The names—Daniel and Maeve Baca. Geoff liked puzzles—crossword puzzles, jigsaw puzzles, anagrams. If you run the names together you get Danielandmaevebaca."

"Okay." But La Joie's tone held doubt.

"Adam, Eve, Cain, and Abel."

"It could be coincidence."

"Maybe."

"Then again, we may never know what his real name was, or where he came from."

"The cabin will be there," I said. "And the pots."

"If they're really there, we'll find them. The families of those men deserve to know what happened."

Except for taking the notebook, mug, and coil pot, we left the cave as we'd found it. I wouldn't be back.

I stood up and took one last look at the mesa. Over my shoulder, the sliver moon tumbled down the ramparts of the western Cadys. The first constellations appeared—Cassiopeia, Auriga, the Pleiades, Taurus, Orion. The Milky Way crossed the sky above the rock corridor. Perhaps, after all, Seth's theory would prove to be right. Perhaps these alignments were built to mark the rising of winter stars and constellations, the paths of the sun and Milky Way on the winter solstice. Would Dora pursue what Seth had started? Would someone else?

At the foot of the mesa, Crank and his crew were nearly ready to leave. "Enough," I said. "Let's go home."

# 48

Philo and I had our Friday, working around my bum knee. Under the circumstances, food wasn't a priority. But we took a break midday to eat, call my insurance agent, buy me a few clothes, and visit Sarah. No guard outside anymore. Her bed was empty and freshly made, awaiting the next occupant. In a panic, I accosted the nurse, the same one I'd spoken to before heading to the Cadys.

"Dr. Barstead woke up a couple of hours ago," he said. "We moved her to a different wing."

I wasn't sure what to expect when I pushed open the door.

"Hey, Frankie," said the mummy in 326-A, the bed closest to the window.

"You know me," was all I could say.

"I remember most things. I'm a bit hazy on the last few days, but I swear I heard you talking to me."

"I was here."

"And this must be your Mr. Dain."

"Philo," he said, pressing her good hand. Sarah responded with a smile, or a good approximation of a smile.

"You heard about Rhys-Evans?"

"God, yes. I'm just sick about it, about everything. A Detective La Joie was here and filled me in on the details. He seemed to know you pretty well."

"That first night I was 'a person of interest' to the police. Did he say anything about Nakata and Rudinsky?"

"They'll pull through, though we'll all be out of commission for a while. Guess Marsh'll have to be in charge—or Rizzo. I'll figure it out."

I hated to ask, but I needed to know. "My defense?"

"We have enough for a committee. How does March sound? End of the quarter? I'll dictate a letter to your college saying I'm issuing a provisional degree so you can keep your job. It won't be worth the paper it's printed on, but they'll accept the delay, given the circumstances . . . How's Zoey?"

"Phil Grover's offered to take care of her. I'll leave Sunday, unless you want me to stick around."

"There's nothing you can do here."

I hesitated to broach the subject, but the elephant was taking up a lot of space in the room. "Your legs . . . ?"

"Lots of pins holding the pieces together, but they think I'll walk again."

Seth had lost another round. "Hell, no," I said. "You'll run."

Killeen and Sylvie tied the knot on Saturday. Philo and I stood with them along with Sylvie's boss, Dr. Noah Forsythe, at a simple ceremony at the Newman Center on campus. Tommy the Ringbearer was healthy again, although he had to be talked out of wearing a plastic elvish blade. He dropped the little satin pillow only twice on the way to the altar.

"Thank you," Sylvie said, kissing my cheek as I prepared to follow Tommy. She looked ethereal in a simple cream-colored silk dress and pearls. She'd walk up the aisle alone. She had no family except the people in that room.

"For what?"

"For bringing him home alive, in good shape, and in time for the ceremony."

"Nothing," I said, "was going to make Killeen miss this wedding."

I thought, looking at the three of them clustered in front of the minister, that sometimes, despite all odds, life does work out. It's a matter of trust. And luck.

People have been looking into this country for a long time, loving it, cursing it, gutting it, changing it, enduring it. Not all have found it to be beautiful. Many have come to know parts of it very well; few have come to know all of it.

—C. Gregory Crampton, *Standing Up Country,* 1964

I sometimes choose to think, no doubt perversely, that man is a dream, thought an illusion, and only rock is real. Rock and sun.

—Edward Abbey, *Desert Solitaire,* 1968

# University of California–Del Rio

A large audience and positive atmosphere greeted me in the lecture hall. Rudinsky hadn't offered credit for attending, so I attributed the change to spring fever. Dee, Zev, Ryan, Cassie, and Dora were there to show support.

Sarah, Nakata, and Rudinsky made up the new committee, though the rest of the faculty was in attendance. It was the first time in ten months we were all together—all, that is, except Dai Rhys-Evans. A picture of him stood on his empty chair. The celebration afterward would include a memorial to him.

Though my bum knee had recovered completely, my committee members weren't as lucky. Sarah was in a wheelchair, her legs still in casts. Her arm, newly released from plaster, was whiter than its mate. But there was nothing wrong with her mind. She'd just taken the departmental reins back from Rizzo, who still lamented the emergency that had kept him from joining the search for Dora. He seemed to feel his presence would have made a difference, that he would have stopped Seth single-handedly.

Nakata was still undergoing physical therapy for the injured shoulder muscles. The arrow had chipped her collarbone, and they'd had to operate to remove the fragments. She still had headaches from the concussion, but she was almost back to normal. Rudinsky, however, was not. The arrow had narrowly missed heart and lungs, but an infection had set in at the hospital. He'd almost died. His body and antibiotics had won the war, but his mind and spirit were still recuperating from the assaults. A student had tried to kill him. A student had almost succeeded. Maybe it was time to examine priorities, he'd said to me when I'd arrived the day before. Coming face-to-face with mortality can have that effect. He was dating a physics professor.

Marsh was in the best shape of all of them. The migraines triggered by the concussion had receded. He was pugnacious as always, but he and Rudinsky had patched things up—for now. Rudy had added Marsh's name to the GSA abstract.

Among the students, Dee and Zev had both moved on to other partners. Ryan and Cassie had hooked up. And Dora was busily writing her senior thesis. She'd already been accepted into grad school in Texas, closer to her daughter and grandchild. Whatever nightmares haunted her she kept to herself or shared with her therapist. Sarah called her indomitable. It fit.

Hard Rock Sam disrupted the proceedings only twice: A large plastic rattlesnake found its way into my briefcase. I jumped. The audience clapped. And HRS had somehow managed to insert a porn site advertisement at the beginning of my PowerPoint presentation. They broke the ice. The rest of the forty-five-minute talk passed like a blur. The questions began—straightforward for the most part. The panel didn't have the heart to be tricky.

Rudinsky was quiet during the session. But apparently he felt obliged to ask at least one question about thrust faults versus low-angle gravity slides. I'd already stated that both were present, pointed them out on the geologic map, and explained the structural and stratigraphic differences. He hadn't been listening. But I couldn't announce that to the room, not if I wanted his signature on the dissertation.

I was gearing up to go through the evidence again, when Nakata intervened. "She's been there, Rudy. Let's move on."

"Any other questions?" asked Sarah.

As the professors went over their notes, a child's voice piped up from the back row. "Is she done yet?"

It was Tommy. Killeen and the family had driven over from Tucson for the event.

The audience laughed. Rudinsky cleared his throat as if in prelude to another question.

"She's done," said Sarah.

It was over. Rudinsky, without demur, added his signature below Nakata's and Sarah's and shook my hand. I felt numb. Here, where the saga began, the aftershocks of violence put a damper on the occasion. Anticlimax.

"Dr. MacFarlane," said a voice behind me. La Joie.

I turned to find him standing with Mulroney, both smiling, which was unusual in itself. "Officer Rivera sends her congratulations," said Mulroney, handing me a card signed by all three of them.

I was touched, and said so. "Would you have arrested them if they hadn't signed off?"

"It's possible," said La Joie. He sounded as if he meant it.

"You're welcome at the party—as long as you hide your badges."

"Thanks, but we have to get back," he said. They slipped quietly out the side door.

While the department members adjourned to a side patio to start the party, Killeen, Sylvie, and Tommy helped me pack up my computer and briefcase and carry them to my nearly new Toyota pickup. Killeen paused on the grassy slope between the geology building and the parking lot. It was quiet here. A scrub jay poked among the leaf litter. Tommy handed me a small gift bag, black and white, with *Congratulations!* printed all over it.

"From the three of us," Killeen said.

"I helped Mommy wrap it," said Tommy. White teeth gleamed in his toffee-colored face. He'd inherited the physical beauty of his Jamaican father. He was five, now, and tall for his age. "I'll help you open it if you want."

"Tommy," Sylvia warned.

"It's okay. I could use some help." I sat down and patted the damp grass next to me. The bag was heavy. Tommy reached inside and pulled something from the nest of magenta tissue paper. It was a block of ice-blue marble cut into a triangular column. The sides had been ground and polished until they glowed. *Dr. Francisca MacFarlane* was carved in one face.

"Daddy made it—all except the letters." Tommy traced the letters with his index finger, reading each one aloud.

Tears pricked my eyes. "It's lovely," I said. "Truly."

"It's local—from Crestmore quarries," Killeen said. "I thought that would mean more. I got a sculpting student to do the engraving."

"I'll treasure it." I gave them each a hug, slipped the gift back in the bag, and locked it in the cab of the truck. I handed the plastic rattlesnake to Tommy, who thanked me with a resounding kiss. One person's treasure is another's nightmare. "I'll see you back at the party," I said, "after I turn in the dissertation."

I watched them walk off, thinking how integral a part of my life they'd become since last summer. Especially Killeen. In Nevada, he'd helped me collect data, helped me regain my trust in people after Geoff's betrayal. He'd picked me up when I was running on empty. We'd saved each other's lives. He'd come through for me again in the Cadys and was now handling Philo's workload while he was on the other side of the world. We'd known each other only eight months. It seemed like forever. How quickly life can change through chance intersections.

I walked slowly to the Graduate Division office to turn in copies of my dissertation. Above me, perihelia, called sun dogs back home, made rainbow parentheses on a threadbare blanket of cirrus. The high sun drove away the shadows between the concrete and brick buildings. Bells rang faintly. Students erupted from buildings. At the center of campus, a carillon player practiced a sprightly tune in the phallic bell tower. I passed a few familiar faces, but didn't stop to talk. My body moved on autopilot, just going through the motions. My mind was detached. I wished Philo were here.

Closing the door on one phase of my life allowed the worry I'd held at bay to rush in like a storm surge. I hadn't heard from Philo since that Sunday in December. He'd warned me to expect that. He'd be in the Middle East, he told me, for six to nine months. Communication would be iffy. He didn't know when or how often we'd be able to speak by phone. Even e-mail would be sporadic.

My cell phone rang. "I only have a minute," said Philo. I heard noise in the background—music, shouting, popping sounds.

"Are you at a party?"

He laughed. "A local wedding celebration. It's a little different from Killeen and Sylvie's."

"As long as it isn't yours," I said.

"Not a chance. Is it over?"

"Signed, sealed, and soon to be delivered."

"Good. We'll celebrate when I get home. How does a trip to the Grand Canyon sound?"

"Sounds perfect. When?"

"Late summer, maybe early fall. Depends on the Boss." I didn't say anything. I didn't trust myself. "Don't worry if you don't hear from me," he said. More pops in the background. They were gunshots. "I love you," said Philo.

"I love you, too." And then I remembered that tomorrow was Philo's birthday. "Happy birthday," I said. But the line was dead.

The woman behind the desk in the Graduate Division office accepted MacFarlane's Opus. I paid my fees. She smiled and congratulated me. I smiled back. She'd never know how much that

246 **Susan Cummins Miller**

smile cost me, how many lives had been changed during the research and writing of that dissertation. It hurt. But then, change always hurts.

"Glad to be finished?" she said.

"You have no idea."

# Acknowledgments

Michael O. Woodburne, Jonathan C. Matti, and Douglas M. Morton shared their thoughts on the geologic history and evolution of the Mojave Desert. Hedley Bond patiently answered my innumerable questions about Type I diabetes. Raymond C. Murray pointed out that the California Department of Justice employed a forensic geologist. William and Gayle Hartmann discussed astroarchaeology and the ages of Mojave Desert rock alignments. Greg Willitts provided information about off-road vehicles. I offer my sincerest thanks to Wynne Brown, Sheila Cottrell, Elizabeth Gunn, William Hartmann, J. M. Hayes, E. J. McGill, Douglas Morton, Liza Porter, and Lou Halsell Rodenberger, who read and commented on all or part of the manuscript.

Many friends and colleagues offered shelter, food for thought, and encouragement while I researched and wrote this book. Of those, I would especially like to thank Wynne Brown and Hedley Bond; the Chapman family; Mike and Janice Woodburne; Hillary and Len Whitten; and Mary Jo, Judith, and David Keeling. I'm also grateful to Dennis O'Leary and the Djerassi Resident Artists Program, Woodside, California, for the "gift of time" to work on this project during the winter of 2004.

Thanks also to Judith Keeling, editor in chief; Katherine Dennis, managing editor; and the staff of Texas Tech University Press, and to John Mulvihill, copyeditor, for their patience, humor, and attention to detail.

One final note: I owe a much belated debt of gratitude to Charles A. Repenning—WWII POW, vertebrate paleontology mentor, friend, and former colleague at the U.S. Geological Survey—who left us tragically and far too soon. I'll miss you, Rep.